RUNNING
FROM
MERCY

RUNNING FROM MERCY

TERRA LITTLE

Q-Boro Books
WWW.QBOROBOOKS.COM

An Urban Entertainment Company

Published by Q-Boro Books
Copyright © 2008 by Terra Little

ISBN-13: 978-1-933967-37-0
ISBN-10: 1-933967-37-4
LCCN: 2007923277

First Printing January 2008
Printed in the United States of America

10 9 8 7 6 5 4 3 2 1

Cover Copyright © 2007 by Q-BORO BOOKS, all rights reserved.
Cover layout/design by Marion Designs
Editors: Tee C. Royal, Candace K. Cottrell, Latoya Smith

Q-BORO BOOKS
Jamaica, Queens NY 11434
WWW.QBOROBOOKS.COM

In Loving Memory of Mary Elizabeth Richie
October 26, 1930–January 3, 2007
I love you, Grandma. Rest In Peace.

Acknowledgments

I must send out big thank you's to the following people: To my advance readers: Theresa Bosslet Biberdorf, Sylvia Little, Donna Adams, and Anita Shari Peterson. To Niecy Davis and the rest of the Foxy 95.5 FM family and to Chaz Saunders & Isis Jones and the rest of the Majic 104.9 FM family for being accessible and for putting a sista out there without the slightest problem. To the good folks over at First World Books, Ujamaa Maktaba Books, Left Bank Books, and Knowing Books & Café. It's all love in the "Lou." To my mama, Lavelma Little, and to each and every member of my family for all the love, support, and encouragement.

Thanks to Anita Shari Peterson for reaching out to a sista, for keeping it real, and for doing what you do, and to everyone at Q-Boro Books for doing what you do too.

And last but never least, much love and gratitude to my daughter, Sierra Hughes. Thanks for always having your mama's back and believing that I really can walk on water, that I have eyes in the back of my head, and that the bird angels actually came and picked up poor little Sam from the balcony. You are my greatest accomplishment. But you know you need to do something about that gym class grade, right?

If I unintentionally forgot anyone insert your name here and hear me when I say, "Thank you."

ONE

From the diary of Pamela Mayes:

May 10th

Dear Diary,

I had the strangest dream early this morning. Paris and I were kids again and we were goofing off in Truman Field, the way we used to do every chance we got back then. We ran after fireflies and rolled around in the grass until our clothes were smeared with grass stains, blew bubbles with big gobs of pink gum, and dug for worms in the mud by the creek. We had so much fun together.

The dream was strange because we were adults and she looked the same as she did when I saw her just three months ago. I imagine that through her eyes I was an adult too. Yet, we were children in our hearts and minds, and there was nothing out of the ordinary about us playing the way we were playing.

I even remember thinking that when we got back home we'd be in serious trouble for ruining our clothes and I was worried about that. Maybe we'd be grounded or given extra clean-up duties. Then I wondered why there were fireflies flitting around in the middle of the day. I felt the brush of her skin against mine as we sat next to each other in the grass. I reached out and touched her hair and felt the smoothness of it under my palm. Over and around the smell of freshly cut grass, I smelled her scent, fresh and wild from the outdoors, but still so uniquely hers. I breathed it in greedily, dizzy from it and deliriously happy.

"I gotta go in a little while, Pam," she said.

By then we were lying on our backs in the grass, staring up at the sky. I'd never seen a sky so still and blue. No clouds or sun in sight, just bright blue as far as the eye could see. I was contemplating where the clouds might've gone when she told me she had to go. I immediately forgot about the sky and focused on her face instead.

"How come I didn't know you had somewhere to go?" I demanded, upset that she was planning to leave me. This was news to me because, as kids, we did almost everything together. I didn't like the faraway look in her eyes.

"You ain't supposed to know about it yet, because it ain't your time to know, sistergirl." She was being sassy, trying to make me laugh and for a while it worked. We grinned at each other and then I remembered what she'd said and my smile fell.

"When are you coming back?"

"I don't know, sis, but you're gonna be okay without me. If you start missing me all you gotta do is look in the mirror. Okay?"

"Okay," I said, not entirely convinced. "But I want to go with you. Make them let me come too."

"I can't. You have to stay." She started crying and watching her, I did too. We wiped each other's faces and sat up to hug. "I'll come and get you when it's time for you to come with me," she whispered in my ear and gripped me tighter.

"You promise?" I buried my nose in her neck and pulled her scent deep into my nostrils. Her skin was sweaty against my cheek, and I thought it was the most beautiful feeling in the world. She was warm and soft, special to me in a way no one else could or would ever be.

"I promise," Paris said. She set me away from her and stared into my eyes for endless seconds. "Come on, let's swear on it."

Our fingers tangled together in a solemn swear and our eyes locked, but it wasn't enough for me. I didn't want a swear, I wanted her not to leave me alone.

"Please don't go," I begged. Through my tears I saw that she was crying just as hard as I was. I fought to separate my words from the saliva, thick in my mouth. "Don't go, don't go."

"I don't want to, but I have to." Her hands clamped around my face, then my shoulders as if she was searing the feel of me into her palms. Her eyes roamed my face like a blind person experimenting with newly given sight. "I love you, sis. You love me?"

"Yes," I nodded slowly, sorrow squeezing my heart. I pulled at the straps on her sundress, tugged on the ends of her hair. "Yes, I love you. More than anything in the world. Please don't leave me."

Paris didn't answer. Not with words, anyway. She

laced her fingers with mine and tugged me toward her until our faces were inches apart. We stared at each other and looked into each other's souls. I smelled her breath, laced with strawberry bubble gum, and mashed my nose against hers. She pressed her lips against mine.

And then the alarm clock went off. I fought my way through piles of pillows and stifling covers to reach it and shut it off, still tasting strawberry bubble gum at the back of my throat, the memory of the dream hovering in my consciousness.

I would swear everything about my dream was real. Even now, fully awake and sitting on the patio, I would swear that I went somewhere last night. I was in my bed, but I wasn't. I was dreaming, but I wasn't. I went on one of those time travel trips and Paris went with me. I'm tempted to call Chad and ask him if his wife was in bed all night last night because I'm convinced she was with me. I have to call Paris sometime today and tell her about my dream. I know she'll get a kick out of it.

May 11ᵗʰ

Dear Diary,

Everything was so hectic yesterday I never got the chance to call Paris like I planned. I was reaching for the phone late last night to call and wake her up when it rang. It was Chad, calling to tell me that Paris was gone, that she'd left me. There was an accident. A really bad one, Chad said. And my sister was thrown from her car onto the side of the road.

He said she died instantly, but I know better. She would never leave me without first saying goodbye.

I have cried so much, I don't feel anything. Except for mind-numbing emptiness. I feel that. I feel lost and alone and angry and cheated and confused. I feel cold and afraid and uncertain about what my life will be like without Paris to help me find my way. She was always the sensible one, the brave one. Me? I'm a coward, and you know that as well as I do. I don't want to go on.

There are pills in the bathroom, left over from the time I broke my toe and almost stroked out from the pain. I'm thinking about swallowing all of them so I can be with Paris again. Waiting for her to come for me is unacceptable.

So I've lied, haven't I? I do feel something. I feel like breathing is too much to ask of me.

The phone hasn't stopped ringing. The doorbell is like a song now, going on and on, never resting, because they keep coming. I sit here and listen, unable to move. I know what they must be saying. That I have nothing now. No one. They are waiting for me to open the door or to answer the phone so they can witness my destruction and whisper about it to the tabloids, who will eat it up.

I think it's been about twelve hours since Chad called, but I don't know for sure. I don't have the energy to lift my head and find a clock. I know it was dark when he called and then it was light and now it's dark again.

How can she be gone?

May 12th

Dear Diary,

   Gillian is here. I forgot I gave her a key to my home and she used it today. I sat huddled in the closet, listening to her go from room to room calling out to me and said nothing. She finally found me.

   "You're starting to smell," she said after she came upon me, still wearing the clothes I had on when Chad called. I forgot to bathe or to brush my teeth. To eat. She stood over me like the workers at the home used to do when they caught me doing something I wasn't supposed to be doing. I looked up into her scowling face and discovered I had more tears. They came from some deep, dark place I didn't know existed. I pulled a rack of blouses down on top of me and let the tears come.

   When I was done, Gillian dragged me out of the closet and forced me into the bathroom. I wouldn't bathe myself, so she bathed me like I was a child. I wouldn't brush my teeth, so she brushed them for me. I wouldn't eat, so she fed me something I don't even remember swallowing. And through it all, she answered the phone and marched to the door to squint through the peephole and make note of who was who. She was brisk and efficient, as she always is, but I thought she scrubbed my scalp a little harder than necessary when she shampooed my hair. Trying to wake me up, I suppose.

   "Snap out of it," she barked at me once.

   "Do you think Paris would've wanted this for you?" she asked another time.

She has been with me almost since the beginning. Thirteen long years she's been my manager, publicist, and friend all rolled into one. She is a pint-sized dynamo with yellow-gold hair and sparkling blue eyes. She never lies, and she never minces words.

"So what, are you just going to hide here and not even go to your own sister's funeral, Pam? I know you can be cruel, but I didn't know you had it in you to do that," she said the minute she had hung up the phone from talking with Chad for the fifth time. We were huddled in my bed, sipping awful Irish tea she brought with her and brewed.

"I'm going," I told her. "I have to find out when it is."

"Saturday morning and Chad needs your help with the arrangements."

The arrangements. Today is Wednesday, which means I have to get myself together soon and I don't know if I can do it. Gillian is making sure I have food in my belly, but I still feel empty. Hollowed out. This must be how parents feel when they bury a child. Except that Paris and I never had parents and she was everything to me. I'm sure I feel ten times worse than any parent has ever felt. I didn't lose a child; I lost the other half of my soul.

"She was so different from me," I said to Gillian. "Did I ever tell you that?"

"I don't think so, no. Why don't you tell me now?"

Suddenly, I remembered that I had told her that many times before, but she knew I needed to tell her again. She let me snuggle in her arms while I told her all I remembered about Paris, which was everything.

✳ ✳ ✳

May 13ᵗʰ

Dear Diary,

  Gillian has made all the arrangements for my return to Mercy, Georgia. The plane ticket, the hotel, a rental car, everything. She's even pulled some strings and arranged for the press to stay off my back for the next little while. Something about an appearance on a telethon and maybe an exclusive interview or two. She knows I hate interviews and I don't do them. But compromise, she says, is what makes the world go round. No, I told her, misery is what keeps the world going.

  I cried this morning in the shower and again while I tried to eat the eggs and bacon Gillian made for breakfast.

  "Is my cooking that bad?" she wanted to know. The expression on her face made me laugh for the first time in days. But, I still looked for the pills later, while she took a nap. And they were gone. Everything except for Pepto Bismol and my toothbrush was gone from the medicine cabinet. I came out of the bathroom and found her staring at me.

  "I have nothing to live for," I screamed at her.

  She didn't say anything, she just let me scream and scream and scream, until my throat was cracked and dry. Then she forced more of that awful tea on me and held me as I cried myself to sleep.

  I don't know what I plan to do or how I plan to do it. I can only move from room to room, following the most basic of instructions from Gillian, when she looks up and notices me roaming around aimlessly. She's all but moved in with me, I think.

We were eating lunch when she answered the phone and handed it to me. I pushed it away and shook my head that I wasn't ready to talk to anyone, but she pressed the receiver to my ear anyway. I was so angry that I opened my mouth to tell her to get out and leave me alone.

And then she spoke.

"Aunt Pam? Are you there?"

The sound of my niece's voice shot through my body like a million electric shocks. I gripped the phone and struggled to control my breath. "Yes, Nikki. I'm here. What's wrong?"

She caught her breath, probably thinking what a stupid question I had asked. What's wrong? Everything is wrong.

"Mom is dead and Dad's making a mess of everything, that's what's wrong. When are you coming?"

I had no answer for her. "What do you mean, Dad's making a mess of everything?"

She started crying then. Deep, shuddering sobs and I felt my own eyes tear up in response.

"He wants her to wear an ugly black dress, and I keep telling him that she should wear pink because it's her favorite color, but he won't listen. You have to make him listen. Why aren't you here?"

"I'm coming, sweetheart." My eyes closed against the accusation in her voice. "I'm coming."

"When?"

I opened my eyes and saw that Gillian had taken my plate away and set a plane ticket in its place.

I have to go back.

May 14th

Dear Diary,

I have to go back today and I'm afraid.

Jasper Holmes heard the knock at his door after ten Friday night and scrambled out of bed to answer it. He'd owned Holmes Funeral Home since he was thirty-two, after his father passed and late-night knocks weren't entirely out of the ordinary. He pulled on his robe and stopped long enough to look through the peephole before sliding the safety chain loose and opening the door. He couldn't be in the business he was in and believe in ghosts, but at the sight before him, his heart thumped double-time. He scratched his balding head and stared.

"How are you, Jasper?" Pam shifted from one foot to the other and let the smile she couldn't hide come. She'd known him since before she was old enough to remember meeting him, and she'd been turned over his knee more than once. She took in his balding head and slightly protruding belly in one sweeping glance and met his eyes.

"*Gal*," Jasper drawled, a smile playing around his lips. "You wake me up just to stare at my head?"

"You used to have hair," she teased. "What happened to it?"

"Worried it all out after you ran off, so now don't you feel special?"

He looked at her and saw the loudmouth little girl he'd scolded more times than he could count, because she was always into something she had no business being into. He'd watched her grow from a child into a teenager, and he'd given her her first part-time job in his funeral home. She'd been like a daughter to him, and regardless of how much time had passed, some things still came naturally to him. He opened his arms and closed them around her when she took her cue.

"I'm sorry about Paris, Pam," he said.

Pam breathed in the scent of Old Spice and tobacco and grinned. "Sorry to hear about your hair. I used to scratch your scalp for you, but I guess you don't need me to do that anymore, huh?" She stepped back and ran a hand across his gleaming dome. His hair had once been thick and coarse, and he'd worn it in a low Afro, even after the style was no longer fashionable.

"I see your mouth is still smart as ever." Jasper left her in the doorway long enough to find his cigarettes and light one. He came back to her with a mouthful of smoke and blew a stream of it in her face. "Still smoking, too?"

"No, but I'll take one anyway." She'd quit four years ago, but who gave a damn about that now? With everything going on, she could've used something a lot stronger than a cigarette. She took the one Jasper was puffing on, parked it between her lips and drew smoke into her lungs.

Jasper saw the frown on her face and cackled knowingly. "Viceroy's too good for you now? I 'spose you used to smoking rich folks' cigarettes, way out in Caleefornia and all." He took his time lighting another cigarette, staring at her through the smoke. "How you holding up?"

"Not too good. I still can't believe it, you know?"

He nodded slowly. "Ya'll was like two sides of a coin, you and Paris. Couldn't see one without the other, 'less you was up to no good. Then you did your dirt by yourself."

"I did do some dirt, didn't I?" It was hardly a question. More like the truth, the whole truth, and nothing but the truth. "The town was probably glad to see me go."

"Not everybody." He picked up an ashtray from an end table and held it out to her. "Put that thang out, gal. You ain't smoking it no way."

"I want to see her, Jasper," Pam blurted out. She put the cigarette out and turned begging eyes on him.

"Thought you might," Jasper said and went in search of his keys.

Alone in the front room of his apartment, Pam took her time looking around. He lived in three rooms over his funeral home, and all these years later, his apartment still looked the same. There was an old floral print sofa and chair, scarred tables, and outdated accessories. The only new additions appeared to be a plush recliner in one corner and a large-screen television. The smell of Old Spice and cigarette smoke clung to the air, strong as ever.

Her eyes fell on the couch and skidded away just as quickly. When she started working for Jasper he'd given her a key that unlocked the funeral home's main door, in case she needed to get in and he wasn't around. Months later, on a fluke, she discovered that the key also opened the back door to his apartment, just off the kitchen. She wondered if he had ever figured out that she'd been inside his apartment more times than she let on. Aside from being uncomfortable to the nth degree, that couch knew more than a few of her secrets.

"Here we go," he said, coming back into the room. He motioned for her to follow him through the kitchen and down the back stairs.

Pam held her breath as she waited for Jasper to unlock the door to the room where Paris was being kept. Inside, it was nearly freezing cold and the odor of embalming fluid was heavy in the air. She was relieved to see that Paris was alone, already in the casket

Chad had dressed her in a soft pink dress, one Pam had ordered and shipped only hours after Nikki's frantic call the day before. It was amazing how fast money could make things happen.

She approached the casket slowly, starting violently when Jasper turned on a table lamp behind her. The light allowed her to gaze fully into Paris's slack face, and when she did, a tortured moan rose from her throat. She wasn't aware of Jasper setting the keys on a nearby table and backing out of the room. He mumbled something about her taking all the time she needed and then locking up when she was done, and then he was gone.

She pulled a chair up next to Paris and sat down wearily. *How can she be gone?* Pam wondered for the hundredth time.

TWO

Chad Greene stood over his wife's casket and wondered if he had taken leave of his senses during the period of time between that very moment and the day before. Paris looked the same, still peaceful and serene, despite the jarring circumstances of her death, but something was different.

Beside him, his daughter was staggering and gripping at him for balance, and his arm shot out reflexively to steady her and bring her closer to his side. She burrowed in, slipping her arms inside his suit jacket and pressing her face into his shirt, and he continued to stare at the woman he had married fifteen years ago and was about to bury today.

Her hair was different, that much was obvious. Just yesterday he'd instructed Glena, the funeral home's cosmetologist, to arrange Paris's hair in a neat bun at the crown of her head. Other than at bedtime, when she'd combed her hair out and pulled it into one thick braid that hung down her back, Paris never fussed with her hair. The bun was simple and low maintenance, she said. So he had given explicit instructions for his wife's hair to be arranged in a bun, and he'd seen it for himself just yesterday. Glena had even gone so far as to arrange little sprigs of baby's breath around the base of the bun, and the overall effect had been lovely.

The baby's breath was gone now, and in its own way, so was the bun. It was looser and slightly tilted to one side. Livelier. Strands of hair framed his wife's face and rested against her forehead, giving her a gently tousled appearance, as if she had been running around all day and was just now stopping to rest.

Then there was Paris's makeup to consider. She hadn't bothered with it since before she'd graduated from college, but lipstick was smoothed onto her lips now and blush was visible along her cheekbones. In his mind's eye, he saw her as she had looked when he'd first decided to marry her.

A lump formed in Chad's throat as he studied his wife. They'd shared fifteen years of life together—fifteen good years—and even if he was never able to give her all of his heart, she had possessed part of it. He'd never known anyone as selfless and loving, hadn't believed anyone so genuinely good existed until Paris. Her generosity and unflagging optimism was what had initially drawn him to her, and then he'd grown to love her for her strength and drive to overcome the obstacles in her life. Theirs was never a passionate love, but it was strong enough that he sincerely mourned the loss of her.

"She looks so pretty," Nikki whispered for her father's ears only. Now that the service was over she and her father were the only ones standing at her mother's casket, and she was glad for the solitude. She hadn't been able to linger the way she wanted to during the viewing portion of the service. "I can't believe how pretty she looks. Did you tell them to put the makeup on?"

"No," Chad shook his head. He studied the lipstick again and felt himself go cold all over. Suddenly he remembered the name of the vivid shade, he heard himself commenting on it a long time ago and then he heard a voice telling him it was called *Glazed Raspberry*. He saw it in motion as familiar lips moved in one watery memory after another. He should've noticed it right away, because God knew he'd seen it enough, though not on Paris's lips.

He closed his eyes and then opened them back up on Paris's hands. Two seconds later, his breath was locking up in his throat and Nikki was patting him on his back like she thought he might be choking. The concerned expression on her face was so like her mother's he had to look away from her until he got himself under control. He didn't know what he'd do if he looked around the sanctuary and saw her, couldn't guarantee that he wouldn't lose his mind if he called her name and she answered. So, he kept his eyes lowered and let himself be led back to the front pew, where he sat like a statue while the casket was readied for transport. Doing anything else was liable to result in there being two funerals instead of just the one, and he figured the town had had enough excitement for one day.

She's here, Chad thought numbly. *Pam is here*.

It occurred to him to share his discovery with Nikki. He was sure she would be relieved to know her aunt was near. She'd been crying over Pam's lack of presence almost as much as her mother's, and she would want to know. But, he couldn't bring himself to push the words past his lips just yet.

Chad scrubbed his hands across his face and admitted to himself that he wanted to sit with the knowledge a little while longer. As soon as his racing heart calmed down, he would share.

Nikki saw her first. She spied her aunt standing at the side of the road talking to Gillian and broke away from her father's embrace to go to her. A few minutes ago, Chad had mentioned that Pam was at the church, and Nikki had been keeping her eyes open for her ever since.

Nikki raced across the cemetery, unmindful of the graves she trampled over, and stopped less than a foot away from her aunt. With her back to the gravesite, Pam was unaware she and Gillian had company until the other woman's eyebrows shot up in surprise. She barely had time to pivot and then her arms were full of heaving teenage flesh. Over her niece's head, her eyes met Gillian's.

"I'll call you," Gillian said and squeezed Pam's shoulder one last time before climbing into her rental car and slowly driving off.

Pam watched the car until it disappeared around a curve, then she pushed her face into Nikki's soft curls. The girl was holding on for dear life, stealing her breath, but she returned the embrace because she needed it just as much.

"There must be a boy in the picture if you're curling your hair." Pam set Nikki away from her gently and pushed her fingers into her hair, careful not to rearrange the style. "Three months ago you were vowing to stick with a ponytail until you were eighty years old."

"You had your hair like this on the BET Awards," Nikki said. "I wanted it like yours." Before she knew what was happening, Nikki reached out and nipped the dark sunglasses from their perch on Pam's nose.

"If you knew how badly I need those, you'd give them back to me right now." The indulgent smile on her face took some of the sting out of her voice. She felt naked without the oversized, round, black glasses on because they allowed her to see out and no one to see in. Without them, she was laid bare for the world to stare at, and it was unnerving.

Right now the world consisted of Mercy, Georgia and its residents. It seemed that everyone who was anyone had turned out for Paris Greene's funeral. Not that that was unusual, Pam reminded herself. Paris was well loved and highly regarded, starting way back when, when she was a quiet and perfectly polite girl. Never a moment's trouble, Paris was. She had cemented her standing in Mercy when, after college, she returned to put her social work degree to use in the children's home where they'd grown up. She and Chad had made a good home here and raised a good kid.

"They're all here," she said.

"A lot of people loved Mom."

Pam brought her eyes away from the crowd at the gravesite and looked at Nikki solemnly. At seventeen, she was taller than Pam by at least three inches and shockingly thin. She had claimed her father's cocoa-brown complexion and his height, but everything else was her mother's, right down to her long, slender fingers. Her hair was long, silky with natural waves, and inky black. She had eyes a make-up artist would fawn over, deep-set and wide beneath thick, naturally arched brows. And they were green, just like her mother's and Pam's were.

A black child with green eyes, a nurse had exclaimed minutes after Nikki was born. She was a beautiful baby. Smooth and pecan-brown with perfectly symmetrical features, big-eyed and nosy right from the start. The nurse had speculated that her eyes would change in time, and then she'd noticed that both the child's mother and aunt were green-eyed, so change was not likely. If anything, Nikki's eyes were a more intense shade of green than her predecessors' were.

"Not nearly as much as we did, though. I wanted to stop breathing when your dad called me. I'm sorry I didn't come sooner, Nikki. I should've been here for you, but I couldn't . . ." Her voice trailed off as tears filled her eyes.

"You and Mom were best friends," Nikki said. "I figured you were spazzing out, Aunt Pam. It's okay. They say it's different with twins."

"Who says that?"

"Dad, for one. He said you and Mom were like two halves of a whole when you were kids. He knew you'd come, said we just had to wait until you could handle it. I'm glad you sent the dress, though."

"Now do you see why I need the glasses?" Pam wiped at tears and grinned. She glanced back into the crowd and found Chad deep in the thick of it, talking with an elderly white woman who was dressed in black from head to toe. She instantly recognized the woman as Moira Tobias and smiled fondly.

Nikki noted the direction of her aunt's gaze and touched her arm softly. "Are you ready to go over there, Aunt Pam?"

"I have to be, don't I?" She slid an arm around Nikki's waist and leaned in. "Will you stay close?"

"I promise," Nikki said and began leading her aunt across the grass.

Pam slipped the dark glasses back over her eyes and allowed herself to be led.

* * *

Miles Dixon wore dark glasses of his own, and behind them his eyes widened as he caught sight of Pamela Mayes coming across the grass. He'd been in Mercy, Georgia since he learned of Paris Greene's tragic death last Tuesday, hoping for the chance to orchestrate a meeting with Pam. Maybe he'd casually run into her in the local grocery store or just happen to be walking down the street when she came outdoors. But apparently her propensity toward reclusiveness extended over into her personal life as much as it did her professional life, because this was his first time setting eyes on her.

On occasion over the years, he'd looked up and found himself in the same room with her, at an industry function where she'd shown her face and then slipped away quietly and quickly. He was as familiar with the force of her presence and the sultriness of her voice as her legions of fans, but that's where his association ended. Many times he had wanted to simply walk up to her and introduce himself, but she seemed to always be in the company of towering, heinous-looking bodyguards, and he'd had no desire to try his hand at crashing the gates. He was nothing if not patient.

Miles had bided his time, waited her out, and now here she was. *The prodigal daughter returns,* he thought as he watched awareness of her presence ripple through the crowd. These were people she'd grown up with and around, and yet they appeared to be star struck. Even as they genuinely mourned the loss of one of their own, they stared at Pam as if they didn't know who she was. He saw teenagers being tapped out of their trances by scowling parents, elderly ladies bending their heads together to gossip, and old men checking their drooling expressions and straightening their ties.

And he saw that she was aware of it all. It was there in the stiffness of her spine, the subtle flaring of her nostrils as she bowed her head to pray, the way she gripped the teenager's hand. Resentment seeped from her pores the same way an expensive fragrance might. Pam, who was comfortable onstage with thousands of fans cheering and chanting to her, who always stopped to sign autographs, even if it meant pushing her food away in a restaurant or cutting her leisure time in half, was uncomfortable.

Miles had started his career as a journalist almost twenty years ago, when he'd taken a part-time job as a second-string metro news reporter. His duties had mainly consisted of picking up the slack where the lead reporter left off and fetching coffee, but periodically, he was thrown a bone and allowed to cover a story with some substance to it. It was during one of those times that he'd aspired to make a name for himself. His chance finally came when the lead journalist was stranded out of the country on the same day as a horrific bombing. A headline-grabbing story emerged, and with the lead journalist out of his way, he grabbed a young, similarly aspiring photographer by the collar and set off to write a kick-ass story.

Barely a year later, Miles was writing his own feature stories and soaking up as much of the business as he could. Then somewhere along the way he developed a fascination with ghostwriting books, mostly biographies and autobiographies, and discovered he had a knack for the undertaking. No one was especially surprised when he scraped up the capital to purchase a small, low circulation newspaper and proceeded to increase the paper's circulation three-fold. By the time he'd purchased a fledgling publishing company and breathed new life into it, his reputation for being tenacious, shrewd, and sometimes ruthless had preceded him, and he couldn't have described himself better.

He was at a point in his life where he was used to doing just about anything he damn well pleased, and he was imminently pleased with the prospect of writing Pamela Mayes's autobiography. Given her considerable fame as a songstress, Miles was certain that he'd have a bestseller on his hands. She was mysterious and withdrawn, she never granted interviews, and she had a hard and fast rule of never addressing the personal questions that were frequently thrown her way. To Miles, all that added up to a woman with secrets.

As he strolled around town his first few days in Mercy, he'd heard many of the old-timers talking about Paris Greene and what a good, upstanding person she was. He didn't doubt that the woman would be truly missed. Pam, on the other hand—and here the voices lowered and turned sly—was another matter altogether. Some wondered if she would come, while others turned toward the horizon, eagerly awaiting her arrival as if she would suddenly materialize from thin air like a flying superhero. Where Pamela Mayes was concerned, the climate was decidedly cooler. He'd heard the word *scandal* more than a few times. *Whore*, too, which had raised his eyebrows in surprise.

His loosely knit plan to print the story of a struggling artist-turned-celebrated-vocalist was rapidly transforming itself into a quest to uncover the truth about a woman the world only thought it knew. *There's a story here*, Miles told himself. He would bet the whole of his media conglomerate on it. He only needed to figure out a way to get Pamela Mayes to open up and tell him all about it.

As Miles watched Pam from behind his dark glasses, he wished he could read minds. His job would be so much easier if he could.

THREE

Chad closed the door on the last of the mourners and sent the deadbolt sliding home gratefully. They were all well meaning, and he could see that they were sincere when they offered to help with whatever needed to be done, but he was glad to finally be able to breathe in peace. Whatever tasks lay ahead, he'd deal with them when the time came. But that was the future and this was now, and right now he needed to be alone with his thoughts.

Apparently, Nikki had felt the same way, because she pled exhaustion after barely an hour of having her hand pressed and her back patted and fled to the safety of her room. He was left alone to wade through clouds of high-spirited perfume and to stand in obligatory silence on the back patio while the men smoked cigars and thought they were offering words of comfort. He'd never quite understood the ritual of returning to the grieving family's home after a funeral. At a time when people would most want to rest and recuperate, they were forced to make smalltalk and to keep up a façade of emotional well-being. That in itself was exhausting; never mind the clean up after everyone left.

It gave him something to do, though. Platters of food needed to be put away, and he attended to the task automatically, as his mind wandered. He stretched out sheets of aluminum foil and covered cakes and pies, sliding them in the refrigerator without really taking note of what he was doing or of how he was doing it. He swept crumbs from the floor, dumped them in the trash can and stood the broom up inside the pantry. He leaned against the counter and devoured a hunk of chocolate cake in three quick bites because, with seeing to everyone's glasses being filled and their plates piled high, he hadn't had time to eat a damn thing all day.

Chad was licking frosting from his thumb when the knock came. Though his eyebrows rose, he stayed where he was and let her knock a second time. Then he walked to the back door and pulled it open. He'd known she would come. The only question in his mind had been when.

She had changed out of the classy black dress she wore earlier, into jeans and a T-shirt. The rubber soles of slightly broken-in Nikes squeaked across the floor as she made her way into the kitchen. She stood in the doorway separating the kitchen from the front room, rubbing her arms briskly, as if to ward off a sudden chill.

"She's really gone," Pam said.

"She's really gone."

"I thought Nikki would've still been awake. How is she doing?"

Chad glanced at his watch as he locked the door. It

was after eleven. "Last time I checked on her, she was asleep. You could've seen for yourself how she was doing if you'd come at a decent hour, Pam."

"You want me to leave?"

She had never visited Paris's home, not in all the years since she'd left Mercy and everything was new to her. The photos she'd seen paled in comparison to the inviting warmth of the real thing. She didn't know what she'd do if he opened the door and told her to get out.

"I want you to turn around and look at me."

Pam turned slowly and met his steady gaze. He stared at her for several seconds before a grin tilted one corner of his mouth. Unsteady hands rose to scrub across his face roughly. "That wasn't so hard, was it?"

"All of this is hard. Paris being gone is hard, being back here is hard. I said I was never coming back here and she *knew* that. I think this must be her idea of a joke, dying on me and forcing me to step foot in this awful little town again. I can't believe she would do this to me."

"I don't think she planned it," Chad said carefully.

"I did, though. I had it all worked out. We'd die together in a boat crash or else our plane would go down over the Atlantic, on our way to a tropical island. We'd be little old ladies when we went and we'd go *together*. But this," she waved her hands in the air, "this feels wrong. Like the world is off balance or something." She caught herself pacing the floor and came up short, pushed her hands through her hair, and looked at him.

"Seeing you again is hard, Chad."

He nodded, considering her. "I feel the same way. This isn't quite like watching you on television or hearing you on the radio. The last time I saw you, you were getting on a bus and mooning the town as the bus rode off into the sunset."

"You're exaggerating," she said, flashing him a shaky grin.

"A little bit, maybe. The concept is the same, though. You left and never looked back."

"What did I have to look back on?" She waited for an answer, but he didn't offer one. She shook her head knowingly and moved toward him. "There was nothing here for me except for a town full of hateful people and an orphanage I was too old to live in. I had nothing here."

"You had Paris," Chad challenged. "She was here. And after Nikki was born you had her too."

"I never abandoned them. They always knew where I was and how to reach me. I didn't have to be here to have a meaningful relationship with them, and I saw them as often as I could."

"You had me."

She dropped her head and turned away from him. "See, I knew this would happen if I came here. This is part of the reason I stayed away. When you and Paris got married I thought things had worked out the way they were supposed to. You had Nikki, and Paris was settled. I knew you'd be good to her and treat her the way she deserved to be treated. I couldn't put myself in the middle of that."

"You could've if you really wanted to. You could've been a part of our family, if you cared enough to try."

She looked at him like he'd lost his mind. "And play what role? Come to visit and do what? Watch you be a husband to my sister and pretend that seeing you with her was normal? Bounce Nikki on my knee and be content with it? I don't think so."

"I needed to be a father to my child. Was that such a bad thing, Pam? Can you blame me for wanting to see Nikki grow up?" He heard his own voice and struggled with lowering it for fear of waking the very person they were discussing. "Besides that, you didn't leave me much choice, did you? You had to know I would go to Paris after you left."

"Don't talk about her like she was second best." She wiped away unexpected tears and pointed a stiff finger at him. "She was a better person than I'll ever be, so don't you dare stand here and talk about her like she wasn't good enough."

"You're right. She was a better person than you are. I won't argue with you on that one. She had spirit and guts and she never backed down from a challenge." He let her stew on that in the seconds it took him to turn on the tap and fill a glass with water. He drank half of it, set the glass down with a soft thump, and gave her his eyes. "While you were flitting across the country making records and living the high-life, she was here raising a child and making a home."

She slapped the shit out of him before she could think about it. One second stretched into the next with them staring each other down. Chad licked his lips and watched her mouth search for words with little success.

"Chad, I . . ."

He reached out, wrapped his hand around her neck, and dragged her closer to him, breathing down into her face like he was winded from running a race. "The truth hurts, doesn't it, Pam? You can't hop on a plane and run from it anymore, can you? Where are those dark glasses you love to wear like a fucking tragic martyr when you need them, huh?"

"I didn't come here for this."

"Then what did you come here for?"

"I came to check on Nikki." She slapped his hand away and replaced it with her own, absently rubbing the spot where his palm had burned into her skin. "I thought she might want to talk."

"At eleven o'clock at night, you thought she might want to talk." It wasn't a question. It's nice to know that at least one thing hasn't changed, Pam. You're still as full of shit as you ever were." He saw the intention in her eyes and quickly put up a hand. "I wouldn't do that if I were you. The way I feel right now, you might get slapped back. Then we'd both be cowards."

"Why are you doing this?" Pam was exasperated. "Did you hear what I said? The only reason I came here was to see Nikki. Can't you just go and get her for me?"

"She's asleep."

"Well, wake her up!"

Chad forced himself to look away from her. "She's not a toy, Pam. You can't just pick her up and put her down when the mood strikes you. So no, I will not go and wake her up simply because you want to talk. Her mother is dead. We buried her today, in case you forgot. I think letting her sleep is the best thing we can do for her right now."

"In case I forgot . . ." Pam stared at Chad with her mouth hanging open in disbelief. "What the hell does that mean? How could I forget?" Angry now, she pushed against his chest and sent him stumbling backward. He barely managed to regain his balance and narrowly missed ramming into the counter behind him.

"Pam . . ."

"You bastard," she hissed through clenched teeth. Then she went wild on him.

Chad tracked the course of her flying hands with his

own and finally caught them just as they came toward his face. He brought them to his chest and held them there, waiting for her to calm down so he could speak. By the time she was done struggling against his hold, she was breathing hard and tiny bubbles of perspiration sat on the bridge of her nose. He watched them catch the light and then he caught her eyes.

"You said you loved me. You said we were best friends and that what we had together was special. We talked about getting married and having children and leaving here together. And then you got on that bus and left me here." He squeezed her hands and made her look at him. "Eighteen years you stayed gone. What the fuck was I supposed to do?"

"Marrying my sister was the best idea you could come up with?"

"She had my child."

"She was my best friend."

"Mine, too," he said softly. "She filled the hole you left behind. Having her was the next best thing to having you."

"That's sick."

He released her hands when she tugged and then spread his arms wide in surrender when she fisted them in the collar of his shirt. "You want to fight me, go ahead. I'm only telling you what you came here to hear, and you know it. You want me to tell you that all these years I still thought of you? Fine, I will. You want me to tell you that sometimes I looked at Paris and wished she was you, looked at Nikki and wished that it was the two of us raising her? Then that's what I'm saying. I'm telling you right here and right now that you damn near killed me when you got on that bus. But hell, you knew that already, because I begged you not to go. And you went anyway." He took both of her hands and held them between his, used them to nudge her back and away from him. "Go ahead and admit it, Pam. Your ego needed to hear that. You got what you came for, and now you can do what you do best, which is run. Only this time have the decency to say a proper goodbye to Nikki, will you? You owe her at least that much."

"Are you leaving already, Aunt Pam?"

Chad's head rocked back on his neck and his entire body stiffened as the sound of Nikki's voice cut through the tension in the kitchen. He wondered how long she'd been standing there and how much she'd heard in the process. He massaged the bridge of his nose with stiff fingers, waiting for the explosion he expected to come.

Pam took a moment to rearrange her expression before she looked at Nikki, and when she did, there was none of the hurt and confusion from minutes ago. Her lips trembled into a gentle smile. "I thought you were asleep," she said.

"I was and then I heard you guys down here." Nikki looked from Pam to Chad curiously. She could've sworn they were arguing and she wondered what they could possibly have to argue about at a time like this. "Is everything all right?"

"Everything's fine," Chad put in evenly. "How are you doing? Do you need anything?"

"Just my mom, but I can't have that, so I guess not." She was silent for a moment. And then, "Are you leaving, too, Aunt Pam?"

"Not just yet, but you know I have to eventually, Nikki."

"I don't want you to go yet."

"Then I won't." Pam reached out and gently smoothed the creases from Nikki's forehead.

"Yet," Chad snapped. Two pairs of eyes trained on him, one irritated and the other surprised, but he ignored the pull of them in favor of concentrating on the simple task of swallowing the rest of his water without choking. "I'm going to bed," he said and left them standing in the kitchen.

FOUR

Was he angry? Hell yes he was angry, and why shouldn't he be? Time had somehow gotten away from him and in the space of thirty minutes, he lost all the ground he'd gained in eighteen years. In stepped Pam and out went his self-control.

Since he was being honest with himself, Chad admitted that his anger had been simmering just below the surface all day. Pam had taken her time about coming home, and when she finally did, she chose to hide out like a thief instead of helping him and Nikki with everything that needed to be done. She acted like she was attending the funeral of a distant associate rather than that of her only sister. And then there was Nikki, falling all over Pam and pleading with her to stay, like Pam was visiting royalty. Like she couldn't see that Pam was itching to be on the next flight, leaving Mercy in the dust again.

It galled Chad that Pam acted like she was the only one grieving over Paris's death. Hell, the whole town was in shock. Nikki had been prescribed pills to help her sleep, and he was having to dole them out one by one on a nightly basis for fear she'd do something stupid like overdose. Meanwhile, he was desperately searching for ways to reconcile himself with his own sorrow and guilt.

For him it wasn't a question of worrying about who would take care of him and see to his needs. His marriage was never like that, and he was never that kind of husband. Paris's death didn't leave him scrambling to learn how to iron or how to boil water. They had lived together for fifteen years and basically taken care of themselves the entire time. Neither of them had been partial to leaning on each other excessively, so they had each simply stood. He thought what he and Paris had shared was a little like having a roommate. A kind and generous roommate, but a roommate nonetheless.

Nikki was already two years old when Chad finally worked up the nerve to ask Paris to marry him. He was going into his junior year at Georgia State University and she her freshman year the day he glanced up from the campus newspaper he was perusing and saw her taking long strides toward the Student Affairs Center. It never occurred to him to notice the way she walked or the anxious expression on her face. Seeing her had stopped his heart and then started it to pounding in anticipation. As he ran to meet her, he called out to her and then tried to keep his smile in place when she turned and he saw that she wasn't Pam, but Paris. For a minute, he was sure that Pam had changed her mind and decided against leaving Georgia after all. But she was gone and Paris was there.

Paris was studying social work and he was studying education, so they found themselves in a few of the same elective courses. They studied for exams together and fell into the habit of hanging out before and after classes, just as they'd done years ago as part of a slightly larger group. Paris was easy to talk to and funny in her own way. Just when you thought her mind was off in space somewhere, she'd interject a witty comment with such bull's-eye accuracy you knew she had only been pretending to be distracted. He began to look forward to talking with her, and somewhere along the way, the evenings they spent together began to take shape and resemble dates.

He thought it began when, after six months or so, Paris brought him home with her to her apartment to retrieve a book she'd forgotten. She lived off campus in a spacious studio apartment, which occupied the entire third floor of a three-story house on the south side of the city. Nikki was six months old then, chubby and dimpled everywhere, with a happy disposition that had instantly sucked him into her tiny universe. If he had occasionally caught himself staring into eyes that he found eerily familiar and kissing little lips that curved just as his mother's did when she was being coy, he never dwelled on it. He told himself that he was drawn to the child by the sheer force of his genuine affection for children.

Chad never pressed Paris for the details of Nikki's birth, thinking that it wasn't his place to ask, but naturally he was curious about the child's father. He wondered how she managed to support herself and an infant on the stipend she received as part of her scholarship from the university. Her apartment was comfortably furnished, and she was never without money the way most struggling college students were. He was curious to know how she made ends meet, but he never pried.

He was given his first peek into Paris's private life

when she revealed to him that Pam helped her with household expenses. That in itself didn't strike Chad as odd, since he assumed that though Pam had moved away, they were still as close as they'd ever been. At the time, Pam was just starting to make a name for herself in the music industry. He'd caught a few of her songs on the radio, and Paris had mentioned that Pam also supplemented her income by singing commercial jingles. Until then he hadn't realized that it was Pam's voice he was hearing in his head as he picked one can of soup or box of cereal over another, though he shouldn't have been surprised to find that he was still under her spell.

Chad didn't really question the fact that Paris had given birth to a child and was no longer with the man who'd made her pregnant. But, he did question the arguments he sometimes overheard between Paris and Pam during their frequent phone calls back and forth. Paris would leave the room to take a call and come back pretending she hadn't been screaming and crying, just minutes before. Yet his own feelings where Pam was concerned were ambivalent enough that he was content to let Paris keep her secrets and to mind his own business. He pretended he hadn't heard anything, reminded Paris what page they'd left off on, and kept studying.

Paris was never much of a drinker, though, and she tended to ramble after she drank more than two glasses of anything stronger than beer. The night Chad finally learned the truth, she was well and truly drunk. It was Nikki's second birthday and Paris had given her a birthday party and invited several of the single parents she knew from school. The party was a success, but Paris was a wreck. No sooner had she seen the last of her guests out of the apartment than she was gulping wine like it was water and crying into her glass. He did what he could to comfort her, but theirs wasn't an intimate relationship. He had never even kissed her or held her hand in a romantic way, so he patted her back awkwardly and said all the things men usually said to crying women when they wanted them to stop.

She was drunk and it was difficult to follow everything she said, but he got the gist of it fairly quickly. She was angry with Pam because she hadn't come to Nikki's birthday party. She said Pam was letting Nikki grow up without taking the time to witness any of the significant events in the child's life. They had talked about things like this, important things, and made a pact. Pam had promised she would be a part of everything, not just send money and silly gifts. Paris told him the money Pam sent was more than enough and that she didn't mind doing anything she did, really she didn't, but it was so unfair to Nikki. Then she had apologized to Chad for losing control of herself and offered him something to drink.

But by then Chad was damn near catatonic, and accepting something to drink was the last thing on his mind. He walked over to the bed where Nikki lay sleeping and stared down at the child, his mind clicking so fast he could barely keep up with his thoughts. Paris had said it was unfair to Nikki, but what about him? Was any of what he was beginning to suspect fair to him?

All these years later, Chad still remembered the feeling of his gut clenching as he turned to look at Paris. He remembered the confusion on her face, the questions in her eyes like it was yesterday.

"Nikki is Pam's child?" he asked softly. Paris nodded hesitantly and he understood that she hadn't meant to tell him. It was a secret between her and her twin sister, something no one was ever supposed to know.

Chad took a week off from classes and went after Pam. He found her address in Paris's phone book and flew to California to confront her. He stood outside the modest apartment building where she lived and waited for her to come out so he could pounce on her. He envisioned himself wrapping his hands around her neck and squeezing until she understood what it felt like to be lied to and cheated the way she had cheated him. He waited for her to show her deceitful face, but she never did. When he finally entered the building and knocked on her door, a neighbor spotted him and informed him that Pam was in New York, auditioning for a small part in a sitcom pilot. He thought about following her to New York and tracking her down, but the idea of spending the rest of his natural life in prison brought his bounty-hunting trip to a screeching halt.

He returned to Georgia and did the one thing still in his power to hurt Pam. He married Paris and gave his daughter his name. Pam was obviously going on with her life, and he needed to go on with his. He banked his rage and considered himself lucky that, even if he couldn't have Pam, he would at least have Nikki.

Chad finished up in the bathroom and padded across his bedroom to climb into bed. Now that Pam was back, so was his anger, and he didn't have the foggiest idea how he was going to keep himself from killing her now.

Dear Diary,

I'm so glad Aunt Pam is here. She makes me not miss Mom so much. I mean, I'll always miss Mom, but having Aunt Pam here helps me not to feel so bad, you know? I think it's because they're twins and looking at her is kind of like looking at Mom. Their voices sound different and they talk differently, but if I close my ears I can pretend, can't I?

Aunt Pam is like a movie star to me. She has the coolest clothes and makeup. And how many kids do you know who have famous relatives? I think I want to do what she does when I'm grown. I might have to take some singing lessons though, because I can't sing a lick and I know it. Maybe she'll help me with that.

When I was little and Mom and I would visit, Pam cuddled me on her lap and sang to me. Silly little songs to make me laugh, but she always added her own touches to them and made them sound like grown-up songs. I would stare into her mouth and wonder if she had a magic box in her throat that made her sound so beautiful. I never realize how much I love and miss Aunt Pam until I see her again. I want to wrap my arms around her and make her stay here with me forever. Mom is gone (sigh) but as long as Aunt Pam is here I don't feel so alone. Dad tries to comfort me, but he's a man and you know how they are (smile). I'm going to make Aunt Pam stay as long as I can.

I hope she'll want to spend time with me. I want us to do stuff together like me and Mom used to do. In California, we went shopping and to the beach, but we can't do that stuff here, so I hope she won't be bored if we spend time just talking and getting to know each other. I wonder why she always seems so distracted and lost in thought? I think I'll ask her about that. I want to be closer to her, like she and Mom were, and I hope she wants that, too.

I'm going to bed now, but I'll try to remember to write tomorrow night.

Nikki

PS: I wonder what Aunt Pam and my dad were arguing about the other night?

FIVE

Miles stayed awake late into Monday night, pulling together his notes and conducting last minute research on Pamela and Paris Mayes. By the time he was finished, his eyes were dry and gritty and he had developed a heightened sense of respect for the Internet. The power of the World Wide Web, combined with the spyware he'd spent thousands of dollars on, had given him an auspicious start on the way to where he needed to be. Plus, there was something to be said for the friendliness of small towns. People talked too much without even realizing what they were saying, and paid even less attention to who they were saying it to. So far, all he'd had to do was put himself in the right places at the right times, open his ears, and keep his mouth shut.

He calculated the time difference in New York as he showered and then made a few phone calls while he was toweling himself dry. If things kept going the way they were, he might not have to stay in Mercy as long as he'd originally planned. As things stood, the first half of his book could pretty much write itself.

It was public knowledge that Pam and Paris were born two minutes apart at a nearby private hospital. Immediately after birth, they were signed over to the state in anticipation of an adoption that never happened. Mercy was a small town full of working-class families barely scraping by, and no one was in too big of a hurry to adopt two additional mouths to feed. Their birth records were sealed and they were placed in Angels of Mercy Children's Home, where they lived until they were eighteen and no longer the responsibility of the state.

It was interesting that the nightshift workers at the home had fought for the right to name the babies and won. They'd each chosen pairs of names, put them in a hat, and pulled out Pamela Anne and Paris Marie. One of the workers had claimed a distant relation to the late great Willie Mayes, and they decided as a group that's what the babies' last names would be. Not exactly conventional, Miles thought, but whatever.

According to the locals, the girls were inseparable. Like night and day, someone told Miles. Paris was quiet and book smart, while Pam was loud and brash. She hadn't especially endeared anyone to her plight with her flippant manner and who-gives-a-shit attitude. A review of her school records had revealed that she was a mediocre student, with no particular proclivity toward mastery of any one subject over another. She had apparently done what was required to get by and spent the remainder of her time brawling or sitting in detention. Notes made by various teachers told him that she was opinionated and combative when challenged, and unconcerned and unmotivated when left to her own devices. Of the two, she was the one who was literally passing time and waiting for childhood to be over.

None of this information particularly interested Miles since he was just about the same in school and he could probably name a hundred other people with similar reports. Pam's grades remained steady in the *B* and *C* range throughout elementary and junior high school. Nothing surprising there.

Toward the end of Pam's high school career was where things started to get more interesting to Miles. She surprised him by earning a 1500 on her SAT, but she hadn't applied to any colleges. Paris applied and was accepted at Georgia State on a full scholarship, but Pam had put forth zero effort in that area. Even with the sharp plummet in her grades three quarters of the way through her senior year, she should've been able to get into college somewhere. Instead, she had skipped graduation all together and hopped on a bus just a week later. Something was missing, something important, and Miles would pay hard-earned money to find out what that something was.

Miles glanced at his watch and shook himself. As if on cue, his stomach growled and he knew just where he would go to feed it. Since she'd arrived in town, Pam had taken nearly all of her meals at the little bed and breakfast on the outskirts of town, where she was staying. He decided to skip the greasy spoon he usually ate in and join her there. It was time to officially make her acquaintance.

On his way there, he spotted a stalled car on the side of the road, about a mile before the turn-off for the B&B. He slowed his own car to see what the problem was. As he came closer, he saw her sitting on the rear

bumper facing the opposite direction with a lit cigarette dangling from her fingers. The grin that took
over his face was triumphant.

Miles swerved across the two-lane road, came to a
stop in front of her car, and climbed out. She heard
him coming and turned to watch his approach from
over her shoulder. She brought the cigarette to her
mouth for a drag as she watched him stroll casually in
her direction.

Her eyes dropped to his expensive loafers and
crawled up his body to his face slowly. She took in his
neatly pressed khakis and polo shirt and the Tag watch
on his wrist. "You don't look like a serial killer," she
said finally.

"That's because I'm not. What does a serial killer
look like anyway?" He propped his hands on his hips
and waited for her answer.

Pam stared at him as she thought about the question. Whoever he was, he was tall and fit, with clear
brown eyes and professionally trimmed brown hair.
His freckled porcelain skin was just starting to tan
under the sun, which told her he hadn't been in town
long. She thought maybe she'd seen him at Paris's funeral, standing apart from the crowd and looking
solemn throughout the entire ordeal, but she hadn't
recognized him then and she didn't now.

"A serial killer looks like someone who doesn't look
like a serial killer," she said.

Miles chuckled despite himself. Up close and without all the makeup, Pam had a pixie-ish look, with her
slightly upturned nose and plump lips. Her eyes were
serious looking, but the corners of her lips were toying
with a grin. "Did they teach you that in school?"

"Right after they taught us never to get in cars with
strangers."

"So you're planning on staying out here all day and night, smoking yourself into oblivion?" He reminded himself to make a note that she smoked cigarettes.

"That wouldn't be such a bad idea if I wasn't down to my last two cigarettes. What's your name?"

"David." David was his middle name, so it wasn't exactly a lie.

"David is a serial killer's name. It's right up there with Sam." She dropped her half-smoked cigarette and brushed off the seat of her jeans as she stood. "You know anything about cars, David?"

"A little. Do you have gas in the tank?" She nodded. "Oil in the motor?" Another nod, this one a little less nice. "What about the radiator? Was it smoking or anything when the car stopped?"

"Nope. But it's a Ford, so it doesn't really need an excuse to be a piece of shit, does it? You know what they say FORD stands for, right? Forever on the road dead."

"Hey," Miles barked, pointing behind them to his car. It was a late model Ford 500. A rental, but still.

Pam leaned around him, looked at the car and giggled. "Sorry."

"I suggest you watch your mouth if you think you want a ride into town. That's where you're going, isn't it?"

"Yeah, I can call a tow truck from town. Right after I buy more cigarettes."

"Aren't you worried that smoking will ruin your singing voice?" His tone was smoothly casual, as if picking up stranded celebrities on the side of the road was all in a day's work. She threw him a surprised look, but didn't say anything. He watched her round her car and pull the driver's door open. She ducked inside and backed out with her purse and a small Gucci traveling bag. "What? Don't tell me you didn't think I'd recognize you?"

"Wishful thinking, I guess."

"You don't like the attention you get from your fans?"

"Are you a fan?"

He thought about lying and then decided against it. "I'm partial to classical music myself."

"Well then what kind of attention will I get from you? If you're not a fan you probably don't want my autograph, so what do you want in exchange for a ride into town?"

"I could probably get a pretty penny for your autograph," Miles smiled at her across the roof of the car. He relaxed a little when she smiled back.

"Fifty years after I'm gone, maybe. But right now I wouldn't bet on it. Did we establish that you were taking me into town or not? It's hot out here."

He fished his keychain from his pocket and hit a button to unlock the doors. Pam folded herself into the passenger seat and stacked her purse and carryall on her lap. "You can put that stuff on the backseat if you want to," Miles told her.

"I have a pistol in my bag, so I'd better keep it handy." She slid him a look. "Just in case."

They rode in silence for several minutes, during which Miles felt his opportunity slipping through his fingers. He cleared his throat and adjusted the rearview mirror. "You grew up here," he said, hoping to lead her into a conversation about the town. More specifically, her feelings about the town.

"You read the tabloids," Pam came back, just as evenly.

"It's not a secret, is it?"

"No, it's not a secret, and yes, I grew up here. I figured out about ten miles back that you aren't from Georgia, so why are you here?"

"Visiting."

"Visiting who? Or is that a secret?"

"I'll bet your fans would be very interested in knowing that you have a sharp tongue."

"You're not one of them, so what do you care?" She fished around in her purse and came out with her dark glasses. After she slid them over her nose, she went back in and produced a king-size candy bar. She was chewing aggressively when she saw him glance at her snack for the third time. Wordlessly, she removed the wrapper and extended the opposite end of the candy bar to him.

Miles stuffed the candy in his mouth and chewed slowly. "Thanks, I'm starving. Haven't had lunch yet."

"Makes two of us, and no, I don't care if my fans know that I eat three meals a day." She let him twist off another hunk and then slipped the rest of the candy in her mouth. Around a mouth full of chocolate she said, "Tell me who you're visiting."

He licked a string of caramel from his front teeth and swallowed. "Moira Tobias. You know her?" He knew very well she did. Moira was his preliminary source of information, though she hadn't agreed to the task and wasn't aware of his intent. The mere fact that she resided in Mercy was the perfect cover for his being there.

Pam's eyes went soft. "Of course I know Moira. Everybody knows Moira. She's been in Mercy forever and a day. You want some gum?"

He looked at the pack of spearmint gum she held out and shook his head. "I'm still finding nuts, but thanks." She dropped the pack back in her purse and zipped it closed. He waited to make sure the next thing she pulled out wasn't a pistol. "Moira was my step-mother. She was married to my father a long time ago."

"I think I remember that she was married something like three times," Pam told him. "Lots of head shaking and tsk-tsking about that, as I recall."

"My father was husband number two. He died ten years ago."

"Sorry to hear that."

"I was sorry to hear about your sister."

She softened even more. "Me too. Thanks."

Silence descended again and they rode into Mercy a short time later. Pam opened her mouth to give him directions to Paris's house and noticed that he was turning off in the opposite direction.

"Where the hell are you taking me, David the serial killer?"

He pulled into a parking space on a McDonald's parking lot and shut the car off. "I don't know about you, but that candy bar didn't do much more than make me mad. I'm hungry, and judging by the sounds coming from your stomach, you are, too."

She looked at him long and hard, trying to determine what he was up to. She still hadn't come to any conclusions when she reached for the door handle and stepped out of the car. But she was starving and a burger didn't sound like a bad idea. Besides that, he was Moira's stepson, a fact she would verify soon enough, so how bad could he be?

"I'm partial to the burgers at Hayden's Diner myself," Pam informed him on her way to the door.

Miles stepped around her and opened the door to the restaurant for her. He caught her eyes as she sailed past him like the diva she was. "We'll go there next time," he said easily.

SIX

Chad was still in the midst of a long-distance relationship with his girlfriend Leslie, whom he was forced to leave when his parents suddenly decided that Georgia was their next destination. His father was in the business of revitalizing failing small businesses and offering his services on a consulting basis when larger ones floundered. The move would make the family's third since Chad's fourth birthday.

Before Georgia, they had lived in Arizona for nearly four years and then in Nevada for six. Chad was just starting to believe they would put down roots in Nevada when his father was summoned to Georgia to try his hand at saving a black-owned communications company from bankruptcy. The company's main office was located in Atlanta, and the plan was for the family to lease a house in the city so Chad's father could be close to work. They were still living out of their suitcases in a hotel room when his mother decided to go house hunting, got her directions mixed up, and ended up in the little town of Mercy, Georgia.

She should have taken a left on Highway 25, but she took a right, and then she exited on the wrong ramp and ended up in College Park. On the drive back to Atlanta she merged onto Highway 205, when she should've stayed on Highway 25 and then she took Chad on a sightseeing excursion that led them to Highway 210. There, they stopped for lunch at a dusty little diner and asked for directions back to Atlanta. They were told to keep straight on 210, that it would put them off on 25 and, from there, they'd be less than an hour outside of Atlanta's city limits. They filled up on gas and set out.

With a full stomach and the certainty that they were finally on course, Chad slept for most of the drive back to Atlanta. He didn't wake until they were in Mercy, and when he did, he found his mother talking to an old woman about the *For Rent* sign she'd seen in the window of a two-story house there. He could see in his mother's eyes that she liked the town and wanted the house. He knew what it meant when his mother got that look in her eyes and he'd started feeling sorry for his father right then and there. What should've been a thirty-minute drive to work every day was suddenly about to be stretched to almost an hour, one way.

Chad was fourteen when they moved into the house on Northrop Lane. He started his freshman term at Mercy High School halfway through the school year and stuck out like a sore thumb, with his designer jeans and funny accent. He talked in clipped, rapid tones while everyone around him spoke slowly, almost musically. More than once he'd had to ask for something to be repeated before he fully understood what was being said to him, which made the other kids laugh and shake their heads at him. They were under the impression that he was the one with the speech impediment.

Finally, Nate Woodberry took pity on him and struck up a conversation with him in gym class. Nate was popular, and through him, Chad gained acceptance. Suddenly, people were coming up to him, wanting to talk, inviting him to sit with them at lunch, and inviting him to come along when they went to their hangout spots after school and on weekends. Apparently, hanging out with Nate meant he was worth the time of day.

He was introduced to Pam and Paris on a Saturday a few weeks later when he accompanied Nate to a pool party a classmate was hosting. Nate came by to pick him up so they could walk together, and Chad had come jogging out the door with a purple towel draped around his neck, his swim trunks slung low on his hips, and his mind on all the havoc he planned to wreak. He remembered every detail of the moment he first laid eyes on Pam. She was riding piggyback on Nate's back, whispering something in his ear as Chad crossed the porch and met her eyes. It had taken him a full ten seconds to get around to noticing Paris, who was busy pulling her sister's hair into a sloppy ponytail and looking anxious about the fact that Pam wouldn't be still.

"Chad, this crazy girl on my back is Pam and the other one is Paris." Nate grinned up at Chad. He slapped Pam's bare thigh playfully. "Pam, get down. You're too big to be riding on my back anyway."

Pouting, Pam lowered her thighs and slid down the back of Nate's body to her feet. Chad thought the contact was uncomfortably intimate and cocked a curious brow. Sensing his thoughts, Pam cocked one in return and they stared at each other as he came down the steps and joined them on the sidewalk.

"How come I never seen you around school?" Chad asked the back of Pam's head. She was walking ahead of him, next to Nate, and they were so close that their arms were brushing as they talked back and forth in low voices. He was trying unsuccessfully to catch the drift of their conversation, but he kept getting distracted by other things. Namely, the shorts Pam was wearing—denim cutoffs that were frayed around the hem and riding high on her thighs, almost like panties. And then there was her hair. It was dangling down the middle of her back in a loose ponytail, the ends trailing across the clasp of her bikini top. He waited for her to turn around and answer him.

"We don't go to the high school," Paris said from beside him. By contrast, she was wearing a one-piece swimsuit underneath an open camp shirt and a denim skirt that stopped just above her knees.

Chad remembered that she was there and looked down at her politely. Her eyes were the same shade as Pam's, sheer green and weird looking, shining out of a honey-toned face. He blinked from the intensity of them, thinking that Paris was cute and then he thought that Pam still hadn't answered him.

"We go to the junior high."

"Oh." He was shocked, but he thought he hid it well. At least until Paris's knowing chuckle reached his ears. He couldn't stop staring at the rhythmic sway of Pam's hips.

"They're best friends," Paris supplied quietly. "Since Beacon."

"Beacon?"

"The elementary school."

"Oh."

"You're a freshman, too?"

"Yeah."

"So you're what, fourteen, fifteen?"

"Fourteen," he said, scratching the back of his head

lazily. In front of him, Nate reached out and hooked an elbow around Pam's neck, catching her in a headlock. The laugh she uttered in response hit him straight in the gut. He tried to picture Leslie's face in his mind and found the image fuzzy and out of focus. Lines of confusion creased his forehead as he looked down at Paris. "Why?"

She shrugged primly. "Just asking. She's thirteen, though. In case you was wondering."

"I wasn't," he lied.

"Oh."

He was busy trying to touch Melissa Henry's breast underneath the water, without seeming to be doing so, when Pam slipped out of her shorts and headed over to the pool. Since they had arrived, she'd helped with setting out food and drinks and then she'd disappeared inside the house with some of the other girls. She'd stayed inside and out of sight for over an hour, but now she was ready to swim and she hadn't so much as looked in his direction all day.

Pam jogged the last three steps to the pool and cannonballed into the deep end. She stayed under for several minutes, then finally resurfaced less than a foot away from where Chad stood in the shallow end of the pool. His eyes locked onto the imprint of her nipples through her bikini top and he forgot all about trying to touch Melissa's breast. He swam to the edge of the pool and climbed out.

She played Marco Polo with some of the other kids. She joked around with some of the boys and seemed completely unaware of the lustful looks she received for her efforts. She swam lap races with Paris and lost two times out of three. She threw her head back and laughed with her mouth wide open and she ran her fingers around the rim of her bikini bottoms to smooth them out five times.

Chad knew because he'd counted while he was staring at Pam. He was perplexed by her face, couldn't seem to figure out the symmetry of it. Her eyes were wide and deep-set, her cheekbones jutted out sharply over hollowed jaws, and her lips were just plain too big. They sat on her face like a ripe peach, split in half and full of juice. She smiled and he saw that her teeth were straight and white, but too large for her mouth. He thought she resembled the Pink Panther with all those teeth. Her nose should've helped balance everything out, but it was narrow and slightly turned up at the tip, which made her look even stranger.

She looked like a cat, he decided. Moved like one, too. Tight little body, small breasts, narrow waist, and a round, plump butt. Her skin was barely brown-tinged, and he didn't know what it was about her that kept his eyes straying in her direction. By the time they left the party and headed back to his house, he was pissed with himself for allowing a thirteen-year-old kid to get his goat.

He took his frustration out on Pam. He walked behind her next to Paris and tried to stare a hole into the back of her head. She continued to ignore him, which made him even angrier.

"What's your problem, Pam?" he asked when he could hold it in no longer.

"Excuse me?"

She stopped walking and turned to face him. At fourteen, he was nearing the six-foot mark and she had to tilt her head back to catch his eyes. "You heard me," he said. "You think you're too good to talk to somebody?"

"I didn't hear you say nothing to me."

"I've been talking all day."

"To Paris and Nate and all those other girls, but you ain't said nothing to me. So what's *your* problem?" She propped her hands on her hips and shifted her weight to one side. Neither of them noticed the look that passed between Nate and Paris because they were too busy staring each other down.

Chad's eyes darted over her strange-looking face rapidly. Somebody must have reached in a bag, pulled out facial features and put them together on her face with no rhyme or reason. He sucked his teeth and looked away. "Whatever. You're blocking my way."

"You got a problem with me, you need to tell me what it is."

"I'll tell you when I'm good and ready to tell you."

"Whatever," she snapped and resumed walking. And Chad resumed staring at the sway of her hips.

They fought like cats and dogs every time Nate had the bright idea to force them together, which was often. She was like Nate's shadow, and Chad couldn't resist temptation. He began to look forward to the times when he could make her face flush red with a few sharp words or make her so angry he could hear the sound of her breath whistling through her nostrils. She pretended to be so tough, but he didn't have any trouble wriggling his way under her skin and taking her attitude down a few notches. It became like a game to him.

He took it a step too far the night he tagged along with Nate to walk Pam home. Earlier in the day the four of them had gone to a movie and then split up. Pam hadn't materialized again until well after ten o'clock, coming out of the shadows at the side of Nate's house like a ghost and jogging up on the porch, where they were kicked back talking trash. She had sneaked out of the home after everyone was asleep and would sneak back in when she was ready to join them.

Chad wondered how she'd managed to get past her parents and out of the house to roam the streets at all hours of the night. He was staying over at Nate's house and Nate's mother was down at the speakeasy, but what was Pam's deal? Plus, they were almost fifteen to her thirteen. She should've been in bed counting sheep, where apparently, Paris was.

He said this to her and she told him to shut up. He kept poking and prodding at her until he had her right where he wanted her, knee-deep in the middle of a heated argument that had Nate shaking his head and cracking up. For him, it was all in fun.

Until he said, "Where's your momma, anyway?" just as they came out of the woods and approached the back of the children's home where she lived. He looked from her to the home, clearly surprised.

"I don't have a momma," Pam said. "A daddy, either. Still think it's funny?" She left them there and disappeared through a window she'd left cracked for the purpose.

They didn't speak to each other for a week, mostly because Pam was giving Chad the silent treatment. If he thought she was standoffish before, it was nothing compared to the way she treated him after the night he put his foot in his mouth. He waited for an opportunity to catch her alone to apologize, but she went out of her way not to be left alone with him. And she was good at it.

When the opportunity finally presented itself, he followed her from the movie theater and caught her before she could turn off into the girls' bathroom. She hadn't known he was on her heels until he cuffed her arm, dragged her down the walkway to the rear of the building, and caged her in a dark corner.

"What's your problem?"

"You said if I had something to say I should say it, right?"

Her back was to the wall and he leaned in. She flattened a hand against his chest and nudged him away from her. His face was in her face and she couldn't breathe without sharing air with him.

"Hurry up and say it because I have to pee."

"I didn't know you lived there," he said softly.

"So what if I do?"

"So . . . nothing, I'm just saying I didn't know, that's all." She pushed him away from her again and he came back even closer. "How old are you?"

"Thirteen, why?"

"I'm almost fifteen."

"So?"

"You're too young for me."

"So why are you in my face, then?"

"That's what I'm trying to figure out. What's up with you and Nate?"

"Nothing. Did he say something was up?" she asked suspiciously, ready to take Nate's head off for lying.

"He didn't say nothing. I'm asking you." He reached up and pressed the pad of his finger into the flesh of her bottom lip, watched it sink and then rise again. She swatted his hand away irritably and he grinned.

"Stop it." She came away from the wall and pushed at his chest with both hands. "Get off me."

Instead of heeding her words, Chad dipped his head and stole a kiss. He drew back and looked into her shocked face and then stole another one. And another one after that. When her lips went slack, he slipped his tongue in her mouth. Pam had never kissed a boy before, and the experience shook her.

"Stop," she pleaded against his lips.

"You ever kiss before?"

She shook her head. "Not like this, not with tongue. I don't know how to do what you're doing."

"Open your mouth wider and put your tongue in my mouth," Chad told her. "Move your head this way."

She did as he said and let him slip his arms around her waist as they kissed. "Your tongue is in the way," she said after they pulled apart for air.

"That's part of the fun, Pam. You have to make room in my mouth for your tongue."

"Oh."

Chad grinned at the silly memory and stepped back from the window in Paris's bedroom. He had been standing there long enough to see Pam get out of a car with a strange man and then he'd heard her and Nikki talking downstairs. They spoke in low tones for several minutes and then the sound of the door closing floated up the stairs to him. Nikki hadn't told him Pam was coming to the house, nor had she told him she was leaving with Pam. He figured it out when he saw the two of them climb into a shiny new rental car, with yet another strange man, and drive off.

Worrying about Nikki's safety was the last thing on his mind. What he did worry about was Nikki becoming too attached to Pam and being let down when Pam disappeared again. No one knew better than he did the pain Pam could cause when she pulled one of her famous disappearing acts.

May 21st

Dear Diary,

Nikki went back to school today. She told me that Chad was going back to work, and since he was, he was making her go back, too. How would it look if the principal suspended other kids for skipping school and let his own daughter get away with it? she said he'd asked. I made sure to make a lot of sympathetic noises when she told me about it, but secretly I agree with him. Sunday will be two weeks since Paris died, and I know she wouldn't want Nikki to start slipping in school. Paris was all about education, and Nikki knows it.

I have spent time with her every day since the funeral, and I've decided that she is the most amazing young woman I've ever known. Talking with her feels different in person than when I called from California to see what she was up to. She tells me her secrets and her dreams and I soak them in like a sponge, thinking that I never thought I'd know these things about her. Paris was the one she confided in, and I was the one who went looking for the latest Prada bag and sent it to her right away. When she and Paris came to visit, I thought I was being the best aunt I could be by introducing her to famous people, bringing her to the studio with me to watch me record tracks, and letting her shop endlessly. But there's more growing between us now, and I don't know if I should be afraid of what's happening or not. We both know I'm not the most emotionally available person on the planet. Even scarier is the thought that I don't know how to be.

Oh, and she looks so much like Chad it kills me to look at her sometimes. She laughs and I catch myself staring at her mouth, at the way her dimples sink into her cheeks like wells, just like Chad's used to do. She has his forehead, smooth and high, with eyebrows that spread out like wings. I look at her and think that Mannie, my makeup artist, would have a field day with her eyes. They are wide, the clearest green, and deep like an ocean. They talk even when her mouth is still and the things they tell me are frightening.

I've seen videos of Nikki running track and I knew she was fast, but in person she is stunning. Whew, can she go! I tagged along with her and Kelli when they went running yesterday, and I was reminded of every minute of my thirty-five years. She is tall and slim like Chad, and I can't believe I have to look up at her when she is standing next to me. Seems like she's grown three feet since the last time I saw her. They say pictures don't really do their subjects justice, and they are absolutely right.

I'm convinced that Nikki has a future in modeling, with her smooth, brown skin and long face. Did I say she is the spitting image of Chad already? Well, she is. Except for her eyes and hair. She has the Mayes's green eyes and black hair, but everything else is purely Chad. Even the way she chews gum and blows bubbles. He has stamped everything she does.

I can't help feeling disloyal to Paris for being happy about this time I have with Nikki, because I know I never would've had it if she hadn't gone away.

I would never have come back to this godforsaken place if she were still alive.

I have to go now. I told David Dixon I would meet him for lunch at Hayden's Diner today. I'm still trying to figure out what the hell he wants with me, but I guess I have to eat, don't I?

Pam

Miles arrived at Hayden's Diner before Pam and chose a booth near the back of the room. The place had been designed to resemble a railroad car, with a Formica counter and cracked plastic stools running the length of one wall and plastic covered booths back-to-back along the opposite wall. Windows along the front of the diner afforded a view of Main Street. As he kept an eye out for Pam he wondered if every small town in America had a Main Street. Mercy's was the town's hubbub of activity, with various shops and professional offices situated in two long rows across the street from each other, like a frontier western town. The diner sat at the end of one of the rows, between a small dry cleaner and a free-standing building that housed the DMV office and a state family services center.

Pam drove up a few minutes later, spotted him through the window, and came inside. From behind her dark glasses she took in the smattering of old men seated at the counter, then angled her head so she could peruse the filled booths. Amused, Miles lifted a hand and beckoned her over to the table.

"Were you looking for the paparazzi?" he joked as she slid into the booth across from him.

A wry smile touched Pam's lips. She plucked the

glasses off her nose and dropped them inside the Cavalli tote she carried. "I don't care about the press. I'm used to them. I was checking to make sure the coast was clear of certain townsfolk, who I don't really want to see and who shall remain nameless."

"How can you get onstage and entertain a hundred thousand people without breaking a sweat and be afraid of a few harmless old folks?"

"Afraid is a strong word, and I know plenty of old folks who aren't all that harmless. Hello, Peaches," she looked up as a waitress approached their table.

"Hey, Pam." Peaches was a short, pleasingly plump woman with a wide smile and mischievous eyes. She and Pam had hung around together for a few months during their sophomore years in high school, before Peaches had gotten pregnant and been forced to slow down. She had six kids now. "How you doing?"

"I'm good. Today anyway. How's them babies?"

At the mention of her children Peaches brightened considerably. "Shoot, the oldest is damn near grown now and the baby is eleven, so they ain't babies no more, thank goodness. They're good, though. You know I hated to hear about Paris."

"Thanks." She remembered Miles and motioned across the table in his direction.

"You remember Miss Moira, Peach? This is her stepson, David. He says he's in here all the time."

"He sure is. You want the sourdough melt with homefries, right?" Her pen was poised to scribble.

"Right," Miles said, smiling. She scribbled his order down and turned to Pam expectantly.

"Does Willie still do that patty melt on marble rye with the Irish potatoes?"

"Sure does, but I thought I read somewhere that you was a vegetarian?"

"That story was in the same rag that reported finding Martians living in the White House, Peach. You know better than that. There probably are a few little green men hiding in the bowels of our nation's capitol, but you know I need my burger fix."

"So you really didn't marry that African man so he could stay in the country?"

Pam cringed good-naturedly. Miles thought she did an admirable job of covering her irritation. "The African guy was a musician. He did the track for one of my songs, and his wife and I were pleased with the results. A lot of that shit they print is lies."

"Oh," Peaches looked stumped for a moment. Then she grinned. "I don't suppose I could get an autograph for my daughter, could I? She loves your new CD."

"I'd love to Peach, but I may not be able to keep my hand steady long enough to write. I'm starting to shake from lack of sustenance. Help a sista out and bring me some food, huh? I'll sign whatever you want me to sign, just please feed me."

Miles watched Peaches move away, then folded his hands on the table. "So what was the real deal with the music producer?" He was referring to another one of the rampant rumors in which Pam had been featured. This one, he knew, had a little more truth to it than most, but he wanted to gauge her reaction.

"Not you too, David? I'm supposed to be hiding out here."

"From the mean old folks?"

"Them and the press. Between the two extremes, I don't know which is worse."

"Which reminds me. Melva Howard still thinks you were the ruination of her son. Junebug, I believe she said his name was."

A while later, Pam picked up the water glass Peaches

set in front of her and took a sip. Done mulling over the accusation, she said, "Gregory Howard was gay long before I got hold to him. All I did was encourage him to be who he really was. It's not my fault he's a male stripper now, is it? Hell, he looks better in full makeup than I do, and he was the one who taught me how to use liquid eyeliner." Melva Howard was full of shit.

His eyes skimmed her freshly scrubbed face lightly. "I just thought you should know what they were saying in the beauty salon before you went to get a haircut or something and got blindsided."

"Melva Howard can be the first in line to kiss my ass. What were you doing in the beauty salon anyway?"

"Picking Moira up. I borrowed one of your CDs from her and listened to it last night," he told her. Peaches brought their food and he dumped a mound of ketchup on a corner of his plate, soaked a fry. "I was pleasantly surprised."

"Moira has one of my CDs?" Moira was every bit of seventy-five, if she was a day.

"All six of them, and I think a poster or two."

"Hmm. And you turned off your classical music long enough to listen to my stuff?" She picked up half of her sandwich, took a big bite, and chewed slowly. Nobody did a burger like Willie. Here was another thing she had truly missed in all her years away.

"Yes, I did. Why does that surprise you? Almost half of your fan base is non-black and your music consistently crosses over. Did you notice that trend starting before or after your torrid love affair with Jose Marillo?"

"After," Pam blurted out. She immediately realized what she'd said and closed her eyes for the space of three seconds. Jose was the music producer he'd asked about earlier, the one who was also married with four children. Just as he had been ten years ago, when he and Pam began working together.

Pam concentrated on eating her food, taking reasonably sized bites and chewing thoroughly before swallowing. "I didn't mean for that to come out," she said after a while.

"It's not like the press didn't have an inkling," Miles said, wanting to put her at ease. Besides the fact that he needed to keep her talking, the haunted look in her eyes made him uneasy. "You haven't scandalized me."

"If you know anything about me, you know I neither confirm nor deny any of the silly rumors that circulate from time to time about me."

"You hardly talk to the press at all."

"Exactly, and there's a reason for that."

"Which is?" He looked at her steadily.

"I don't have anything to say to them. My life is my own, and I'd just as soon not have the world know everything there is to know. Just because I sing a song and you like it enough to buy it, does that mean you have the right to know everything about me?"

"I wouldn't say so, no."

He wiped his mouth with a napkin and processed what he'd confirmed so far. The affair with Jose Marillo was true, and he knew he could pull together at least a chapter's worth of information on that subject alone. Marillo was a hit maker, savvy and powerful, and he recalled the man's vehement denials of an affair with Pam, saying that they were just good friends and industry associates. Miles hadn't believed it for a minute, and he was more than a little satisfied that his instincts were on the mark. Marillo and Pam had worked together on three of her albums over a six-year period, and Miles was willing to bet their affair had lasted just as long.

"I read somewhere that your favorite dessert is banana pudding," he teased her. Something in the set of her shoulders warned him not to ask any more questions.

"That's probably one of the few things you read about me that's actually true. Willie makes the best banana pudding this side of the Mason Dixon."

"That's what I know. You want to split some with me?"

"No, but you can order your own," Pam said, pushing her plate away and smiling at him. "Some things I won't share, and banana pudding is one of them."

SEVEN

Pam parted ways with Miles outside the diner and set off on foot toward Holmes Funeral Home. She hadn't seen or talked to Jasper since the night before Paris's funeral, and she had a sudden inspiration to visit him. A few times over the years she had called him. Other times she'd written him short notes and mailed them or sent him a postcard from wherever she was vacationing at the time. He'd never written back, but she hadn't needed him to. It was enough that he knew she was thinking of him, which was usually the extent of her notes. *Doing okay. Thinking of you. Love, Pam.*

A blast of cool air greeted her as she walked into the home and she lifted her hair off the back of her neck to cool the skin there as she made her way to his office. She found him sitting behind his desk, feet propped up on a corner and a newspaper spread open in front of his face. A smile curved her lips.

"Don't you have some work to do, old man?"

The paper lowered slowly and his eyebrows shot up.

"Just got done tussling with Wilma Thomas. Even in death that woman won't cooperate. Got her in the back. You want to take a look at her?"

"I don't think so. She'd probably rise from the dead just to point a shaky finger at me and call me a whore." She left the doorway and dropped into a seat on the couch against the wall. "She finally keeled over, huh?"

"The good Lord couldn't put off taking her home any longer and not have a good excuse," Jasper said dryly. "Got some hogshead cheese and some crackers in the refrigerator upstairs."

"And that's where it's going to stay, too. Nobody eats that shit but you. A beer would go down good though."

He dropped his feet to the floor and came to a sitting position as he folded the paper. "Got that in the refrigerator right next door," he said and left the office. A few minutes later, he returned with two bottles and handed Pam one on his way back to his desk. "Saw you racing around town with Nikki earlier in the week."

"Uhhmm. She needs the distraction. I do too, come to think of it."

"And what about Chad? How's he doing?"

"Okay, I guess. I've been avoiding going over there to see for myself, but I have to go today. After I leave here, as a matter of fact." She tipped the bottle up and took a long drink. "Can't put it off any longer."

"Been what, two weeks?"

"Since Paris died, yeah. Chad wants me to help him go through her things." She looked at the floor, then brought her eyes back to Jasper's face. "I don't want to." She set her beer on the floor by her feet and fished around in her bag for her cigarettes, lit one. "Packing up her stuff makes everything real."

"It's real whether you pack up her stuff or not. How come you ain't been over to the house before today?" Bushy brows rose toward the ceiling as he leveled a serious look at her.

"I go by and pick up Nikki." She caught his look and didn't pretend not to know what it meant. "Hell, Jasper, you know why."

Jasper knew what a lot of people didn't know, and his question was loaded with the knowledge. For Pam, it wasn't as simple as going to the house where her sister had once lived, though that was part of it. Her reasons for keeping her distance had more to do with what the house represented and who was still there.

"Seems to me the time for running is long gone, Pam. You gotta go over there and help your sister's husband pack her stuff up, whether you want to or not." Jasper swallowed the last of his beer and set the bottle on his desk with a click. "You might as well go through all that other shit and pack it up too, while you at it."

"Can I come here and hide out if things get ugly?"

"Hell, you used to come here and do everything else, I don't see why not." The startled expression on her face had him throwing his head back and cackling with laughter before he could catch himself.

"Where's Nikki?"

"She went over to a friend's house." Chad closed the door and locked it. "She didn't want to be here. I'm supposed to call her after we're done."

Except for a dim light in the kitchen, the house was dark. Pam's eyes darted around nervously, looking for some place to land other than on his face. He was still dressed for work in khakis and a navy blazer. Underneath it an oxford cloth shirt was unbuttoned far enough to reveal the neckline of his undershirt. He looked tired.

"Long day?"

"It's about to get longer. You sure you can do this?" He took his glasses off and swiped the back of his hand across the bridge of his nose.

"You don't think it's too soon?"

"Is there a timetable?"

"Isn't there?" she snapped, meeting his eyes, then looking away again.

He took a long time looking at her, silently willing her eyes to stop skipping around and stay on his and slightly angered that she wouldn't let them. When his fingers itched to reach out and touch her, he smoothed them over his head instead. "I didn't buy the handbook for this kind of thing, Pam. But somehow I don't think maintaining a shrine will help either."

"What if I can't do it?"

"Just do what you can do, okay?"

She followed him up the stairs on stiff legs and crossed the threshold into the first bedroom on the left, the one Chad gestured to wearily as he continued down the hallway. From the doorway, she watched his back until it disappeared from sight and then felt along the wall for the light switch. Both nightstand lamps flickered on and the room came alive for her searching eyes.

Pink. Nearly everything was some shade of pink. The drapes and duvet were a deep rose, the chaise and walls a soft pink. The furniture was white washed oak, contemporary in style and functional looking. There was a stack of paperback books on one nightstand and a cordless phone on the other. On the dresser, Paris's jewelry box was open and various pieces of jewelry spilled out, as if she had been rambling through it just minutes ago trying to decide between a silver pendant and a gold brooch. Pam went over and lifted a slender gold chain from the box. She held it up to the light and noticed Chad leaning against the doorjamb. He had changed into jeans and a polo shirt.

"You haven't changed a bit."

"Gained a little weight here and there. I could say the same about you."

"It's different with me. You've seen me on television or wherever." She put the necklace back where she'd found it and looked around the room. "I didn't know what to expect with you. Didn't know if you'd gotten fat or gone bald or what. You weren't in many of the pictures I got, the videos either."

"I wish I could describe for you what I felt the first time I saw you on television or heard your voice on the radio." He came away from the doorjamb and moved deeper into the room. "Nikki would be having a fit, jumping up and down and screaming at the top of her lungs and I'd be sitting there like a block of ice, stunned. I always thawed out long enough to tell her to be quiet, so I could hear, though."

"She still has the tape I gave her from the time I took her in the studio with me."

Nikki was seven and bursting with energy, asking every five minutes to *do* something. As if walking around the zoo for hours on end until Pam's feet were throbbing was nothing. After ten o'clock had come and gone and Nikki still wasn't asleep, Pam had carted her off to the recording studio with her; Snoopy house-shoes, ballerina pajamas, and all. They had spent an hour in the soundproof booth, singing Stevie Wonder's

"I Just Called To Say I Love You" before Nikki finally conked out on a couch and Pam could get down to business.

"She played it every night for a month. I thought I saw Stevie coming out of her room one night, it got so bad," Chad joked. They laughed together and some of the tension eased away. "Paris was so proud of you."

"I was proud of her," Pam said. "Out of the two of us, she was the one who stuck it out and made a life for herself."

"You have a good life."

"Not the one I wanted."

That gave Chad pause. He didn't know what to say, so he didn't say anything and Pam didn't seem inclined to elaborate. There was so much she wanted to say and so much he wanted to ask, but time and distance divided them, kept their eyes away from each other's. Finally, he suggested they start the process of sorting through Paris's clothing by emptying the closet and drawers and making stacks on the bed. Pam slid the closet door open and stepped inside, grateful for the distraction of having something purposeful to do, even if doing it might kill her before she was done.

Paris's tendency toward obsessive neatness and order was evident in the structure of the closet; the arrangement of the clothes hanging on the rack. Pants, then skirts, then jackets, and then blouses. Shoes lined up neatly on the closet floor by pairs, sneakers in the far left corner and dress shoes on the right. Loafers and casual flats front and center.

Pam brought an armful of pants over to the bed and glanced at Chad, who was doing the same with a stack of shirts from a drawer, and turned to retrace her steps. At the one-hour mark, Chad reached over and turned on the bedside radio to keep them company.

Pam caught herself humming along and singing under her breath and stopped abruptly. She shot a look at Chad and found him leaning against the armoire, watching her.

"What?"

"What kind of life did you want?"

Pam dropped the shoes she was carrying on the bed and wiped her palms on the seat of her pants. "I don't know, the same as everybody else, I guess. I figured I'd have a couple of kids, a husband, and a pain-in-the-ass mother-in-law. The whole deal."

"You never met a man in California you wanted to marry and have kids with?"

They looked at each other. "I didn't go there looking for a man, Chad."

"So you went there to get away from one?"

"Is that what you thought?"

"What else was I supposed to think? Paris couldn't or wouldn't tell me why you left and you never answered any of my letters. I came to the only logical conclusion there was. You no longer wanted what we had and you left to get away from me."

"I had . . . there were . . ." She struggled to grab hold to the right word and came up empty. "Things I needed to straighten out."

"Things," he said slowly, looking confused.

"Yes, things," she snapped anxiously. "Things that had nothing to do with you. Why would I need to get away from you when what we had was one of the best things going on in my life?"

"Why couldn't we talk about whatever those things were and still find a way to be together, Pam?"

"By the time I was ready to talk to you, you were married to Paris. There was nothing to say after that."

"What are these things you're talking about? Tell me . . ."

She put up her hands as if the action had the power to physically stop his words and sighed disgustedly. "Come on, Chad. Could we just . . . can we just . . . do this and get it over with?"

"Just tell me this." He came away from the armoire and towered over her. "Did you ever really love me like you said you did? Was I the only one who felt that way, or were you there too?"

"What's the point of answering that question now?"

"The point," he hissed, "is that I'll finally know if the last fifteen years was worth what I gave up to have them."

She took her eyes from his and stared at his chest, suddenly mute.

She watched him walk out of the room, leaving her surrounded by pink, and cursed under her breath. She told herself to let him go.

Yet . . . "Chad . . ."

She didn't know which room he'd disappeared into. There were four other doors off the upstairs hallway and they were all closed. She opened the first door and saw that it was a bathroom. The second door led to Nikki's room. A jumbled full-sized bed with clothes strewn across the mattress greeted her and she closed the door on the mess. The guest bedroom was quiet as a tomb and obviously hadn't been used in quite some time. He wasn't there.

Pam turned the last doorknob and stepped into the room hesitantly. The color scheme was masculine, the bed huge and neatly made. Cologne bottles were lined up on the bureau, and a wallet and spare change were tossed carelessly next to them. Chad sat on the bed, watching her take it all in.

"What is this?" Then it began to make sense. A completely pink room, containing all of Paris's things and none of Chad's. She hadn't stopped to wonder where his clothes were while she was milling through Paris's. Hadn't stopped to question the lack of male presence in the space down the hall. Shocked, she looked at Chad as her mouth worked to form words that wouldn't come.

"My room," he said, remembering another room, in another time and place. The look on her face told him that she was fighting it and him, trying to pull her eyes away from his but unable to do it. She was remembering too.

The curtains were pulled closed, the lights were off, and the bed was squeaking. It wasn't the rhythmic sound sometimes heard coming from grown folks' rooms after dark, so you knew they were inside doing something that they knew how to do, but rather the frantic dip and sway of bedsprings unused to the vigorous activity being forced upon them.

Pam was pressed to the mattress beneath Chad's clumsy weight. He was trying to hold his weight off of her and coax her panties down at the same time, and she was trying to see what he was doing in the darkness. Their foreheads collided and they both gasped, then giggled.

"Leave my panties alone. Just 'cause you always want your *thing* hanging out don't mean mine has to be," she whispered.

Months ago they had progressed past the heavy petting stage to a point where Chad now pulled out his *thing* for her to touch as they kissed. A few times she had let him touch her inside her panties, but she'd never taken them all the way off. That was going too far.

"What do you have against my *thing*?" He shifted his weight to one side and propped his head on his hand, staring down into her face. "I thought you said you liked it?" He took her hand and brought it down to where his *thing* lived, thick and hard, a bead of moisture sitting on the tip.

"I do like it. I just don't want it anywhere near *my thing*. That's how trouble starts. You heard about Iris Taylor, didn't you?"

Iris was a freshman, just like Pam was, and pregnant, like Pam didn't want to be. Letting Chad put his mouth on her breasts wouldn't make her pregnant. Letting him touch her *down there* and touching him the same way wouldn't make her pregnant. But if his *thing* got near her *thing*, there was no telling what might happen.

"Come on, Pam," he pleaded, easing his tongue in her mouth as his hand slipped inside her panties. She gasped as his fingers raked through the mound of coarse hair there, then moved lower, where she was wet. A while back he had discovered the wonders of her clitoris and now he knew what to do to make her forget to think. "Ain't nobody gonna know. I won't even put it in. You tell Nate or Paris you was coming here?"

"No, did you?"

His finger slid inside her and her thighs parted all by themselves. Her hips rocked against the palm of his hand, searching for something she couldn't name. He'd made her come like that before, and she wanted to experience the feeling again.

"No, so you know I ain't gone tell nobody nothing else. You can't get pregnant if I don't put it in."

"I might," she said, still not entirely convinced of the gospel as he told it. What did boys know?

"You won't. Trust me."

She lifted her butt and let him slide her panties down and off. Then he climbed off the bed long enough to quickly step out of his pants and his Fruit of the Looms. He settled himself on top of her in the middle of the bed and braced himself on his hands. She was warm and wet and Chad sighed as he coaxed her *thing* into allowing his *thing* to lay within its soft folds. He rocked against her and watched her face, transfixed by what he saw there.

Pam rocked with him and came minutes later. It was like having his fingers touch her down there, only better. She didn't know what she was feeling was called an orgasm, she just knew that whatever it was, was indescribable. Her legs shook, her mouth fell open, and her fingers tightened around Chad's waist. During all the friction, Chad entered her and once there, he stayed. It was an accident, and he knew he should've immediately fixed the mistake, but he couldn't believe how good it felt to be inside Pam.

Pam's eyes flew open. "Get out," she hissed urgently, pushing at his chest. "You have to get out."

"It feels good, Pam." Never in his wildest dreams had he thought it would feel this good. His hips rotated automatically, pushing forward though his mind screamed for him to stop. "*Shit*, it feels *good*. You're squeezing me."

All Pam felt was pain. Every time his hips pushed forward a sound of distress filled the room. He wasn't stopping and she scared herself by not really wanting him to. He came fully into her and sank down to rest his damp forehead against hers.

"You okay? Does it hurt real bad?"

"At first it was bad, but it's not too bad now. We have to stop though, Chad. What if you get me pregnant?"

"I won't, Pam. I promise I won't. *Shit* . . . you feel that?" The expression on her face said she didn't, so he put his lips on hers and began kissing her deeply as he rocked against her, hoping to give her some of the pleasure he felt.

One kiss melted into another, until they were kissing with an intensity and depth new to both of them. Now that he had discovered the feel of her, he had no intention of rushing through what they were doing. He rose and pulled his T-shirt over his head, then helped Pam shrug out of her top. When they were both completely naked, he went back up on his hands and made love to her for the first time.

The memory still had Pam in its grip days after Chad subtly reminded her of its existence. She carried it around with her everywhere she went and it tipped up on her at the oddest moments, stealing her breath and snatching her train of thought from the present to the past. She was having lunch with Nikki when it crept into her consciousness yet again, possibly for the thousandth time. Nikki couldn't help but notice the change almost as soon as it happened.

"Aunt Pam?"

Nikki stared across the table curiously, wondering at the faraway look in her aunt's eyes. A few minutes ago, she'd frozen right in the middle of spooning up shrimp bisque and now she sat there with one hand wrapped around the stem of her spoon and the other pressed to her chest, as if she had been caught off guard by something only she could see. She wondered if her aunt was having some sort of allergic reaction that she didn't know enough to recognize.

"Aunt Pam," she repeated with more force. Pam still didn't respond and she reached over and squeezed her shoulder gently. *Please don't let her start choking,* Nikki prayed. She threw an appraising look around the dining room of the B&B, hoping to catch someone's eye, but the other diners were caught up in their own meals and for once, not staring at Pam.

Pam felt the contact on her shoulder and shook herself out of the past with a low moan. She looked at Nikki and let a smile curve her lips, though it was the last thing she felt like doing. The concerned expression on Nikki's face turned the phony smile into a genuine one in seconds.

"Stop looking like that. I'm fine, I promise." She spooned up more bisque to prove her point.

"Where did you go?"

Pam was seriously considering the best way to answer the question and still be as truthful as possible. But, she still noticed Nikki's hand inching across the tablecloth toward the glass of chardonnay she'd ordered for herself. She'd made the mistake of letting her have a small sip earlier, and now Nikki seemed to be taken with the light, crisp wine. She angled a look toward the offending hand. "Don't even think about it. I'm sending you home with alcohol on your breath as it is. Any more and Chad will have me arrested. Plus, you're underage." On her way to moving the glass out of Nikki's reach, she paused to take a sip. "I was just thinking about when your mom and I were kids. Not too much younger than you. We had some good times."

"You miss Mom a lot, don't you?" Pam held out her hands and Nikki immediately placed hers inside them. She gave her aunt's hands a squeeze and sighed as she felt a squeeze in return.

"I miss her like I would miss an arm or a leg and I know you do, too. She'll always be with us though."

"How? Everything she left behind is gone. It's like her presence is being erased or something."

"You weren't ready for her things to be put away?"

"I mean, I know it had to be done, but I would've been happy to leave her room like it was for the next twenty years. It's sick to want to do that, isn't it?" She searched Pam's face intently.

"It's not sick to feel that way." A sneaky smile crept across Pam's face. "But if you had actually done that, I would've had to put a sign up in the yard, advertising a vacancy at the Bates Motel and then start calling you Norman."

"Aunt Pam!" Nikki gasped, and then burst out laughing. She took her hands away from Pam's to cover her mouth.

They laughed together for a moment and then Pam was serious again. "She's still with us, Nikki, just not physically. I don't know about you, but I'll never forget the way she sounded when she laughed or how she looked when she was happy about something."

"She was beautiful," Nikki said softly.

"I guess I can take that as a compliment, huh?" Pam desperately wanted to lighten the mood. If they kept going like this she'd be crying in her food in no time.

"You can if you want to, but you and Mom kind of looked different to me."

"Excuse me?"

Nikki noticed the look on Pam's face and laughed again. "I didn't mean it like that, Aunt Pam. You're beautiful, too. I just meant that if you looked really closely, you could see different things about you and Mom."

"We were alike in a lot of ways, too. After you came along it was like we suddenly had a third twin, if that makes any sense. You got a lot of our mannerisms and personality traits. It was a little scary."

"Really?" She was pleased by the thought of having noticeable similarities to her mom and her glamorous aunt.

"Really. Is that your mother's charm bracelet I see on your wrist?" Pam reached across the table and fingered the delicate silver bracelet.

"Yeah, I got it out of her jewelry box. She never let me wear it when I was little because she always thought I'd break it or lose it. I won't lose it now, though."

"She'd want you to have it."

"You still wear yours?"

"Since I was sixteen." Pam pulled up her sleeve and held out her arm to show that she was wearing an identical bracelet.

Nikki noticed something different about Pam's bracelet right away. "Where's the charm I like, the one with the little hearts next to each other and the diamond in between?" It was her favorite.

Pam chose her words carefully, spoke slowly. "When your mom died, she took part of my heart with her, so I buried the charm with her."

"Oh . . . Aunt Pam. You want me to cry, don't you? Why only part of your heart?"

"Because you have the other part," Pam said simply.

Tears filled Nikki's eyes and she rushed to wipe them away. "I love you, but please don't say things like that. You'll make my mascara start running."

"You're wearing mascara now? When did this happen?"

"I'm seventeen now," Nikki said as if it should be obvious that she was now a woman. She rolled her eyes toward the ceiling, thinking that a lecture was coming.

Pam caught her breath. "I know exactly how old you are, Nikki. Right down to the minute. Oh, before I forget, I have something for you." She reached under the table and pulled her Gucci tote in her lap. "And no, it's not the bag," she said with a smile. She lifted Paris's diary out and handed it across the table.

"What is it?" Nikki stared at the floral-print cover curiously.

"Your mom's diary. I know she'd want you to have it, and I'm hoping it'll help you feel close to her when you need to."

Several minutes passed before Nikki spoke again. She spent the time staring at the book, stroking the cloth cover and fighting back tears. She swallowed and looked at Pam. "You should have this, Aunt Pam. I know how close you and Mom were. You'll need something to help you feel close to her, too."

"I have other things to help me do that. Plus, I have thirty-five years of the best memories saved up. You didn't get to have that, so you should have this. Keep it safe for me, okay?"

"I will. I promise I will."

"Here." Pam held the wineglass out to Nikki. "One more sip. You look like you need it more than I do."

Chad chose that moment to walk into the dining room. He hung back long enough to see his daughter take one, then two sips of wine, then he approached the table like he was outraged.

"First, staying out all times of the night and now drinking? Nikki, I can't believe this. I thought I taught you better?"

Nikki's head shot up in alarm. She was poised to offer every flimsy excuse she could think of. Then she saw the playful gleam in her dad's eyes. She knew when to take him seriously and when he was teasing her. "It was only one sip, dad, and Aunt Pam let me have it."

Pam's mouth dropped open. "Oh, now see that was just wrong. If he was the police I'd be going to jail right about now, thank you very much. In my day kids knew how to keep a secret."

"They sure did," Chad seconded, catching Pam's eye. "What is the world coming to?"

Pam snatched her eyes from his and put them back on Nikki, where they were safe. "Well, since we're telling on each other. Nikki went over her limit on your charge card today, Chad." The gasp Nikki uttered was comical and Pam smiled wickedly. "By a hundred dollars, too."

Nikki dropped her head in her hand as if to say, *no she didn't just go there.* "Aunt Pam let me drive ninety miles an hour on the interstate."

Pam nodded that everything was fine. She pushed her bowl away and downed the rest of her wine. "You got me there, Nikki. I'm so ashamed about that, it almost makes me forget I paid the three speeding tickets you already had and got them changed to non-moving violations, so your dad would never find out that you drive like a bat out of hell with or without me. God, I'm so absentminded." She smacked her forehead dramatically.

This time Nikki's shocked gasp stole her breath and made her cough. Chad took it upon himself to pat her on her back none too gently. "Three tickets?" he asked softly. Too softly.

Pam recognized the look and the tone instantly. A little clean up was definitely in order. "Actually, Chad, it was more like one ticket. Something about parking too close to a fire hydrant, I think."

"Thanks a lot, Aunt Pam. You probably just got me grounded."

"No probably to it," Chad told her. He glanced at the

shopping bags stacked next to her chair. "Why don't you take your bags out to the car and wait for me? I'll be out in a minute. I want to yell at your aunt a little bit."

Pam and Nikki got to their feet slowly, staring at each other across the table. *Are we in trouble*, Nikki's eyes asked? *Hell if I know*, Pam's responded. Pam shrugged and leaned in to kiss Nikki's lips. While she was close enough, she whispered to her that she'd work on Chad and for Nikki not to worry.

"I'll see you later," she said, hefting her bag and squinting meaningfully at Nikki.

Chad watched Nikki until she was out of sight, then he turned on Pam. "You paid her tickets?" He was incredulous.

"Only one," she lied smoothly. "And she only drove for a split second. You know she's exaggerating about the speed, right?" She waved a hand distractedly, on purpose. "And like, one sip of wine, just to take the edge off. I gave her Paris's diary and we were both worked up and . . ."

He cut in. "Pam?"

"What?"

"Are these your bags?" He pointed to the two bags she had as a result of her shopping excursion to Atlanta.

"Yeah, but you don't have to . . ."

"I'll carry them upstairs for you." When she didn't move, Chad motioned for her to start walking. "Lead the way."

Left with no choice, Pam led him up two flights of stairs to her room. Hers was the only room on the top floor, a converted attic that resembled an efficiency apartment. It was normally billed as the honeymoon suite and it had come equipped with its own bath-

room, a sitting area with a modest entertainment center, and a table and chairs. The sturdy lock on the door
was the main draw, though. She used her key to let
them in and gestured for him to set the bags by the
door.

"This is nice," Chad said, looking around leisurely.

"It serves the purpose. You won't be too hard on
Nikki, will you?"

"Oh yeah, I plan on beating her to within an inch of
her life. She knows I could never stay mad at her for
more than two minutes, and it's been longer than that
now, so I would say she's safe." He pushed his hands in
his pockets and rocked back on his heels, considering
her. "I wanted to thank you for helping me out the
other day. I appreciate it."

"I would've regretted it if I hadn't helped you. I
needed to do it." She dropped her bag on the table and
stepped out of her shoes. Her height was significantly
decreased and she tilted her head back to catch his
eyes.

"I know. How are you doing otherwise?"

"Okay. You?"

"Okay. I better give you this before I forget. I've been
carrying it in my pocket since I found it." Chad pulled
something from his pocket and held it out to her. She
looked down at the earring blankly, unable to place it.
"It must've fallen out of your ear when you ran from
the house." Ten silent seconds passed. "Not long after
you came to my room."

"Oh." She reached out for the earring, fisted her
hand around it in the palm of his hand and felt his fingers close around hers. The contact had her eyes sliding closed and her head shaking slowly.

Chad tugged once, then again on her hand and she
came forward one, then two steps. He tugged again

and dipped his head in search of her lips. His tongue shot out and licked her lips lightly, then he reached up and palmed the back of her head. She gasped and it was all the invitation he needed.

His tongue was inside Pam's mouth like the past eighteen years had never happened. He took her head back on her neck and pressed into her as far as his lips would allow, hungry for the feel and taste of her after going without them for so long. She kissed him back just as greedily and opened her mouth wider with each passing second.

"Stop, Chad," she eventually whispered. She pressed cold fingers to his lips to stop their progress when they would've come at her again.

"I got you out of the habit of saying that a long time ago," he murmured. His arms snaked around her waist and pulled her against him. He dropped soft kisses on her neck and teased the skin there with the tip of his tongue. "Ask me how long I've been sleeping in that room, Pam."

"I don't want to know that." Her own hands slid up his back and flattened against his shoulder blades. She rested her forehead on his chest and breathed deeply.

"Don't you want to know why?"

She shook her head and fit her body to his. A groan rumbled in Chad's throat as he scooped her up in his arms and squeezed her tightly. She squeezed him back just as tightly and made him curse viciously.

"This is why," he whispered close to her face. "This is why, Pam. Damn, I missed you."

EIGHT

Nikki took the diary with her to her room and closed the door. She hadn't known that her mom kept a diary and now, actually holding the heavy book in her hands, she felt like she had a piece of her mother that no one else had ever had. Her mom's private thoughts and feelings were inside, her secret hopes and dreams, and just thinking about it made Nikki want to cry.

She laid the book inside her nightstand drawer, where she kept her own diary, and flopped back on her bed. She could pretty much guess what was inside her mom's diary. Paris Greene was probably the most predictable person in the whole world. Growing up, Nikki found comfort in the routines her mother had kept to. Dinner at six-thirty, always, unless there was an emergency, which there never was, and laundry on Mondays, Wednesdays, and Fridays. Meatloaf with red sauce on Thursdays and pot-roast on Sundays after church. She'd always known what to expect from her mom;

what she could get away with and what she shouldn't even bother trying to get away with.

Nikki guessed that the book was filled with Paris's thoughts and feelings about her work and about their home life. There were probably a hundred pages about the stunts she'd pulled and the gray hair she'd caused. Just thinking about a few of those stunts brought tears to Nikki's eyes. She'd give anything to have her mom standing over her, shouting at the top of her lungs right now. To walk into the kitchen and see her mom standing at the stove, making dinner.

Whatever her mom had written about, Nikki wasn't sure she could ever bring herself to open the diary and look. If she had a question about something she read, she couldn't go to her mom and ask her about it. She'd never be able to talk with anyone about what she read, and that would only magnify the loss she felt. It was enough that she had the book. She could press her nose to the cover and smell her mom's perfume, rub her hands across the cover and know that her mom's hands had done the same thing. It was a way to connect, just like Aunt Pam said it would be.

Nikki rolled to her stomach and stacked her hands under her head, deep in thought. Almost three weeks had passed since Pam had arrived and Nikki was holding her breath, waiting on the day her aunt announced that she was leaving. She didn't know what she'd do when the day came. It didn't even bear thinking about. Her dad was great, but having him around wasn't the same as having another woman around to talk to.

Aunt Pam was the complete opposite of her mom in a lot of ways, and Nikki didn't feel shy about bringing up certain things to her. They had talked about sex a few days ago and Pam hadn't started talking in riddles and turning red in the face as she answered questions.

Nikki remembered that her mom had had trouble getting past talking about the purpose of menstruation, let alone discussing the actual mechanics of sex, and in the end, her dad was the one who'd explained everything to her. But Pam talked freely and openly about it, and even Nikki had blushed at some of the things she'd said. That was Aunt Pam for you, though.

She'd made Nikki promise not to have sex until she was absolutely sure she was ready to handle the consequences, whatever they were. And there were always consequences, she said. The only time she'd clammed up was when Nikki had asked her how old she was when she'd had sex for the first time. That question, Nikki suddenly realized, was never answered.

Nikki was sure that her Aunt Pam had a lot of knowledge to pass on. Her mom had been there every day in boring Mercy, Georgia, but Aunt Pam had traveled all over the world, done a lot of things and she knew a lot of people. She'd seen her in magazines, looking glamorous and with super fine men. She kept up with all the gossip and she knew that her aunt had had a few high-powered boyfriends. And she listened to the songs she sang about being in love and how great it was. You couldn't go through all that and not know some things.

Nikki hadn't yet mentioned it to anyone, but her future was all planned out. As soon as she graduated from high school she was planning to get the hell out of Mercy. She wanted to go to college, but she wanted to do it in California, where Pam lived. She'd never broached the subject with her parents, but she knew she would have to bring it up to her dad soon because it was getting close to time to start talking about college and applying to schools. Her mom had always said that Aunt Pam had itchy feet and that's why she left Mercy all those years ago. Well, Nikki guessed she had the same itchy feet, because she was waiting on the day she could do the same thing.

Mercy wasn't so bad that she'd stay away forever, though. Unlike Pam, she wouldn't let a death be the only reason she came back. She'd come back to visit her dad and her friends, and to visit her mom, so she wouldn't get lonely out there in the cemetery by herself, but she was leaving. That part wasn't up for negotiation. She hoped her dad didn't blow a gasket when she told him.

She looked up at the knock on her door. "Come in."

Chad opened the door wide enough to stick his head inside the room. "You coming down for dinner?" He looked around the cluttered room like he thought something might jump out and bite him. Discarded clothing covered almost every available surface. "This room gives me a migraine every time I see it."

"Yours doesn't look much better."

"I pay the bills, so mine doesn't have to look better. Come on down and help me eat some of the casserole Ms. Harrison forced on me," he said. "I don't want to have to look her in the face and lie about eating it the next time I see her in the grocery store."

Nikki's face wrinkled knowingly. "Mom always brought Ms. Harrison's cakes in the house and put them straight in the trash. You should work on being a better liar, dad."

"It's either the casserole or sandwiches and at least the casserole is hot. And lying isn't the best habit to be perfecting, I don't think. Tell you what, help me eat some of it and we'll go out tomorrow."

She pushed off the bed and straightened her shirt on her way to the door. She was a tall girl, but her dad was even taller. She looked up at him and smiled. "Can we invite Aunt Pam to go with us?"

Caught off guard, Chad looked at Nikki for more seconds than were necessary for such a simple question. "She might have other plans," he finally said.

"She might not. Why don't you want to ask her?"

"I didn't say I didn't want to ask her. I just said she might be busy." He released the door so she could move past him into the hallway.

Nikki turned to study his face shrewdly. "You don't like Aunt Pam very much, do you, Dad? That's why you hardly talk to her and why you guys argue all the time."

Surprised, Chad's mouth fell open. "What?" was all he could think to say. Anything else would've given up the ghost, providing his daughter with more information than was really necessary for her to have. Still though, he couldn't help but think back on the origins of her question. For a long time hatred was the very thing he felt whenever he thought of Pam; that and incomprehensible anger. He'd held himself in check for as long as he could, thinking that he'd mastered his emotions and made peace with his life, but it hadn't taken him long to discover that he was only fooling himself.

Paris hadn't known what to think when he finally did blow up, and for his part, he hadn't been thinking at all. He'd only been feeling. The day came back to him as he stared at Nikki, the cause of it all.

He beat Paris to the phone by scant seconds, snatching up the receiver and punching in numbers like he was possessed. Paris was pulling on his shirt and whispering for him to hang up and the longer he held the phone to his ear, the more agitated she became. Tired of her antics and oblivious to her distress, Chad yanked his shirt out of her grasp and stalked over to the door to slam it shut. Nikki was down the hall in her room, watching another one of those goddamn tapes she was fascinated with, ones of Pam prancing around onstage like she didn't have a care in the world and he didn't want her to overhear.

The phone dragged across the floor with each step he took, knocking against furniture and stretching the cord, but he was beyond caring. He stared at Paris's tear-drenched face and felt nothing but anger.

Pam answered the phone on the other end and he sucked in a sharp breath before saying what he had called to say.

"What the fuck were you thinking, Pam?" He fought to keep his voice even and reasonable, but it was damn hard to do.

"I don't know what..." Pam began.

"You don't know? You don't *know*, Pam?" He took two steps backward and pinched the bridge of his nose. "You're a selfish bitch, do you know that?" He heard Pam's shocked gasp and thought about going through the phone. "There's a little girl here who has no clue just how selfish you are. You send all those silly presents and all that other bullshit, but it doesn't mean a fucking thing. And it doesn't make up for the fact that you abandoned your child."

Finally able to speak, Pam's voice floated through the phone softly. He could hear that she was crying. "Please don't do this to me, Chad. Not now. I can't . . ."

"Don't tell me what you can't do, Pam. You can do whatever the fuck you want to do. You can sneak away to have my child and you can give her to your sister like she's a purse you don't want anymore, but you can't tell me anything?" He waited for her response and silence reigned when none was forthcoming.

"Chad . . . please . . ." Paris begged pitifully. She was still confused as to what had set him off. Everything had happened so fast. One minute he was in the kitchen pouring himself a glass of juice and the next thing she knew, the glass was sailing across the room, crashing into the wall and juice was flying everywhere. Then he was racing off, searching for the phone to "call the lying bitch."

She tugged on his shirt one time too many and Chad lost it. He smacked Paris's hands away roughly and sent her stumbling backward with fear in her eyes. "This is too much," he said to Pam. "Both of you, plotting and scheming to keep me away from my child. I could accept that you left if that was all there was to it Pam, but this shit you pulled is over the goddamn top. You don't give a shit about how you've fucked up Paris's life, you don't give a shit about how you've fucked up Nikki's life, and you don't give a shit about what you've done to me. Did you think about any of that when you thought up your fucking master plan?"

"It wasn't supposed to be like this," Pam whispered. The call had come through in the middle of a recording session. She was huddled in a corner, trying to keep from being overheard and hoping that Chad's voice didn't carry too far. "You don't understand."

"Oh, I think I understand perfectly. I understand that we were together and you left. I understand that you were pregnant and you didn't tell me. I understand that you gave my child away without so much as asking me how I felt about that and I understand that you are a sick, self-absorbed bitch."

"You married my sister and you're calling me sick?"

"What else was I supposed to do?" Across the room, Paris started at the tone of his voice, and across the country, Pam pressed shaky fingers to her eyelids and held in a sob. "What the fuck was I supposed to do, Pam, huh? How else would I have had the chance to raise my child? What other options did you give me?"

Pam was silent.

"Answer me!" Chad shouted and both Paris and Pam began crying. He looked askance at Paris and uttered a harsh string of curse words in Pam's ear. "I came there looking for you once. Did you know that?" He didn't notice the shocked expression on Paris's face. "I came there looking for you, to see if you had the guts to look me in my face and lie to me. You weren't there, though, and now I know that's a good thing because I would've fucking killed you, you bitch."

Paris leapt off the bed and came toward him. "Chad, that's enough. Give me the phone."

"Fuck you, Pam," Chad kept talking. "Fuck everything we had, fuck everything we were, and fuck you. I hope I never see your fucking face again." With that, he dropped the phone on the bed and scrubbed his hands across his face.

Paris grabbed the receiver and pressed it to her chest, staring at him. "You went there?"

"Hell yes, I went there. Did you think I wouldn't? You tell that bitch her shit is done. She comes here and I'll kill her with my bare hands." He went in the adjoining bathroom and slammed the door behind him.

Six long months had passed before he was able to pick up the phone, hear Pam's voice on the other end asking to speak with Paris or Nikki and not hang up on her.

Too many years had passed for his feelings to still be as raw and inflamed as they were back then. Yet Nikki had picked up on them easily and accurately, making him wonder just how much she'd sensed when he thought she was too young to be aware of everything that was going on over her head. She had enough on her plate to deal with, without the added worry of strife among her remaining family. And wasn't it his responsibility to see that she was as happy as she could be under the circumstances?

"Call your aunt and ask her about dinner tomorrow night," Chad told Nikki. "You're right, she might not be busy." He passed the salt across the kitchen table and forced himself to pick up his fork and eat.

NINE

Miles left his hotel room intending to enjoy an early evening drive around Mercy and then to stop by Moira's to visit. The truth of the matter was that he was becoming restless and just a little bored with Mercy, Georgia. Even though the town wasn't far from Atlanta, where there was always something interesting going on, it was trapped in a time warp. Old men still sat outside playing board games and sipping from bottled sodas, old women still met on the sidewalks and spent interminable minutes gossiping, and kids still preferred playing outdoors as opposed to gluing themselves to the nearest television screen.

There was exactly one nightclub, which was still called a speakeasy, on the north end of town and it did a brisk business, exactly four sit-down restaurants, one of which was a buffet, and a bowling alley that doubled as a hotspot for local teens on Saturday nights. For anything more exciting than a movie that had premiered everywhere else at least a month prior, and a mediocre meal, the sixty-seven-mile drive to Atlanta was absolutely necessary. He could go crazy here, with little to no effort on his part.

As he slowed his car to a crawl in front of the barbershop, Miles wondered if he had stepped out of the twenty-first century and back into the fifties. A rousing game of checkers was in progress at a sidewalk table and he saw that Clive Parker was one of the contestants. Three or four spectators crowded around the table and he contemplated parking his car and joining them. He'd chatted with Clive several times since coming to town and he was suddenly in the mood to do more chatting this evening. If he hung around long enough, he could probably talk Clive into joining him for a beer after the game. There were still a few questions he needed answered.

Miles had run into Minnie Peoples in the grocery store and shamelessly used Moira's name to put the woman at ease about talking with him. All he'd had to do was pretend to be awed by the fact that Pam was in town, ask Minnie if she enjoyed Pam's music, and open his ears. She was long-winded and leaning toward senility, but from her he'd learned that Pam was considered to be what Minnie had delicately referred to as a "loose girl."

Minnie shared that she, like a lot of other town women, was shocked when Pam left and made something of herself, even if it was as a singer, because anybody could be a singer these days. But Pam seemed to be doing pretty well with it, so go figure. Maybe that's how she was able to sing all those songs with the suggestive words, Minnie speculated as she squeezed tomatoes and ruined them for anybody else. Lord knows the girl had taken her turn and a few other people's turns, where the boys were concerned. By the time he left Minnie, who didn't seem to notice that he hadn't

filled a cart with groceries but only gone through the
checkout with a bottled soda, Miles had names.

The names were circling around in his head a few
days later, when he managed to finagle a seat across
from Clive at the checkerboard table. While getting his
ass kicked in checkers, he was subjected to Clive's version of the third degree, which had mainly consisted
of answering questions about where he was from, who
he was related to, and why he was in town in the first
place. He was a white man in a predominantly black
town, which was cause for suspicion in itself, and Miles
didn't pretend to be unaware of that fact. Once again,
he'd used Moira's name and affiliation with the town
to put Clive and the rest of the old men at ease.

After the game, he'd pretended to be in need of a
stiff drink. He hadn't lived forty-four years without
having learned to observe people, and Clive was a clas-
sic case study. His shaking hands and the broken blood
vessels in his eyes, coupled with the fact that the liquid
in his soda bottle was a tad bit lighter than true Dr.
Pepper, had alerted Miles to the fact that Clive was a
heavy drinker. He was also a talker when his tank was
full.

Miles had sipped on the same beer all evening, treated
Clive to three refills of Jim Beam, and opened his ears.
Clive told stories of Pam running around town half-
dressed, purposely enticing men and laughing about
it, said she'd never had too much tolerance for women,
other than her twin sister, and that she was always
traipsing around with boys. Miles had casually mentioned the names Minnie had given him, and Clive was
off and running, sipping on his fourth glass.

Pam had mainly kept company with three boys back
then. Nate Woodberry, James Humphries, and Scooter
Wright. No one knew exactly what the four of them

had done when they were together because they had
always disappeared from sight the minute they con-
gregated. Hours later, they'd come storming back into
town, talking loud and looking worse for wear. No
telling what Pam was up to with those boys, Clive said.
A prevailing rumor, even today, was that Pam and
Nate were lovers, starting as early as grade school.

Miles wanted to know if Pam had started singing
early on, maybe in church as many other performers
claimed. He ran the suggestion by Clive only to have
the man throw his head back and burst out laughing.

"That gal ain't never set foot in a church the whole
time she was here," Clive declared, his speech slightly
slurred. "That's like asking if the devil splashes on holy
water for perfume."

Miles had come away from the conversation deter-
mined to track down Pam's childhood cohorts. He
hired a private detective, and within days, his portable
fax machine was humming with details.

James Humphries lived in Mesa, Arizona, where he
supported a wife and four children on a postal
worker's salary. Twenty thousand dollars had loosened
his lips enough, so that Miles now knew that Pam had
liked to walk on the wild side. He confirmed that
James was the one who'd taught her how to drive, as
she'd mentioned once during lunch. What she failed to
mention though, was the fact that she and James had
regularly experimented with drugs. Mainly marijuana,
James disclosed somewhat hesitantly, but a few times
they'd tried small amounts of cocaine. Apparently,
Pam hadn't liked the numbing effects of the drug and
she'd quickly vetoed it. The marijuana was obtained
locally, while the cocaine had come by way of his older
brother, who was in college at the time.

James revealed that he and Pam were never sexually

involved, but that he thought maybe she and Scooter had messed around a few times, though he couldn't say for sure. And Miles would never be able to say for sure either, because he learned that Scooter Wright had moved to Shiloh, Illinois, where he was shot and killed by his wife eleven years ago.

He moved on down the list to Nate Woodberry and paused. Of the three men, Nate was the most difficult to pinpoint. Even without the information he'd obtained, Miles was aware of Nate's reputation as a daredevil investigative reporter. Rather than be affiliated with any one newspaper or television outlet, Nate contracted himself out on a freelance basis. He consistently assigned himself to the pieces many conventional reporters were afraid to touch; wartime coverage and the like. He hadn't attended Paris Greene's funeral because he was currently in Iraq, putting his life on the line as he acquired the photos and interviews that very few were willing to seek out, the ones that disturbed peaceful sleep and earned him six figures in the process. It was unlikely that Nate was even aware that Paris was dead.

The best Miles could do was to put in a call to Nate's publicist and wait for a response. Apparently, Nate checked in with the man once a month and was due to make contact within the next few weeks. His message would be passed along then. As an afterthought, he remembered to relay the news of Paris's death to be passed on, as well.

The waiting was starting to grate on Miles's nerves. It had been three days since he'd left the message with Nate's publicist, but it felt more like three weeks. He tried to stay busy, making nice with the locals and gathering peripheral information on Pam, but he was anxious to start tightening up his manuscript. He thought he had a decent composite of Pam's childhood and he'd have no trouble writing about her professional career. But it was the hole—the black hole, he called it—that kept him from being able to make real progress.

The last few months of Pam's senior year in high school remained a mystery. Something had happened to Pam at a time when she should've been looking forward to graduating and moving on with her life. Something important enough to stall her progress. Instead, her grades went to hell, she skipped more school than she attended, and she was seemingly unconcerned with the consequences of her actions. She hadn't shown up for her own graduation, and she'd sneaked out of town on the fastest thing smoking at the first chance she got. Though her twin had gone with her, Paris had returned to Mercy to settle down. Meanwhile, Pam never came back, not even to visit.

Why, was what he wanted to know. And once he had the answer to that final question, he'd be ready to get down to the business of writing.

A car horn blared behind him and Miles glanced in the rearview mirror. He noticed Clive regarding him curiously and waved before pressing on the gas to speed up. He decided against stopping to play checkers and continued down Main Street.

He figured the gods were smiling down on him as he spotted Pam and her niece, along with a tall black man he vaguely recognized as Paris's widower, crossing the street at the next corner. Pam was deep in conversation with the girl and didn't notice him sitting at the stop sign, which was fine because he didn't want to be noticed just yet. The trio disappeared inside the restaurant they were headed for, and Miles debated for the space of five seconds before pulling into a parking space on the lot next door.

He entered the restaurant, saw the trio being led to a corner booth, and carefully chose a seat at the bar. If Pam happened to see him sitting there, she would assume that he was simply enjoying a meal while he watched a baseball game on the big screen television across from the bar. He ordered a barbecue platter and a beer and stared.

Chad Greene was a good looking man, and Miles wondered if he'd ever looked at Pam and found himself thinking of his dead wife. He felt sure he would've, in Chad's place, since the likeness was uncanny. He thought he remembered hearing that Chad and Nate were good friends and that he and Nate, plus Pam and Paris, had often been seen together. It made sense, he guessed, given that Pam and Nate were rumored to have been involved and Chad had gone on to marry Paris.

He watched Chad touch Pam's hand softly and lean across the table to say something to her, and felt his eyebrows climb his forehead. Pam leaned in too and their heads were unusually close as they talked. Whatever it was Chad said made Pam throw her head back and laugh, and while she indulged herself, Chad's eyes were glued to her face, with a perfectly blank expression on his own. The girl, Nikki, he thought her name was, was quickly drawn into the conversation and she, too, had a flair for laughing out loud and freely.

Miles waited until they were eating dessert to settle his check and approach Pam's table. He sidled across the restaurant casually, hands in his pockets and a reluctant smile on his lips. Despite it all, he genuinely liked Pam.

"Pam?" he asked, as if he wasn't sure he had the right person. He came to a stop at the edge of the table and sent a friendly smile in Chad and Nikki's direction before focusing on Pam's face.

She looked up and smiled. "David, hi. How are you?"

For a moment, he wondered who David was and then he remembered. He was David. The three beers he'd drunk must've been going to his head. "Better now that my stomach's full. I was over at the bar and I thought I'd come by and say hi before I left." He looked expectantly at Chad and then Nikki.

"Oh," Pam said, remembering her manners. "This is my brother-in-law, Chad Greene, and my niece, Nikki. Nikki and Chad, this is David Dixon."

"Hi," Nikki said, looking from Pam to Miles curiously.

Chad came to his feet and extended a hand. "You dropped Pam off at the house once, if I'm remembering correctly."

"You are. She was sitting on the side of the road pouting and I picked her up. That's how we met. I'm sorry for your loss, by the way."

"I appreciate that." Chad released Miles's hand and resumed his seat.

"David is Moira's stepson," Pam said. "Chad, you know Moira Tobias. You should too, come to think of it, Nikki."

"She makes the best chocolate chip cookies," Nikki piped up.

Pam was surprised and Miles was too, though he hid it well. "Is Moira still feeding the kids cookies in exchange for helping her out around that big old house of hers?" Pam asked Nikki.

"I went there once with my friend Kelli. I think she

was organizing the library or something, I can't remember. But I do remember the cookies," Nikki laughed. "She's nice."

"I remember when I would sit and talk with Moira for hours at a time. Your mom and I ended up on her porch a lot when we were kids." Pam smiled fondly.

"She doesn't get into town very often. Is she feeling okay?" Chad remembered that Paris had visited with Moira often, too.

"She's old and cranky," Miles said. "And she has arthritis, but other than that she's fine. I know she'd love to see you, Pam."

"I've been meaning to make some time to get out there. Tell her I said hello, will you, David?"

"You can tell her yourself. I mentioned to her that we've gone out to lunch a few times and she made me promise to tell you that she still keeps the cookie jar full."

"I'll definitely get out there before I leave. I've missed talking with her," she said, realizing that she actually had.

"Sometime next week would be good. I don't think I told you, but I'll be out of town then. Would it be all right if we changed our lunch date to the following Tuesday, instead of this one coming up?"

Pam nodded and crunched ice noisily. "I can live with that."

"Good. Then I'll see you next Tuesday. It was nice meeting you," Miles said, looking at Chad and Nikki. He gave them one last wave and left the restaurant. Minutes later he was in his car, feeling pleased with himself.

Inside the restaurant, Nikki aimed a speculative look at her aunt and cleared her throat. "You didn't tell me you were dating someone, Aunt Pam."

Pam was concentrating on scooping up the last of her apple crisp and she looked up, genuinely taken aback. "What?"

"That man said you two have been going out to lunch. Is that a sneaky way of saying you two are dating?"

"Me and him?" Pam looked over her shoulder in the direction Miles had disappeared. "Nikki, please. David is nice, but hardly my type. We've met for lunch a few times, but that's it. I think he's hoping he'll get his picture in the paper or something."

"What does he do?" Chad asked. He spotted their waitress and lifted a hand to signal for the check.

"I don't know. I'll have to remember to ask him sometime."

"What exactly is your type, Aunt Pam?" Nikki wanted to know. "*The National Tattler* said you only date rich white men and Mr. Dixon is white."

Pam sucked one last ice cube in her mouth and crunched into it viciously. She set her cup down with a sharp thump. "Don't believe everything you read, Nikki. Over half of the men they paired me with were only business associates."

"What about that producer?"

"God, you're worse than the media. What *about* the producer?" She looked at Chad, whose face was blank, and rolled her eyes. "Are we ready?"

He nodded and she got to her feet briskly. But she couldn't help sliding one last look at Nikki.

"And just for the record, the producer isn't white, he's Mexican."

TEN

Pam reached across the bed and snatched her cell phone from the nightstand. Underneath two pillows, she put the phone to her ear. "Please tell me you have a good reason for calling me at three o'clock in the morning."

"You're never asleep at this hour," Gillian chirped. She was wide-awake and in her home office tending to business. "What's going on down there?"

"Things are different in this backward town. If you aren't in bed by seven, they call the police on you. What's up?" She pushed the pillows aside and sat up, sweeping her wild hair back from her face.

"Personal tragedy is making you a hot ticket, Pam. Sharon Templeton's people called me today. She wants you on her show like yesterday." Gillian was referring to the queen of daytime talk shows. "They're willing to let you write the script, as long as you agree to talk about your loss."

"You woke me up for that? Come on, Gil, you know

I don't do interviews and shit. Tell Templeton's people thanks, but no thanks. Can I get back to sleep now?"

"Sure, but first tell me when you're coming home. I need to know so I know what to book and what to toss in the trash. Dynasty Entertainment is putting together a nineteen-city tour, and they want you on the ticket."

"What tour and what cities?" She hadn't done a tour in quite some time and a diversion might be just what the doctor ordered after she left Mercy. She listened intently as Gillian gave her the preliminary details of the tour, providing the names of the artists who were already signed on. "Sistahs of Soul, huh? Sounds interesting."

"If you decide to do it, you'll need to be ready to go on the . . ." Gillian searched around on her desktop and found the paper she needed. "Twentieth of next month. That gives you a couple more weeks down there and then you need to haul your ass home so you can get ready. The tour kicks off in Houston, Texas."

"I think I want to do it." Pam could feel the thrill of anticipation flowing through her blood.

"It'll be a great start for your latest CD. Sales are good now, but with a tour to help promote it, they'll go through the roof. Your call, though. Think about it and let me know."

Pam exhaled on a long breath and squeezed her eyes shut. "Do it," she said several seconds later. "Sign me up, Gil."

"You're sure? Because with everything you've been through you . . ."

"I'm sure. Something like this is just what I need. I can't stay here forever and I don't want to. Nikki will have to let me go if she knows I have definite work lined up."

"She's still clinging, huh?"

"Not that I blame her and I'm enjoying spending time with her, but I think she has this fantasy that I'll stay in Mercy, and I just can't do that. It's been almost a month as it is and I'm starting to go stir crazy. This place depresses me."

"That bad?"

"Worse. Everywhere I go, the old biddies are whispering and clinging to their husbands like they think I'll run off with them."

"Women do that everywhere you go, Pam," Gillian joked. "What about the other thing?"

Pam was quiet a long time. "Nothing that I know of. I try to steer clear of that area all together and so far I've been successful. I keep a paper bag handy though, just in case."

"I was hoping you'd be able to get some closure."

"I'd have to open that door again to get some closure and I'm not doing that. It's over and done with, which is why I'm telling you to sign me up for the tour. I need to start planning my escape, so give me a reason, okay?"

"If you say so. I'll do some follow-up and get back to you."

"I'll be waiting." Pam folded the cell phone closed and dropped it on the nightstand.

Fully awake now, she climbed out of bed and headed to the bathroom. She emptied her bladder, washed her hands, and picked up her guitar case on her way back across the room. She sat on the side of the bed and flipped the case open, stroking the guitar lovingly. It was the same one she'd been making music with since the days of recording demo tapes to shop to major studios, and she couldn't imagine having to replace it.

She was as attached to it as some people were to their pets.

Pam closed her eyes as she settled the guitar across her lap and let her mind take her to the stage. She strummed her fingers lightly over the strings, re-acquainting herself with the chords, then she began playing. Her voice came out softly, joining the music hesitantly at first and then growing stronger the longer she played. She forgot about the other guests at the B&B as she played and sang. It was a song she'd started writing a few years ago and had only recently re-discovered, scribbled on a sheet of paper and tucked inside a book she'd started reading and quickly grown bored with. Over and over, she sang the lyrics she re-membered writing, until they flowed into a melody she could work with. More lyrics came to mind and she weaved them into the fabric of the song. She had started off freestyling and playing around with the song, but she ended up scrambling off the bed, searching for a pen and paper to write the lyrics down.

She was still making music when the sky lightened and the sun began peeking from behind the clouds. Before she spread out to sleep, she named the song "Have Mercy On Me."

The sun was peeking from behind the clouds on the morning Paris Greene rolled over in bed and realized that Chad was no longer lying beside her. She cracked her eyes open and looked around the bedroom slowly. She saw him sitting on the very edge of the bed, knees spread, hands dangling in the space between them and staring into space.

Paris recognized the defeated slump of his shoulders and wrestled with the choice to pretend that she was asleep and ignore him or to open her mouth and say something. Eventually she rolled to her side and propped her head on her hand, touched his back softly. Chad glanced back at her over his shoulder, then looked away quickly.

"Did I wake you up?"

Her eyes slid over to the alarm clock and noted the time. 5:40 AM. "It's almost time for me to wake up, anyway." She took a deep breath. "This is the third time this week I've opened my eyes and seen you looking like that, Chad. Tell me what's wrong. Is it something with work?"

"No, it's not work, Paris." He scooted around on the mattress until he was sitting sideways and could see her face without having to crane his neck. "Is everything all right with you? Are you happy?"

"Where did that come from?"

"I'm just wondering if you're happy and if you are, what is it that's making you happy?"

"What if I say I'm not? Will that make you feel better about the fact that you're not happy? Is that what you're trying to get at?"

"We've talked about this before," he said carefully.

"Yeah, we have. Three times. I don't know about you, but I'm sick of talking about it. We're married. Is this what married couples do, sit around talking about how unhappy they are?"

"I don't know what married couples do." He blew out a harsh breath. "But somehow I don't think they do what we've been doing."

"What do you want me to do? What can I do to make you happy?" The beginnings of anger were in her voice. She spun away from Chad's probing eyes and rolled to a sitting position on the side of the bed.

She rooted around on the floor for her slippers and pushed her feet into them.

"It's not that you make me unhappy, Paris. Why is it that every time this subject comes up, you immediately assume that the problem is with you?" He watched her come around the bed and storm past him to the bathroom.

"Why is it that this subject keeps coming up, Chad? It's like an every three-month thing now. Everything is fine for a while and then, wham, you hit me with this. Why can't we find a good place and stay there?"

Chad rose from the bed and went to stand in the bathroom doorway. Paris squeezed a line of toothpaste on her toothbrush and looked at his reflection in the mirror. The first time he'd told her in that roundabout way of his that he was unhappy she hadn't known what to do with the information, so she'd stored it away and ignored it. Maybe he was having trouble adjusting to married life, she thought. He just needed a little more time to get used to the responsibilities of a new house and a family.

But they were settled into a groove by now. He was teaching at the high school and coaching the girls' volleyball team, and he said he enjoyed working with the kids. She was working as a social worker at the children's home right outside of town and she loved her job too. In another year or so she planned to apply for a supervisory position, and they had already discussed his intention to apply for the position of school principal after the current one retired, which was expected in the next five years. They lived in a nice home, spacious and tastefully furnished, and one they had picked out together and decided on buying. Nikki was almost five and flourishing, looking more like her father every day and reading already. And he still wasn't satisfied.

Theirs was an easy relationship, mainly because Chad didn't mind sharing in the household chores and he insisted on being a hands-on parent. He started dinner as many nights as she did, he did laundry, ironed most of his own clothing and helped Nikki with her homework, all without having to be asked. When she'd discovered that he also left the bathroom as neat as he found it, Paris had considered herself lucky to have him. She didn't nag him and she gave him plenty of space to move around in. What else did he want?

"Something's missing, Paris. Don't you feel it?"

Paris turned on the tap and dampened the bristles of her toothbrush, then bent over and went to work brushing her teeth. She used the time to consider his question carefully.

She recalled the first time she'd ever laid eyes on Chad, coming across his porch and jogging down the steps casually. Though she didn't think she'd had a crush on him all those years ago, she did remember thinking that he was nice to look at. Like a painting that drew the eye back to it time and time again, but you couldn't really say why. For a fourteen-year-old boy, she had thought him surprisingly appealing to the eye. He'd had none of the unchecked scruffiness the other boys she knew had, and he was always meticulously groomed. She had always believed that was part of what Nate had initially liked about Chad, too. The two of them running around together had attracted more than a few appreciative feminine glances, from both young and old.

In high school and then again in college, Chad played basketball and his body was well-formed and leanly-muscled as a result. Long hands and feet, once dangling

from his extremities awkwardly, now fit his frame perfectly. He treated himself to a manicure once a month
in Atlanta, while he was receiving a pedicure, and he
was fastidious about keeping his hair shaped and
trimmed. He never skipped out on his biweekly barber
appointments and his infatuation with clothes and
shoes rivaled that of any woman's. He had what some
would call presence. He turned heads just by walking
into a room. Paris knew of at least two women who
regularly flirted with her husband, despite his married
status, but she tried not to let it bother her.

She couldn't blame those women for noticing that
Chad was easy on the eyes. When he was fourteen he
was cute, but as a fully-grown man he was magnetic.
She thought it had something to do with his eyes and
the way they stared out of his face like lasers. They
were an average shade of brown, except they were re-
markably expressive and framed with long, thick
lashes. If he allowed himself to give in to anger, which
he rarely did, they could cut like knives. When he was
passionate about something or someone, they could
made you lose track of your train of thought, and
when he was indifferent, their affect was flat, almost
like he was in a trance.

His smile, when it came, was wide and slightly tilted
to one side, sandwiched between deep slashes in his
jaws and flashing brightly out of a longish cocoa-
brown face.

She liked to see him smile, liked to come upon him
in the middle of laughing about something silly, and
thought with more than a little sadness that she hadn't
had the opportunity to do so in quite a while. Maybe
in years.

"Yes, I feel it," Paris eventually said. His eyes were
expressionless now, which meant that he was indiffer-

ent and seeing it made her angry. Her hands shook as she replaced her toothbrush in the holder.

"What do you think it is?"

"Don't try to turn this around, Chad. You're the one who brought the subject up, so why don't you tell me what you think is missing?" She reached for a tube of facial cleanser and squeezed a dollop in her hand, smoothed it into her skin with small circular motions as she caught his eyes in the mirror. "What about sex? That's something that's noticeably missing. Do you miss that?"

Chad's eyes widened slightly. He shifted and leaned against the doorjamb. "Of course I do."

"Just not with me, right?"

"Paris, I . . ." He trailed off, unsure of what he wanted to say or of how to say it. This was another topic that they discussed often, but he wasn't in the mood to tackle the issue right now.

"What, Chad?" She looked around for her towel and snatched it off a nearby rod. "Do you realize I could probably count on one hand the number of times we've made love? And that includes our wedding night and the night you rolled over, calling out for . . ."

He cut her off tersely, his eyes going from blank to hard in seconds. A hand went up to push her words back. "Don't," he snapped. "I've apologized for that a hundred times, and I wish you wouldn't keep throwing it in my face."

Paris came toward him and he stepped back to let her pass. Belatedly, he realized that she had intended to initiate some sort of embrace and, still, he didn't attempt to right his fumble. He stood there staring at her, hating himself for causing the pain in her eyes, but unable to prevent it.

He was the first to look away, dropping his head and

massaging the bridge of his nose as he retraced his steps to the bed and sat down heavily. She went over to the closet and stood in front of the open door, visually choosing her outfit for the day.

"Are you seeing someone else?"

Chad's head shot up. He was expecting to find her hovering over him, ready to do battle, but she hadn't moved from her place in front of the closet, hadn't turned to face him. "No," he sighed. The lie was like a bad taste at the back of his throat. "Are you?"

"I've gone out to lunch with Ben Nolan a few times, but nothing more than that."

He searched his mind for information about Ben Nolan and eventually came up with what he knew. He was an older man, average looking and nice enough, as far as Chad could tell from the one time he'd had occasion to cross his path. He remembered being introduced to Nolan at the home's annual Christmas party, remembered shaking his hand and making casual conversation. Nolan was in an upper level social services position and part of his duties included making the trip to Mercy several times a year to inspect the children's home where Paris worked.

He sat there and waited for anger and jealousy to come and when neither of those feelings surfaced, he sighed again. This time loudly.

"He's asked me out, too," Paris added. She decided to bypass skirts all together and pulled a pair of slacks and a blouse from the closet.

"Do you want to go?" She threw him an "are you serious" look before bending down to grab a pair of heels from the closet floor. "I just meant . . ."

"Do you *want* me to go, Chad?" He didn't answer, and she grew tired of standing there waiting. When she was certain he didn't intend to look at her or to address the question, she left him in the bedroom and went to shower.

Paris was dressed and standing at the dresser, rifling through her jewelry box in search of an illusive earring when Chad spoke next. Across the room, his head was bent to the task of sliding a belt through the loops of his slacks. He called her name and she looked up and locked eyes with him in the mirror, her eyebrows raised expectantly.

"Nolan seems like a decent guy," he said.

Though they had discussed many of the issues living within their marriage, Chad's decision to set up a separate bedroom down the hall from Paris's bedroom was never discussed. It was something that happened gradually, until all of his belongings were transferred and he was firmly ensconced there.

Ironically enough, it was Nikki who had unwittingly started the process. She was five when she caught the chicken pox from one of her kindergarten classmates and was sent home to wait the illness out. Her insistence on scratching ferociously sent Chad to another room to sleep, so Nikki could sleep with Paris and Paris could keep an eye on her through the night. A little at a time, his things were transported down the hall until there was nothing left of his in Paris's room. After Nikki returned to school, Chad saw no reason to move back.

"You want a divorce?" Paris asked him once as they were working in the backyard. He'd gone to a conference in Atlanta the week before and brought back a sapling. He and Nikki were planting it on the side of the backyard Paris hadn't laid claim to for her flowers and he'd just sent Nikki inside to bring him a glass of water when Paris approached him. She stood over him, blocking the sun from his eyes, with dirt-caked gardening gloves on her hands and a wide brimmed straw hat on her head.

Chad propped an arm on his bent knee and met her gaze straight on. "If we get a divorce, I take Nikki."

She sucked in a sharp breath and shook her head. "That's not an option. I had her when you came along and I'll still have her if you decide to leave."

"She's my daughter, Paris."

"You wouldn't even know that if it wasn't for me."

"You're right. But still . . . I'm not leaving her, so you can forget that. Is this about Nolan? Are things getting serious between you two?"

"Ben has nothing to do with this. I asked you if you wanted a divorce."

"You brought it up, so I think it's you who wants one. Am I right?" He eyed her curiously, then shot a glance toward the house to make sure Nikki was still inside.

"It's either that or keep on doing what we're doing. Putting on a charade for Nikki, who realizes that we have separate rooms by the way, and smiling like idiots for the town." She dropped down on her haunches and stared at him. "How long can we keep this up?"

"You want to marry Nolan?"

She thought about it and shook her head. "Not really, no. I care about him, but I don't love him. I love you."

"I love you, too," he said and meant it. Then, "Are you being discreet?"

"You know we are."

"And he treats you well? Because if he isn't, I'll break his neck. You know that, right?"

Despite the hurt squeezing her heart, Paris smiled. "Yes, I know."

Chad looked deeply into her eyes for several seconds. "If a divorce is really what you want, then I won't fight you for it. But I will fight you for Nikki. I feel like shit for saying that, but it's the truth, Paris. I don't want us to have to go there with each other."

"I don't either."

Out of the corner of his eye, Chad saw Nikki tipping across the yard balancing an overfilled glass in her hands. She brought the glass to him, splashed water on his leg, and shimmied her way onto his lap, all at once. He bent an arm around her tiny waist and pushed his nose into the silky hair at the crown of her head, inhaling deeply. Then he looked at Paris over the rim of his glass as he drank. His eyes spoke to her and she read them loud and clear. She nodded slowly and rose to go back to her flowers.

Another night he went to her room after Nikki was asleep and stretched out next to her on the bed. She was snuggled under the covers watching television and he fit a pillow under his head and settled down to join her. He lay on top of the covers, with his feet crossed at the ankles and his hands folded over his abdomen. Three sets of commercials came and went, the show she was watching went off and another one came on before he spoke.

"You remember when all of us used to sit around Nate's house watching television when we were kids?"

Paris giggled at the memory. "Nate's mother would have to run us out of her front room with a broomstick. Those were the best times."

"The best," he agreed.

"You and Pam always spent the whole time arguing about silly things. I think that's really the reason we kept getting put out. All that arguing got on Miss Merlene's nerves."

"Got on my nerves, too. I don't know why I let her get under my skin like she did."

She picked up the remote and surfed through the channels. "I do and Nate did, too. We pretty much figured you two were sneaking around behind our backs and breaking the code of the foursome."

His head rolled around on the pillow and he looked at her. "Word around town is that she was running around with Nate."

"That was the cover story. Me and Nate knew the real story, and even if we didn't, Nikki is proof enough."

"Pam told you?" He was genuinely surprised. He'd never told anyone about his time with Pam, and she always said she hadn't either.

"No, she didn't tell me. I sneaked and read her diary one time and saw it for myself. She told me she wasn't a virgin anymore, but she wouldn't tell me anything else. I had to invade her privacy to get all the juicy details." She glanced at him and returned her attention to the television. "*Sex in the City* reruns or *Law and Order* reruns?"

"*Law and Order*. She put all the juicy details in her diary?"

"She was seventeen, Chad. That's what seventeen-year-olds do."

It occurred to him then that Paris wasn't as informed as he first thought. He reached up and scratched his head, thinking. "And you think she lost her virginity when she was seventeen?"

Seeing the shit-eating grin on Chad's face had Paris's eyes widening. She took a hand from under the covers and pushed at his shoulder. "Before that?"

He pretended to be concentrating on the television screen and said nothing.

"When?"

"Way before then, and that's all I'm going to say." He had a thought. "We really shouldn't be gossiping about this, anyway. Is this awkward for you? Because I'm starting to feel a little twitchy myself."

"Too late for that. Come on, tell me."

"It's none of your business. It's between me and Pam."

"I told you all kinds of stuff when we were kids." She was indignant. "I told you stuff I didn't even tell Pam!"

"Like what?"

"Like about the time with Rick Moony out at Truman Field. And the time I helped Mike Robins steal his mother's car and we almost got caught."

Chad waved his hand negligently, a lopsided grin on his face. "Rick Moony was a punk, so that doesn't count. And you *did* tell Pam because she told *me* about it not too long after *you* told me about it. Plus, riding in the passenger seat *does not* constitute helping someone steal a car."

"Oh, come on, Chad!"

He unlaced his fingers and turned his palms toward the ceiling. "Okay, okay, but you have to promise not to tell Pam I told you. It's old news, but at the time it was a secret."

"Okay."

"She had just turned fourteen and I was about to be sixteen."

"But she didn't get pregnant with Nikki until she was eighteen . . ." Paris's voice trailed off as the implications of what he'd said sank in. "I'll kill her for not telling me."

"You just promised not to say anything."

She sat with a thunderstruck expression for a few seconds. "So you guys were . . ."

"Pretty serious for a while."

"For how long?"

"Pretty much from the day we met up until the day she got on that bus and rode off into the sunset."

"Exclusive?"

"Damn right."

"I can't believe she never told me. All that time and she never said a word, the sneaky little bitch," Paris hissed. There was no heat in her voice, but disbelief and hurt were strong. "We told each other everything."

"It was a big thing for us to wrap our minds around at the time. Neither of us knew what to do with what we were doing, except to keep doing it." He interpreted the expression on Paris's face and laid a hand on hers. "We both knew we were way too young to be doing what we were doing, but we couldn't seem to stop."

"You were in love with each other."

Chad looked at his wife a long time. He was nodding his head when his mouth opened. "I was, anyway."

"She hurt you badly when she left."

"A little bit, yeah, but finding out about Nikki crushed me."

"That's why you married me, so you could have Nikki?" She tried to slide her hand from under his, but he wouldn't let her.

"I saw you caring for Nikki and doing what I felt Pam should've been doing and I cared too much about you to let you keep doing it on your own. Plus, I had a responsibility toward Nikki, even if Pam didn't think so. Finding out that Nikki was my child only made me love you more than I already did."

"But not like you loved Pam." She would've snatched her hand away if he hadn't tightened his hold and refused to release her. She thought she had a clear understanding of what everything had been about and it galled her.

Silently, they watched three consecutive episodes of *Law and Order* with his hand still clamped around hers. A fourth episode was coming on when he rolled to his side and made her look at him.

"You can go on hating me if you want to, but I won't let you stop being my friend," he told her.

"What am I supposed to do with that?"

"I don't know. Why don't you think about it and let me know what you decide?"

ELEVEN

June 17th

Dear Diary,

I told Nikki that I was leaving next month and she took it harder than I expected her to. She knew I wasn't planning to stay in Mercy forever, didn't she? With school out for the summer she wanted to know what she was going to do and how she was going to pass the time. I told her I didn't know. Maybe Chad would allow her to come and visit me after the tour was over, but she'd have to ask and see. Either way, I have to go. It's time.

I've been taking Gillian's advice and venturing out more. Mercy is actually a lovely little Town, and it's nice to see that not much has changed. Except for the fact that I've been asked to pose for pictures with several of the teenagers and even a few of the parents. I somehow managed to get out of the habit of being stopped every tenth step I took to auto-

graph something or to answer obnoxious questions, but it all came crashing back after I went into the grocery store out on the interstate. Nikki got a kick out of all the attention when we went shopping in Atlanta, but I grew tired of it very quickly. I'm sure there will be a photo of the two of us in one of the gossip rags in the coming days, and I know she'll love seeing it. She's still too young to know the true value of privacy.

Chad and I are getting along surprisingly well. Since the day he kissed me, he hasn't touched me again and I'm thankful for that. All the tension between us complicates things, and I would rather pretend it doesn't exist than deal with it. It's too late anyway. We can laugh and talk now, but there are still questions in his eyes that I won't answer. I hope he's decided to leave well enough alone.

I think of Paris every day. She is like a cloud I walk around with, floating above my head, waiting to pour down any minute. Sometimes I can feel her presence hovering around me and I catch myself talking to her. I reach for the phone to call her and then I remember I can't and why. It's hell living without her. The sun isn't as bright when it shines, and the rain is colder against my skin. I hope that once I leave I'll feel more optimistic about the future. That's always been the case in the past. I can't grow in Mercy.

Nikki is badgering me about going with her to the town festival at the end of the month. There will be carnival rides and funnel cakes and lots of other greasy foods to gorge on, she says. I told her I didn't need to go because they had all that shit when I was a kid and I went to plenty of festivals. I think she just wants me to go because she thinks Chad will let her stay out later if he knows she's with me. I'm not so sure about that, though, especially after the wine-drinking, tattle-telling incident. She really put her foot in it that time, and I didn't help matters any.

What's on my agenda for today? Moira.

More next time.

Pam

Pam found Moira in the south flower garden kneeling in a flowerbed, yanking at weeds and muttering under her breath. She crossed the grass slowly and came to stand over her. Moira was so intent on her task it took her a few minutes to realize she was no longer alone. Surprised, she pressed a hand to the top of her head to hold the straw hat in place and looked up. A slow smile spread across her face, and her eyes widened with pleasure as she pulled her gardening gloves off and came to her feet.

"Pamela?"

"I'm the only one left, Moira," Pam said softly. "You know it's me." She reached out to help Moira to her feet, but her hand was graciously ignored. Even at seventy-five, Moira was still slim and physically fit, only slightly larger than she had been when she was thirty-five.

"Even if that wasn't the case, I never had a bit of trouble telling you and Paris apart." She opened her arms and wrapped them around Pam, squeezing tightly. "How have you been?"

"Better than I thought I would be. You look wonderful, Moira." Moira reached up and removed her hat and Pam's eyes widened. "What happened to your beautiful red hair?" Without thinking, she stepped forward and ran her fingers through the silky white hair flowing around Moira's shoulders.

"I worried it all gray after you took off for parts unknown," Moira quipped, only half teasing. She hooked an arm through Pam's and turned them toward the house. "Paris kept me updated on what you were doing, so that helped, and now I have that lovely niece of yours to tell me all the gossip. But before that, I had no idea where you'd gone or what you were doing. Not that it was any of my business, but I still missed you."

"I missed you, too," Pam said.

They climbed the steps to the back porch and sat across from each other at a patio table. As Pam situated herself in a chair and set her sunglasses on the table between them, she let her eyes take Moira in. In her mind, whenever her thoughts had wandered to Moira, the image was always the same. Pam remembered Moira as she'd looked when she saw her last. She knew she should've been prepared for the inevitable changes, but she wasn't. The idea that Moira had aged was startling.

Gone was the flowing, fire-red hair, and in its place was a head full of wispy, silver strands. The same green eyes stared out of her face and the freckles were still there too, but wrinkles and age spots had joined them. Pam was reminded all over again of how long she had been away, and the thought of all she'd missed suddenly made her sad.

"I know what you're thinking, Pamela," Moira teased gently. "You're thinking that I've gotten old. I know this because I'm sitting here thinking the same thing about you. I remember when you were running around in pigtails and blue jean shorts, before you had breasts and hips. Now look at you. You went away from here and grew up on me."

Moira's long-time housekeeper poked her head out the back door and came up short when she saw Moira wasn't alone. "I thought I heard you out here, Miss Moira. I didn't know you had company." Her name was Janice and she had two teenage daughters at home, which meant she recognized Pam immediately, even if she did live in a neighboring town and hadn't been very familiar with Paris. She smiled brightly and tried not to stare. "Aren't you . . . ?"

Pam put an easy smile on her face and nodded, though the last thing she wanted to do was be drawn into a lengthy conversation about her career. Thankfully Moira intercepted the faintly frozen look on her face and stepped in smoothly.

"Yes Janice, this is Pamela Mayes," she drawled. "Now that we've gotten that out of the way, I believe we'll have some lunch." Janice disappeared as quickly as she had appeared. To Pam, Moira said, "I remembered that you used to love my chicken salad, so I made some this morning. You will stay for lunch, won't you?"

"You won't take no for an answer, will you?"

"You know I won't." Moira's eyes searched Pam's face. "You don't like it very much, do you?"

"Like what?"

"All the attention you get from people. I think it drives you a little crazy. Am I right?"

"What makes you say that?"

"Just a feeling, I guess. A few minutes ago you had the same look on your face as you did the time I suggested you try the broiled octopus I had prepared. Like you didn't want to be rude, but you really wanted to throw up."

Pam chuckled at the memory and sat back in her chair. "I won't lie and say it wouldn't be nice to be able to shop for groceries and not have to sign thirty autographs before I check out, but I love what I do."

"You're good at it, too. I came to one of your concerts once, in St. Louis I think. I really enjoyed it, seeing you onstage and everything. Of course, one or two of the songs made me blush." Moira looked around as Janice came back out onto the porch carrying a tray with a pitcher of iced tea and glasses perched on it. "Janice, what was the song I told you I was going to have to speak with Pamela about?"

Janice's face split in half with a grin. She winked at Pam as she poured the tea. Tongue in cheek, she said, "I think it was called "Touch Myself," Miss Moira."

"Yes, that's it. It was . . . interesting." A flush crept up Moira's neck as she sipped at her tea. She set her glass down and cleared her throat. "In my day young women didn't speak of such things. And with such . . . clarity."

"Things change, Miss Moira. My girls can't get enough of your music," Janice told Pam. "At least you ain't doing all that cussing and going on."

Pam sipped her own iced tea. "How old are your girls?" Some of her songs were pretty explicit.

"Sixteen and seventeen. They'll have heart attacks when I tell them I met you today, too. I'll be right back with lunch."

"She listens to your music just as much as those girls of hers," Moira confided when Janice was gone. "Every now and again I leave and come back, and catch her in the library with the radio blasting."

"Do you think her girls would like an autograph?"

"They'd love it, and come to think of it, I would, too. I know just the album I want you to sign."

"David told me you have all of my CD's," Pam said, smiling.

"David?"

"Your stepson."

"Oh." Moira's eyebrows met in the middle of her forehead. David was Miles's middle name and she couldn't figure out what his reasons were for introducing himself to Pam as such. She made a mental note to question him about it when he returned. "His father was my second husband. The one with the sticky fingers."

"He didn't tell me that part of the story."

Moira thought about it, then shook her head. "He may not even know what actually happened between his father and me. He was just a little boy when we divorced, around eight or nine, but he looked me up the minute he was old enough to use the telephone on his own."

"I wondered why I'd never seen him in Mercy before now. He said you two always visited and kept in touch." Janice brought out two covered plates and silverware and Pam spread her napkin in her lap before scooting all the way up to the table. She smiled her thanks and turned her attention back to Moira.

"I mainly went to him," Moira confessed. "In the beginning he was in boarding school and it was easier for me to go there from time to time rather than have to deal with his father. Then, when he was in college, he decided Mercy was too small and insignificant to bother making the trip. After that, I backed off and only visited him when I knew I'd be in the vicinity of where he was. Is he treating you kindly?" Her eyes narrowed on Pam's face.

"We're not dating, Moira," Pam said after she had chewed and swallowed. "He must've told you about my car stopping and him giving me a ride into town. We've met for lunch a few times and yes, he's been a perfect gentleman each time."

"Still, I don't want him bothering you. Especially after everything that's happened." She sighed tiredly and flattened her hands on the table. "I said I wasn't going to bring that up. The last thing I want to do is upset you any more than I'm sure you already are. I'm sorry, Pamela."

Pam set her fork down and reached across the table for Moira's hand. She gave it a squeeze. "I'm fine, Moira. We can talk about Paris if you want to. I promise I won't get hysterical on you, if that's what you're worried about."

"It's not you I'm worried about. I'll confess that I didn't take her death very calmly myself. Part of me still doesn't want to believe it. I keep looking for her to come zooming up the drive, ready to dig around in my garden with me, but she doesn't come. That sounds so selfish," Moira chastised herself, swiping at the stray tears that gathered in her eyes.

"No more selfish than me wanting to pick up the phone and call her or wanting to ask her about something and getting angry because I can't do it. It'll take me some time to get used to being alone in the world." She gave Moira's hand one last squeeze and went back to her lunch. "She was all I had."

"You two were inseparable as children. I remember how you would comb each other's hair and paint each other's toenails." A wistful smile took over Moira's face as she searched her memory. "You split everything right down the middle, like two little old women. It was adorable to watch, and you were the most beautiful children."

Speechless, Pam could only nod as she drank her

tea. She remembered all of those things too. And more. "When I left Mercy I wasn't ever planning to come back. I never thought something like this would be the thing that forced me to eat my words."

"Why did you leave, Pamela?"

"Do you realize that you're like, the only person who calls me *Pamela*? You never say Pam, always Pamela. Why is that?"

"Pamela is your name, isn't it? Pamela Anne Mayes. I never liked the way people desecrate a name by chopping it up or cutting it off. I think it should be illegal to do that." Moira took one last bite of her food and pushed her plate away. "It occurs to me that you haven't answered my question."

Pam spent several minutes looking out over the massive backyard. Not very much about it had changed since the last time she'd run across the grass barefoot toward the stables, looking for Moira. In the distance, the converted barn still stood, and she knew that there were horses inside, waiting for someone to ride them. A gated training area was next to the stables, and she recalled many times when she was allowed to lead a horse inside the circle and ride until she grew sore between her thighs, while Moira stood at the gate watching and waiting patiently.

She was waiting patiently for Pam's answer, when she decided to offer one a little while later. Pam shrugged listlessly and met her eyes. "I don't know why I left, Moira. I just knew I had to get away from here. I felt like there was nothing here for me anymore. Not that there ever was," she chuckled. "Me and Paris were just floating along, living in the home with all the other unwanted children and waiting to grow up. What would I have done if I'd stayed? Married some man I didn't love? Gotten a job at the dry cleaners? What?"

"Was the home so bad? Did they mistreat you there?"

"Not that I can recall. If anything, they let us run wild," Pam replied. "I was never there when I was supposed to be, but you probably know that already since I was here often enough. It was really just a holding place for us until we were old enough to get out on our own. Not exactly the kind of childhood a kid would choose for themselves."

The back door opened and Janice poked her head out. Seeing that they were done eating, she came across the porch to collect their plates and refill their glasses. She glanced at Pam and smiled. "You're prettier than on television."

"Janice!" Moira was scandalized.

"I just meant that you're pretty without all the makeup and stuff. Not that you don't look pretty with it on, don't get me wrong, but . . ." she floundered visibly.

"Thanks," Pam said, letting her off the hook. "I think. I was telling Moira that I wanted to send your girls an autograph before I go. If you have something I can write on, I'll—"

Moira cut her off with a wave of her hand. "I have an idea, Janice. Get my camera, too. We'll take a few pictures to go along with the autographs."

"Oh God, not the camera again." Growing up, Moira had always snapped pictures of her and Paris. It was from her that they had received photos of themselves as children and then as teenagers. Otherwise, they might not have had any visual proof of those times in their lives, since no one else had thought to do it. There were group photos with the other kids in the home and the requisite school pictures, but the candid shots of the two of them clowning around had come courtesy of Moira.

"Of course, the camera," Moira said, shooing Janice off to fetch it. "You've been away for eighteen years. This is a momentous occasion."

"I should've come back sooner," Pam decided and Moira's head whipped around on her neck in surprise. "I didn't realize how much I've missed you until I saw you again and all that beautiful hair was white. I didn't get to see it change."

"You didn't miss much, believe me. I woke up one morning and this is what I saw. I cried for a week over it. I won't even tell you how long I cried after you left me."

"Moira, please don't do this," Pam pleaded. "I told myself I wasn't going to cry."

"Okay, I won't do it," Moira said. She rounded the table and pulled a nearby chair close to Pam's. "But I did miss you, you know. You did good and made me proud, though. Both you and Paris did. Come on, scoot closer for the picture. This one's mine."

Later, as Pam was preparing to leave, Moira studied her profile intently, committing it to memory. Pam looked up from zipping her purse and caught her staring. She looked away and cleared her throat, swallowing tears.

"You have that faraway look in your eyes again," she said. "When are you leaving?"

"You could always tell when I was up to something, Moira. Am I that obvious?"

"You forget, I've known you since before you were old enough to climb out of the window and make your way here, Pamela. When?"

"You knew about the window?"

"The window was the stuff of legends. I don't think they ever figured out how you rigged it so the lock would never catch."

"I have a tour starting around the middle of next month, so I need to leave Mercy sometime around the first. I've been here long enough as it is."

"It took you a month to get around to coming to see me." Moira reached for Pam's hands. "Please don't let it take another eighteen years before I see you again. Come see me before you go?"

Pam swallowed and nodded. "All right, I will. I promise." She was surprised when Moira tugged on her hands and brought her forward to press a kiss to her lips.

Miles looked up from the reports he was scanning when his assistant poked her head in his office and told him he had a call holding on line three. He asked her to please close the door on her way out and snatched up the receiver the minute she was gone. He had been expecting this call.

"Miles Dixon," he said into the phone. He listened for a moment and then filled his office with the sound of his disgusted groan. "Did you relay the message to Mr. Woodberry?" A few more seconds of listening. "Well, did you tell him that I needed to speak with him immediately?"

Nate's publicist wasn't sounding very sympathetic to Miles's plight, which only angered him more. The man's high pitched nasal voice grated on Miles's nerves, especially since he wasn't hearing what he had hoped to be hearing. Nate was still in Iraq, caught up in a story he was trying to finish, the man said. He expected to be done by the end of next month at the latest, and he would be in touch with Miles following his return to the States.

No, there was no number where Nate could be reached. *No*, Nate wasn't interested in taking Miles's contact information. And *no*, Nate hadn't made any significant comment upon learning of Paris Greene's death. Miles was no further along than when he had first tried contacting the man. With a strangled sigh, he bid the publicist a terse goodbye and slammed the receiver into the cradle.

He was planning to return to Mercy later in the week and when he did, he decided to take a more aggressive tack with Pam. His time in Mercy was coming to an end, and there were still a few questions that needed to be addressed. He'd get the answers he sought if he had to choke them out of Pam.

Dear Diary,

Me and Nate are convinced that something is going on between Pam and Chad. Nate says he can tell by the way they look at each other that something is up. Plus, they are always fighting, like they like each other, but don't want to admit it. Sometimes it really gets on my nerves. Because of them we got put out of Miss Merlene's front room again yesterday.

Me, I can tell by the way Pam acts that she likes Chad. I catch her watching him sometimes and the look in her eyes scares me. We haven't talked about boys yet, and I don't know if I'm ready to.

Chad is cute, though.

Paris

Chad passed by Nikki, sitting in the family room watching television and reading at the same time, and did a double take. A quick glance at the kitchen clock told him it was after two in the morning, and he wondered what she was still doing up. His thoughts were leaning toward pouring himself a stiff drink and enjoying it in peace out on the back porch. He hadn't counted on having a witness to his edginess, and he didn't really want one.

"What are you still doing up?" he asked Nikki as he splashed a healthy amount of Cognac in a glass. She looked up from the book she was engrossed in and smiled at him. He caught his breath and added another splash. The curve of her lips was all Pam.

"I started reading Mom's diary and I guess I got caught up," Nikki said. A few seconds later she giggled and snapped the book closed. She came to her feet and crossed the room to enter the kitchen. She leaned a hip against the counter and watched him fix himself a glass of ice water to go with his drink. "I didn't know you had a crush on Aunt Pam way back in the day."

He completely missed the teasing in her voice, and his was a little sharper than it needed to be. "What?"

"I said," Nikki drawled. "I didn't know—"

"I heard what you said. Who told you that?" He was slicing a lemon now and hoping his hands were steady.

"Mom wrote about it in her diary. She said that her and Uncle Nate suspected something was going on between you and Aunt Pam. I think it's kind of sweet."

"Her and Uncle Nate, huh?" Chad dropped a lemon wedge in his water and took a box of sandwich bags from a nearby cabinet. "So you decided to read the diary?" He wasn't quite clear on how he felt about that yet.

"I was just flipping through it. It's mostly about all

the running around her and Aunt Pam did when they were kids." She took the wrapped lemon from him and carried it over to the refrigerator. "They were pretty footloose and fancy free."

"A lot of it was your aunt. Paris was usually the one going along for the ride and preaching a sermon the whole time."

"I can see Mom doing that. So . . . is it true?"

"Is what true?"

"What mom wrote about you and Aunt Pam?"

"It's too late at night to be subjected to the third degree, Nikki. She had to be thirteen or fourteen at the most when she wrote that, so I'd take it with a grain of salt, okay? You remember how you used to fantasize at that age." He picked up his drinks and turned toward the back door. "I'm going out to the porch for a while, and you should go on up to bed. It's late."

"That was pretty smooth, Dad," Nikki told him, smiling.

"What was?"

"The way you answered my question without really answering it. But I guess I'll let you off the hook this time." She moved closer and offered her lips for a good night kiss. Chad leaned down and pecked quickly. "You coming in soon?"

"In a while. Hit the lights on your way up."

He escaped to the darkness of the back porch a few seconds later and took a seat at the wrought iron table. Behind him, the kitchen light went off and he sighed with relief. Not that he didn't enjoy his daughter's company, but he was less than fit to be around right now. Hell, Nikki would probably be shell-shocked if she knew where his mind was wandering anyway. Nothing about his thoughts was innocent or pure.

Chad was horny and wanting Pam so badly he'd

been driven to fixing himself a drink to calm his nerves. His yearning for her had started the day he realized she was in Mercy, and it had only gotten worse since then. Suddenly, he was remembering all the time they'd spent together, the ways they'd made love, the techniques they had discovered together and perfected with each other. After the first time, when their coupling was strictly an accident, both he and Pam were curious and comfortable enough with each other to seek answers to their questions. Over time, they had found and mastered sensuality in its purest form, been so damn good together that it gave him a headache just thinking about it.

He closed his eyes and pressed stiff fingers to his eyelids as an image of their bodies naked and slick with sweat flashed through his mind without his consent. He chased the image away with a mouthful of cognac and gritted his teeth as it snaked down his throat. He saw like it was just yesterday the first time he'd brought Pam to orgasm. And then again for the first time with his lips and tongue. Thought about how she'd run her fingers all over his body and make him desperate to have her and then torture him with those sultry lips of hers. For a long time after she'd left, he was unable to think of anything else.

Life had eventually crept in, though, and he'd tried to push Pam to the back of his mind. But the intensity of what they'd shared was always with him. Once he'd believed she was the woman he would marry and have a family with, but she had proved him wrong, yet again. He ended up marrying the twin he liked and respected, but had never loved in a romantic way. Life had a funny way of kicking you in the ass when you least expected it.

Chad rolled his head around on his neck and rotated

stiff shoulders to release some of his pent-up tension. In fifteen years, he'd slept with his wife a handful of times and then only in the very beginning, when he was still convinced he'd done the right thing by marrying Paris and had told himself that they could make a happy life together. Pam was always there though, hovering between them and he had imagined her eyes on him every time he went near Paris, until eventually he'd had no choice but to admit the truth to himself. Pam was the one he wanted. It would've been criminal to go on misleading Paris and worse, using her body to satisfy his physical needs when he couldn't even look her in the face while he was doing it, couldn't even sustain an erection long enough to give either of them any real pleasure.

Turning to other women seemed the lesser of two evils, and it was the route he had opted to take. His first affair was with a woman he'd met while attending a teaching conference in Atlanta, and theirs was a week-long, mutually satisfying fling. After that, he had carried on a three-year affair with a woman from East Point and then she'd decided she wanted more than he was willing to give and they had parted ways. The last woman he'd been involved with was a recent transplant to the area, a teacher at the high school he was inexplicably drawn to. She lived forty miles away in Juilienne, was single, and had gone out of her way to let him know she was interested. He was seven months into an affair with her before it dawned on him that he was drawn to her because of the way her hair flowed down her back when it was loose and because of her lips. They were large and plump. Like Pam's.

She hadn't demanded any more of Chad than he could or would give and, just six months ago, she told him she'd met someone and wanted to see where the relationship might go. Chad had wished her well and backed off.

He swallowed another mouthful of liquor as he thought of the woman now, recalled that she had approached him after Paris's funeral and suggested he call her sometime. But by then he knew that Pam was nearby, and all thoughts of other women had gone flying right out of his mind. They were all nice women and he'd cared about each of them in his own way, but he was reasonable enough to admit that having them had been a means to an end. For him, Pam was always the beginning, the middle, and the end. And now she was back and just as unreachable as she'd been for the last eighteen years. Close enough to touch, see, and smell, but still so far away.

Lust was eating at him when he rolled out of bed this morning, was sinking its teeth in his flesh as he went to work and tried to concentrate on deciding which extracurricular activities he would approve and which ones would have to be cut from the budget. It was wriggling around in his gut by the time he returned home and debated with Nikki over what to have for dinner. Finally he'd narrowed his options down to either locking himself in his room and relieving himself, driving out to the B&B and throwing himself on Pam's mercy, or fixing himself a drink and drowning his lust until it went away. He'd finally settled on the drink.

Chad found himself chuckling over his predicament. He swallowed more cognac, chased it with water, and threw his head back as the liquid slid down his throat. He rocked back on the hind legs of his chair and stayed that way for several seconds, studying the slatted porch ceiling and noticing a crack that he needed to repair.

Then he came forward in his chair, set his glass down with a soft thump and saw her standing on the steps outside the storm door, staring at him. In the here and now, his senses went on full alert, but his mind took him back in time. He stared at her and remembered . . .

"Come on, come on, come on," a twenty-year-old Chad chanted impatiently. He was yanking at the hem of Pam's halter-top, anxious to have it up and over her head.

"Hurry *up*, Pam. Damn, I think I'm dying here."

Pam giggled as she shimmied out of her skirt and kicked it out of the way. She slipped her fingers inside the rim of her panties and lowered them slowly. "You act like you're starving." She gasped as he dropped to his haunches and took her panties with him. His mouth fastened on her crotch, her head slammed back against the wall, and a long hiss escaped her lips. He knew just what to do to make her come quickly and violently.

Chad stood and pulled his T-shirt over his head. His jeans were barely unfastened and out of his way when he pressed Pam against the wall and lifted her for his entry. As she sank onto him, his mouth fell open in ecstasy. He held himself still and helped her out of her halter-top and then he palmed her breasts to bring to his mouth.

"I *am* starving," he growled, then sucked her breast deep in his mouth. "All damn week I've been thinking about this. I missed you, baby. You miss me?" He was a freshman in college and she was a junior in high school, so he made the drive from Atlanta back to Mercy at least twice a week to see her. This week he'd had finals and could only come on the weekend.

"Yes," Pam shrieked as he began moving inside her.

She lifted a leg and hooked it high on his waist, rocked forward to meet his powerful thrusts. "Oh, that feels so good. Don't stop."

"I'm never stopping," Chad vowed hoarsely. Sweat beaded on his brow, a signal to Pam that his release was near. She reached up and smoothed it away with the palms of her hands, then gripped his shoulders to steady herself. "You hear me, Pam? I'm never stopping."

Pam took his tongue in her mouth when he offered it to her and went with the orgasm as it smacked into her and left her breathless. Seconds later, Chad was shouting into her mouth, telling her that he had arrived, too.

They were spread out on the couch with Pam straddling Chad's lap, making love again, when Jasper entered his apartment and caught them in the act. He came up short, looked from Chad to Pam, and then averted his eyes as he walked across the living room and into his bedroom.

"Oh my God," Pam cried, covering her breasts with her hands, though she was a day late and a dollar short. She hopped up and raced around the room, gathering her clothes and trying to pull them on at the same time.

"Okay, so, I'll go in there and talk to him." Slightly irritated at being interrupted, Chad stood and stepped into his jeans. He was still hard and it took a few seconds of shifting around before he was able to situate himself and yank the zipper up. He hustled Pam toward the door. "Go downstairs and find something to do. I'll be down in a minute."

"He said he wouldn't be back until tomorrow morning." She paced in a small circle and pushed her hands through her hair. "I can't believe he saw my tits. *God, Chad. Shit*. I'm probably fired now."

Chad cupped a hand around her neck, brought her mouth to his and kissed her softly. "I know, and his timing is really fucked up on top of that. I was just about to come." He opened the door and nudged her out of it. "Fix your hair. Go downstairs and wait for me."

Twenty minutes later, Chad came jogging down the steps and met Pam in the hallway. She hopped up from the bench she was sitting on and damn near knocked him over. "What did he say?"

"He said you're not fired, but that he *is* getting his locks changed first thing in the morning," Chad said and burst out laughing.

Back from his trip down memory lane, Chad was chuckling to himself as he rose from his chair in slow motion and went to unlock the storm door. Pam heard the lock slide free and hesitated before pulling the door open and stepping onto the porch. She'd been out driving around and had somehow found herself here.

"Where's Nikki?" she whispered.

"I hope she's asleep. Did you park in the driveway?"

"Down the street. I came through the back way."

"Up the alley?"

"Yeah. Damn cat came out of nowhere and scared the shit out of me. I'm out of practice for sneaking around in the dark."

"You used to be so good at it." He slid his arms around her shoulders to lock the storm door and then used them to pull her into his body. "Why are you sneaking around in the dark anyway?"

Pam slipped her hands underneath the hem of his

shirt and skimmed her fingers along the waistband of his pants. He sucked in a sharp breath and let his head fall forward to rest against hers. They stared into each other's eyes.

"This is wrong," she finally said.

"Is it?" He caught her lips with his own and spread them wide for his tongue, walking her around in a circle as he kissed her. He backed her against the wall and pulled her skirt up around her waist. He hissed from behind his teeth when he discovered she was wearing thongs rather than panties.

"Nikki might wake up, Chad."

"Damn, I hope not. I might have to kill her." Chad dealt with his pants and pressed into Pam urgently. "We'll be quiet. Damn . . . make love to me, Pam."

TWELVE

The festival at Truman Field was in full swing by the time Pam pulled her car into an illegal parking space on the dry cleaner's lot across the street and climbed out. She slipped dark sunglasses over her eyes and leaned her butt against the car door to watch the commotion. The mood of the crowd would dictate whether she crossed the street and ventured into the fray or went scurrying back to her room.

The setup was just as she remembered it: carnival rides spaced out all over the field with food carts in between and children running wild, from one ride to the next. Parents trotting along behind them, glancing at their watches and counting the hours until bedtime. Until it was time for the real fun to begin. After dark and their children weren't around to bear witness, the adults swarmed to the rides, swapped bullshit stories from yesteryear, and cackled like idiots the whole time. Free-flowing beer and wine kept anyone from noticing the mosquitoes or the teenagers sneaking off into the woods in pairs. It was the one time of the year when hatchets were buried and people kicked back and let loose.

The smell of roasting hot dogs and barbecue was heavy in the air, and a nose full of the tantalizing aromas had Pam's stomach growling. If her nose was telling her right, Jasper and a few of the other old heads were manning the grills and putting their feet in them in the process. She knew she wouldn't leave without indulging in at least one hot dog and maybe two cups of homemade ice cream. If Miss Loretta still made it using her secret recipe, she might have to have three cups.

An involuntary smile curved Pam's lips as the Ferris wheel swung up in the air and spun a load of screaming kids around. She remembered quite clearly the rush of being hoisted into the air, suspended for long seconds before excitement took over and the big squeaky machine started rolling around in circles. Other kids had always looked down into the crowd and picked out faces to wave at, but she and Paris had held on to each other for dear life and whispered back and forth inside their cage. For them, there was no one in the crowd to search for and wave at.

Pam crossed the street slowly and skirted the crowd gathering near the curb patiently waiting in line for cotton candy. Several heads turned in her direction, and she pretended not to see them as she moved deeper into the flock of bodies. She followed her nose over to the barbecue grills and studied the balding heads stooped over them until she found the one she was looking for. It was almost the only one with sprigs of hair still attached to it. Just as she had suspected, Jasper was surrounded by smoke, flipping slabs of ribs and dabbing on sauce like he had eight hands instead of two.

"You save me a hot dog, old man?" Pam asked across the dome of a giant smoker.

Jasper looked up and grinned around the cigarette parked between his lips. He speared a blackened hot dog, held it out for her to bite into and then popped the rest in his own mouth. "Took you long enough to get here, gal."

"Nikki wouldn't let it rest, so I figured I had to at least show my face," she said. "How come you're not wearing the Uncle Sam costume you always wear to the festival?"

"Ain't wore that thing in five years," he grunted. He pulled his apron over his head and called out for someone to take over his grill, then came around to meet Pam. "They got me doing the announcements now. You want a beer?"

She shook her head, looking at him in shock. "You mean they actually talked you into being the emcee?" He rolled his eyes at her and took off walking toward a nearby concession stand. She ran to catch up with him and hooked her arm through his. "That means you have to sing the anthem, Jasper. Damn, I'm glad I came now."

"I'll let you do the singing, if it's all right with you. You know I can't hold a note." He ordered a beer and slid a sideways glance at her.

"How many beers have you had?"

"This is my first one." He watched her squirm around as he slurped foam from the rim of his cup. She looked in one direction, then the other, touched her glasses and swallowed no less than three times. Her mouth worked, but no sound emerged. He knew he'd put her on the spot, but he couldn't bring himself to care. The idea to ask her to sing had been in his head all day and now that she was here, he planned to see to it that she did. "You can do the Negro National Anthem. Always liked to hear you sing that when you was working at the funeral home."

"You eavesdropped on me?" she croaked.

"Every chance I got. You gonna do it or not?"

"Jasper, you know the last thing these people want is to hear me sing. Half of them won't even speak to me."

"These people are your people, Pam. That's why they so pissed off at you. Well . . . most of 'em, anyway. Pearline Dennis probably still mad about her husband chasing you around town like he didn't know he had a wife and seven kids at home, but that's neither here nor there." He took a hefty sip of beer and swallowed it slowly. It was ice cold and smooth going down after a long morning behind the grills. "Most of the old folks is giving you the cold shoulder 'cause they think you done forgot where you came from and you done forgot them. You gotta kiss a little ass to make it up to 'em."

"Can you blame me for wanting to forget, Jasper?" Pam hissed.

He put up a hand to ward her off. "I didn't say *I* felt that way. I just said some of the old heads was a little up in arms over the fact that you never came back. You sing their song for 'em and they might be willing to forgive you."

"Oh please," she flapped a hand, irritated. She turned away from him and looked over the crowd, noticing almost every pair of eyes that skirted away when hers shifted toward them. "I'm leaving next month. Did I tell you that?"

"Ask me why I ain't surprised? What's that got to do with you singing for me, Pam?"

"I need to get out of here, Jasper." She stepped closer and searched his eyes. "You know it's not the people. They don't know, but you do. This place is making me crazy."

"Okay, so you gotta go and you will. I understand that, but they don't. All they want to do is hear you say you're from Mercy. That's it. Sing for 'em a little bit, so they can stop pestering me and leave me the hell alone."

"What are they bothering you about?"

"Let me think for minute." He looked around when someone called his name and lifted his beer in greeting. "Verna mentioned something about thinking you would've at least came in and let her see to your hair while you was here, but you haven't so much as darkened her doorstep, even though she used to see to your hair all the time when you was a girl. Willie been bitching about the fact that you done ate at Hayden's round about twice now and he ain't had to run you out of his kitchen once, like he used to have to do. And Merlene going around talking about how she used to have to run you out of her front room back in the day, but you ain't came by to sit a spell with her, yet."

"They're mad with me about silly shit like that?"

Jasper nodded. "And you walk around with them dark glasses on, like you ashamed of where you're at."

"That's bullshit." But she reached up and snatched the glasses off of her face. She hooked them in the vee of her shirt and looked away from him. "And I can't believe you're listening to it."

"Small as this town is, you can't help but listen to gossip, gal. You know that yourself."

Her face was turned away from him, but he didn't need to see it to know that she was pissed off. He poked her in her side gently and made her look at him. "But you know I don't contribute to it, Pam. Quit acting like you mad with me and look here. I ever told you something wrong?"

"No," she sniffed reluctantly, not quite ready to give in.

"I'm telling you right now, too. You left 'cause you had to leave, I know that. They don't, so show 'em you ain't forgot about them whilst you was off in big old fancy Cal*ee*fornia."

"I didn't bring my guitar," she said several seconds later, and Jasper knew he had her then.

Wisely, he hid the grin threatening to take over his lips and concentrated on drinking more of his beer. "I think Willie brought his, if I ain't mistaken. That old tired-ass band of his is playing later on. You ask nicely and he might let you use it."

"I might just use it to conk his old ass over the head," she snapped.

Jasper shook his head and cracked up, his gut bouncing with the force of his laughter. "That's the Pam I know," he said, still chuckling. "Now things is back like they used to be." He gave her a gentle push away from him, tipping his head in the direction he wanted her to look. "Go on over there and tend to your fans. I'm going back to my grill, but I'll call you when I'm ready for you, so don't pull no disappearing act on me."

Pam glanced over her shoulder and did a double take. A small group of teenagers were standing around trying to look like they weren't waiting for her to look in their direction and failing miserably at it. She winked at Jasper and then took casual steps over to them. Halfway there, she stopped and stared at one of the teens like she was seeing a ghost.

"You're the spitting image of Josephine Henry," Pam told the boy she was staring at. She took in his pecan-brown skin and close-cropped hair, his dimpled cheeks and wide smile and shook her head. She'd know that face anywhere. She and Josie Henry had gotten into their share of trouble together in high school and had a ball doing it. His face was so exactly like his mother's that it was like seeing double.

"Yes ma'am, I'm Jon. I go to school with Nikki." He stepped forward and thrust a CD case at her. "She gave me a CD she said you signed, but I want to make sure I got the real deal. Could you sign this one, please?"

"Planning on auctioning it off on eBay?" Pam teased as she unfolded the paper insert and scrawled her name across her picture. She slid him a look from the corner of her eye and saw him blush to the roots of his hair. "I'm just kidding, Jon," she laughed and looped an arm through his. He swallowed loud enough for her to hear and be flattered. "You're precious. Introduce me to your friends."

As she stood there signing autographs, posing for photos, and talking with the kids, more kids and a few adults approached her. One of the more mannish boys asked Pam for a kiss, which necessitated her having to give him a quick peck on the lips after warning him not to slip her any tongue. Over an hour passed before Pam was able to excuse herself and by then, she had pecked a total of seven boys on the lips and eleven more shy ones on the cheek. She smoothed on more lipstick and decided to go in search of Josie Henry.

Jon pointed her in the right direction and she found her old childhood buddy right where he said he'd left her a little while ago. Pam walked up behind Josie and plopped down beside her in the grass. "So what did you do, pay someone to clone you and out came Jon?" she asked, then gave up a lopsided grin when Josie's head spun around in shock. They flew into each other's arms for a warm hug.

Other than Paris or Nate, when she'd had a mind to be devious, Josie was always willing to be a partner in crime. In high school, they'd spiked the punch at more than a few dances, skipped classes whenever the mood struck, and stolen candy and cheap cosmetics from the A&P with frightening regularity. They had also sneaked cigarettes together between classes and cheated on more tests than she cared to count. Now, nearly twenty years later, they strolled around Truman Field, sneaking ride tokens off the roll when the attendants weren't looking and going from ride to ride like idiots. Josie nabbed a stuffed zebra from one of the prize booths, even though she hadn't played any games and then goaded Pam into sharing not one, but two cherry topped funnel cakes with her. They carried on just as they had as teenagers, and Pam was hard-pressed to figure out which of them was the worst influence on the other. She left Josie to see to her newborn and sneaked off to repent for the sins she'd knowingly committed during the last few hours.

She was standing on the edge of the field leaning against a tree, feeling sick to her stomach and smoking a cigarette, when Chad found her. She flicked a glance at him, took in his faded jeans, brown polo shirt, and brown leather sandals, and shifted her attention back to the festivities.

"Your toes are out." She blew a thin stream of smoke through pursed lips and darted another glance in the direction of his feet. He'd always had nice feet and she liked to think she was partly responsible for that. Before he'd learned to appreciate pedicures, she was the one who had pampered him. Kept his toenails cut and neatly shaped and convinced him that it was okay for him to bare them every once in a while. It was only one of the many ways she'd spoiled him.

Chad lifted the cup he was holding and sipped deliberately. "So are yours." He wondered if she remembered that he had loved to tongue the soles of her feet as they were making love. Wondered if she'd ever lain awake at night remembering. Instead of asking, he said, "You've been avoiding me since the last time we were together." It wasn't a question, and he didn't let it sound like one.

"You make it sound like what we did the last time we were together was a good thing."

"Wasn't a bad thing. I mean, as far as bad things go, I've heard of worse. I was under the impression that you enjoyed making love with me as much as I did with you."

Pam shot nervous glances over her shoulders and frowned up at him, meeting his eyes for the first time since he'd walked up. "Lower your voice, Chad. Somebody might be listening. Matter of fact, knowing Mercy, somebody probably *is* listening."

He scanned the area where they were standing at length. "I think we're safe. In case you're wondering, I've wanted to do that for the last eighteen years and I'm glad we did. Both times."

"Yeah, well if the rumors about me being a whore weren't true before that night, I guess they are now, aren't they?" A frustrated groan pushed past her lips as she fell back against the tree and dropped her head in her hand wearily. She massaged the wrinkles from her forehead with stiff fingers. "Nikki could've come out and seen us. Anyone could've walked up those steps and seen us. A mistake like that could've cost us both a lot."

"Couldn't have cost me any more than I've already paid."

"I wish you would stop hinting around about your

life being so damn bad because I just don't see it. You always wanted to be a teacher and that's what you are. You wanted kids and that's what you got." She looked him from head to toe. "You don't look like you're suffering to me."

"What about the part where I wanted to do all that and have all that with you?"

"Chad, please, okay? Right now all I can concentrate on is the fact that I slept with my sister's husband and I feel like shit about it, so please don't make me feel worse by shoving the past down my throat on top of that." She dropped her cigarette and stepped on it, then bent to pick the butt out of the grass.

Chad considered her curiously, wondering if he should just come out and say what was on his mind or let the subject die a slow death. Even in profile, she looked tortured, like she was beating herself up at that very moment and hating herself for what they'd done. He, on the other hand, was feeling nothing but the calmness that came along with hot, hard, long-awaited release. The stirrings of anticipation were in his gut, too. Given the chance, he'd make love to Pam again and again, as mány times as he could without causing himself bodily harm. He didn't feel the slightest tinge of either guilt or remorse. More like contentment, if he was being completely honest.

Realizing that he was staring at her and that there were probably several pairs of busy eyes turned in their direction, Chad shifted away from Pam and looked out over the field.

"Fourteen years," he said suddenly. He looked up at the sky and noticed that it was darkening slowly. The Tilt-A-Whirl was doing a brisk business, as was the Ferris Wheel and he thought he saw Nikki ducking into the Bouncing Ball House. He shook his head sadly, thinking that she was too old and much too tall, even if she was still a kid at heart.

"What?"

"You heard me, Pam. I said fourteen years. That's how long it's been since I was intimate with Paris." She sputtered and he rushed ahead before she could interrupt him. "Longer, if you count the months in between, during that first year. Paris and I were never about the same thing you and I were about."

Pam's eyes grew wide as she stared at Chad's profile. He was studying the goings-on at the festival as if he was totally engrossed in them. One hand was pushed casually in his pants pocket and the other held his cup loosely, dangling at his side. "I don't believe that."

"You should, because it's the truth." Chad downed the last of his beer and belched discreetly behind the cup. "Drop your butt in here," he told her, holding the empty cup out to her. She did and he left her standing there long enough to take the cup over to a nearby trash can. When he came back the distance between them was noticeably shorter. "We had separate bedrooms from the time Nikki was five."

"You have to be lying. Paris never told me about that and I know she would have. And Nikki never mentioned it to me, either."

"Nikki was raised not to discuss what went on in our home, not even with you. I can't say why Paris never told you, but it's the truth. I think you know me well enough to know that I wouldn't lie about something like this. I don't think I've ever lied to you about anything, as far as that goes."

"You have to admit it's a little hard to swallow." Unable to stand still any longer, Pam came away from the tree and paced back and forth. She pushed her hands through her hair and fisted them at the nape of her neck. Her eyes darted around restlessly. "God, what is it about this damn town? It's like I'm in the Twilight Zone. First Jasper tells me that all the old folks are mad with me because I haven't gotten my hair done or been run out of Willie's kitchen. And now you . . ." She released the hold she had on her hair long enough to wave a distracted hand in his direction. "What am I supposed to do with what you're telling me, Chad? First of all, how am I supposed to believe it? Would you be telling me this if Paris was still alive?"

He thought about the question and shook his head quickly. "Probably not since you undoubtedly wouldn't be here if that was the case. I'm telling you now so you can finally understand the legacy you left behind."

"You told me once years ago that I'd fucked up everybody's life. I don't need to hear that shit again."

"Then at least stop beating yourself up about what happened between us the other night. Hell, Paris would've been the first to tell you that none of us is perfect. I couldn't be the husband I'd promised to be, so she found what she needed somewhere else, and that was fine with me. I encouraged her to be with someone else. And I never told her, but I'm sure she knew I had other relationships, too. It was an arrangement that worked out for us because we were never meant to be together in the first place. The being together part was for you and me."

"This is crazy." Pam met his eyes and stared into them long and hard. "Why would either of you want to live like that? And why didn't she tell me?"

"We talked about divorce a few times, but whenever the subject of who would get Nikki came up, we left it alone. I told her I would fight her and drag you into court right along with her if it came to that."

"Why didn't she tell me?"

"What would you have done, Pam? Would you have come back?"

Pam opened her mouth to respond, but she never got the chance. Nikki chose that moment to come rushing over to them, a look of relief on her smiling face. As if sensing the tension between them, she looked from Chad to Pam before grabbing hold to Pam's hand.

"Aunt Pam, Mr. Jasper said for you to come on. The band is setting up and he told me to come and find you."

"He's ready for me already?" Pam looked up at the sky and frowned. "They didn't used to start the singing and shit until it was completely dark."

"You're singing?" Chad asked, eyebrows high on his forehead.

"Yep," Nikki jumped in. "They're starting early because Mr. Jasper told everybody and their mama that Aunt Pam was singing."

"I said I would sing *one song*," Pam protested. Nikki tugged on her hand until she was reluctantly skipping along behind her. She threw Chad a slightly alarmed look over her shoulder, to which he only smiled. As they came closer to the stage, she saw that a wooden stool was sitting on the stage behind a freestanding microphone and that was all. The band was nowhere in sight.

Jasper saw her coming and damn near ran up the steps along the side of the stage. The look on his face told her that he had accurately intercepted the look on hers. She was seriously considering strangling him with her bare hands and he knew it. He adjusted the microphone and sent a high-pitched squeal out over the field, then cleared his throat. Pam stood at the bottom of the steps with her arms folded protectively around her middle.

"This is ridiculous," she spat out of the side of her mouth to Nikki, whose arms were draped around her shoulders possessively.

"Shhhh, listen," Nikki whispered back, lifting a hand like she intended to place it over Pam's mouth. She missed the glare Pam shot her.

"Okay, so ya'll know little Pam Mayes finally brought her tail back to Mercy," Jasper was saying. He held up his hands to hold the crowd off as catcalls rose up in the air. "I told her she was gon' have to sing for us if she wanted us to look over her being away so long and all. Seems to me she's got a lot of making up to do. Am I right?"

"I'm going to kill him," Pam hissed to Nikki. She glanced over and locked eyes with Willie and couldn't help the smile that curved her lips. He was tuning up his guitar and looking at her expectantly. She eased away from Nikki and went over to him. "You getting that thing ready for me?"

"This here thing 'bout old as you, gal." Willie looked at her sternly from under bushy brows. "Don't be too rough with it 'less you wanna deal with me, and you ain't too old for me to turn over my knee, either."

"You spanked my butt a few times, as I recall."

"You remember that?" A chuckle rumbled in his throat.

"Nobody forgets your spankings, Mr. Willie. I remember everything." She took his hand and squeezed it warmly.

"Don't be tryin' to butter me up, gal. Always was a shyster." He pretended to be twisting his hand free of hers as he frowned at her. "And still ain't gave me no suga, either." He beamed after she leaned in and pecked his cheek.

Then Nikki was there, poking and prodding at Pam

until she was up on the stage, taking slow steps across the wooden surface to the microphone. She spent a few minutes simply staring out at the crowd, collecting her thoughts as she smoothed her hair back and away from her face. She reached behind her to pick up the stool and set it to the side before she brought the microphone closer to her mouth.

"I've sang in a lot of places and for a lot of people," Pam told the crowd, "but none of those people knew me when I was flat-chested and missing my front teeth." A smattering of laughter reached her ears and some of the tension in her shoulders dissipated. "Never sang in Mercy before, and I'm a little nervous, so please bear with me. Nikki?" She looked toward the steps and caught Nikki's eyes. "Would you get Auntie some water, please?" Scant minutes later, Nikki handed Pam a bottle of water and she turned it up gratefully. Then she spoke into the microphone again. "Now, can someone over eighteen please get me a beer?"

The crowd howled with laughter and Pam began to sing. She didn't need the guitar for the Negro National Anthem. She sang it a cappella and encouraged the crowd to sing along with her, which they did. After the final verse ended and the clapping and cheering died down, she pulled the stool close, sat down and adjusted the microphone. Willie handed her his guitar and she settled it across her lap reverently.

Pam strummed the guitar strings softly and closed her eyes as she found her rhythm. While she allowed her fingers to warm up, she hummed along with the chords and let the music roll through her body.

"Miss Verna, I'm coming to get my hair touched up real soon," she said and laughter was her response. "Nobody shampoo's hair like Miss Verna, and ya'll know it. Got that whole scalp scratching thing down to a science. And Miss Merlene . . ." she strummed a few more strings absently, "next time I come over don't run me out of your front room with a broomstick, okay?" More laughter, this time stronger and louder. She let it die down, then cleared her throat. "I wrote this song a while back, but this'll be the first time I've ever sang it in public. It's called 'Have Mercy On Me.' This is for you, Mercy, and for you, Paris, wherever you are. I love you."

Pam sat still with the lump in her throat and the crowd stood still with her. Then she took a deep breath and pretended she was thousands of miles away in concert and let loose.

Three songs and many hugs and kisses later, Pam slipped away from the crowd and made a hasty bee-line for her car. She locked herself inside, put the key in the ignition, and rested her forehead against the steering wheel. She took several deep, calming breaths and scrubbed half-dried tears from her cheeks roughly. She reached to turn on the headlights and ended up with the windshield wipers swishing across the glass instead. It took her shaking hands several tries to locate the switch to turn the wipers off and then find the correct button for the lights. She turned them on and pulled out into the street slowly.

Two miles down the road, her hands were still shaking, and Pam leaned over to feel around in the passenger seat for her cell phone. She flipped it open and dialed with one hand steering the car. The phone rang ten times on the other end and then a sleepy voice answered.

"This is Pamela Mayes. Is this a bad time?" she said into the phone. Just hearing the familiar voice instantly calmed Pam's nerves. She pulled over to the side of the road to talk and then to listen.

* * *

Miles drove straight from the airport to the B&B where Pam was staying, hoping to find her there and persuade her to join him for a late dinner or maybe drinks, if she'd already eaten. She wasn't in her room and he'd forgotten about the annual festival until the owner of the B&B reminded him that most, if not all of the town, was probably there. That explained why Moira hadn't answered her phone, he thought. She would be there, too.

He entertained the idea of tracking Pam down at Truman Field, but decided against it, since he wasn't really in the mood for socializing on that grand of a scale. He preferred to have Pam all to himself, without all the distractions other people would provide. He thought he knew the best way to approach her with the questions he wanted answers to and he was anxious to get to it. He declined the offer to wait for Pam in the main parlor and returned to his car.

He was checking the messages on his cell phone when Pam's car skidded to a stop not far from where he was parked. Had she glanced around she would've seen him, but she didn't. She hopped out of her car before it came to a complete stop and disappeared inside the B&B as if she thought she was being chased. His eyebrows shot up curiously. He reached for the door handle and froze as a second car pulled into the lot and parked. He watched Chad go inside after Pam.

Miles glanced at his watch and noted the time. 8:47PM. It occurred to him that he should go and check in at his hotel, perhaps grab himself some dinner, since hadn't eaten anything in hours. He could catch up with Pam sometime tomorrow, when she was more relaxed and approachable. Something had obviously upset her, if the way she'd driven into the parking lot and run inside the building was any indication. Now probably wasn't the best time to go tapping on her door suggesting dinner.

"To hell with that," Miles told himself. Even more pressing than the need to check into his hotel was the question running around in his mind: How long would Chad stay in Pam's room? There was only one way to find out the answer and that was to wait and see. Miles loosened his tie and slid down in his seat to do just that.

Inside the B&B, Chad knocked lightly on Pam's door and stood back to wait. "Who's there?" She stood on the other side of the door, close so her mouth was almost pressed to the wood and she didn't have to raise her voice.

"It's me," Chad murmured.

Pam turned the lock and pulled the door open a little at a time. She peered out at Chad through an inch wide crack. "Where is Nikki?"

"Spending the night with Kelly so she can stay at the festival longer than she knows she's supposed to." He used two fingers to nudge the door open wider. She didn't protest and he kept nudging until there was enough space for him to slip inside the room. She stepped around him to lock the door and he stepped with her, moving up close behind her and opening his mouth on the back of her neck. Pam's eyes closed on a long sigh. She sucked the sigh back into her mouth as his hands came around and cupped her breasts.

Chad's tongue flickered along the line of Pam's shoulder, up her neck and dipped into her ear. His breathing was heavy and erratic. "Do you want me to leave, Pam?" Even as he asked the question, he was pulling her shirt over her head and dropping it on the floor. Her bra was next, and then his fingers were teasing her nipples. Pam swallowed and shook her head. She turned in his arms and opened her mouth for his tongue.

Miles didn't check into his hotel room until 4:52AM, twenty minutes after Chad left the B&B.

THIRTEEN

Dear Diary,

Today I learned the true meaning of knocking before opening a closed door. This was even worse than the time me and Pam walked into Lisa Hennigan's room and caught her and Leslie Mayer in bed together, kissing each other on the mouth. Everybody was embarrassed then, but today just takes the cake. I guess me and Nate can stop asking ourselves what's really going on between Pam and Chad because now we know. A little bit, anyway because neither one of them is saying much.

Chad's parents are out of town (big surprise there, right?) and we all planned to meet over to his house and hang out. I met up with Nate at the A&P and we waited around to see if Pam would show up, but she never did. Where was she? I'm getting to that. Nate bought some sodas and talked old Mr. Tommy into letting him have a bottle of wine, too. We walked over to Chad's house and went on in *since the back door was unlocked. It was real quiet and Nate thought maybe Chad was in his room playing with himself or something, so he told me to be quiet going up the steps. He thought it would be funny to bust in Chad's room and catch him. I thought so too, but at the same time I was wondering how Nate figured that's what Chad would be doing. Did he play with himself, too? Hmmm.*

Anyway, Nate eased the door open and we peeked inside the room and there was Pam and Chad in bed together. Oh my God! So that's where she disappeared to. Thank God they had clothes on and were lying on top of the covers or else I would've really had a heart attack. From the look on Nate's face I could tell he was just as surprised as I was. I mean, we pretty much figured that they liked each other, maybe even kissed a few times. We suspected some stuff, but not this. Pam was lying on her back and Chad was lying on top of her, between her legs with his head on her chest. They were both out cold, Chad with his arms pushed underneath Pam and Pam with one arm around a pillow and the other around Chad's neck. It gets worse, though. We were still peeking in the room, watching, when Chad woke up and shook Pam, so she could wake up, too. I guess she didn't come to fast enough because then he started kissing her like crazy. Next thing me and Nate knew, he was lying full on top of her and they were sucking face like people on television do, mouths open wide, so you just knew they were tonguing. I felt my mouth drop open and looked at Nate. His mouth was open, too. Pam pretended like she was so sleepy, but she was kissing Chad back and squeezing his butt as he pressed into her down there.

Nate gasped when Chad went up on his hands and rolled his hips into Pam's private area and I gasped when she gasped. I can't believe Pam never told me any of this. We tell each other everything, but she's been holding out about Chad, and about lying in his bed with him and kissing like she's thirty instead of fifteen. Oh my God! I can't stop saying that.

Nate pulled the door closed and we stood there a long time, listening to them talk in low voices and hearing Pam giggle. She was laughing as she told Chad to stop doing whatever he was doing because she had to pee. We heard her climb off the bed and come walking toward the door. I'm glad Nate is a quick thinker because I was still in shock. He hurried up and knocked on the door, so they would think we had just gotten there.

I wonder what they would've done if me and Nate hadn't showed up when we did? Pam keeps saying she's a virgin, but now I'm not so sure. Are they having sex? When I find out (and I will find out) you'll be the first to know.

Paris

Nikki closed the diary and raised enlightened eyes in Pam's direction. Her dad had dropped her off at the B&B this morning on his way to the high school, so she could spend the day with Pam rather than moping around the house by herself. They'd gone out for breakfast and then returned to the B&B to swim before lunch. Nikki stretched out on her lounge chair and watched her aunt swim. She'd been trying to keep track of Pam's laps, but she lost count somewhere around lap twelve because that was when she had opened the diary and started reading. These days she carried the diary around with her, mostly everywhere she went, in the Gucci tote she had finally talked Pam into parting with.

Aunt Pam and her dad? The idea of the two of them together, kissing and who knew what else, gave her a funny feeling. Like she was on the outside looking in on something she would never be able to completely figure out. Mercy was a small town, and everybody knew everybody else's business, but she had never heard the slightest whisper about anything going on between her dad and her aunt back then. And she'd heard plenty about Aunt Pam running wild and being a hooligan. The gossips had always put her and Uncle Nate together, saying they were the ones who were sneaking around and doing . . . things.

Still, her mom wouldn't write about Aunt Pam and her dad if there wasn't something to it. She rationalized that if anyone had cause to know the inside scoop, it would've been her mom. The one time she'd asked her dad about something her mom had written he'd gone all stiff and started snapping Nikki's head off, which was just as bad as coming right out and telling her to mind her own business. She knew she couldn't go to him asking more questions about him and Aunt Pam, and Aunt Pam probably wouldn't be any better with answering questions either.

I guess I'll just have to keep reading, Nikki thought.

Pam finished her laps and left the pool. She padded across the slippery concrete and dropped onto the lounger beside Nikki with an exhausted sigh. "You decided to have a look, huh?" she asked as she scrubbed a towel through her hair and shook it out with her fingers.

Nikki couldn't help herself. "Yep, and there's some

pretty interesting speculations about you and my dad, Aunt Pam. I think you ought to just come out and tell me if what my mom suspected was true."

"What did your mom suspect?" Pam was careful to keep her voice even and light.

"You and my dad were kind of hot and heavy back then. What's up with that?"

"What's up with that is that your mother had a very active imagination and it looks like you do, too." Pam stood and playfully tapped Nikki's thigh. "I thought you were supposed to be taking comfort from having that book, not looking for clues."

"So there *are* clues to look for?" Pam was gathering up her things so Nikki starting gathering her own things. She dropped the diary in her tote and threw her towel over shoulder. She stood and pushed her feet into her flip-flops, watching Pam's face closely.

"Nikki, please. I told you before not to believe everything you read. And anyway, even if your dad and I did have a crush on each other back then, which I'm not saying we did, he married your mom. Mystery solved. Can we go and eat now?"

I don't think so, Nikki thought to herself as she followed Pam to her room. They took turns in the shower and got dressed. Pam changed into drawstring silk pants and a matching sleeveless top and pulled her wet hair into a sloppy ponytail at the nape of her neck. She was pushing earrings into her ears when Nikki emerged from the bathroom, looking freshly scrubbed and bringing the scent of lilacs with her.

"I see you found my shower gel," Pam chuckled and shook her head. "Your mom used to help herself to my stuff, too."

"You mind?" Nikki perched on the edge of the bed

and slathered some of Pam's shea butter cream on her long legs.

"No, I don't mind. I love you and I share with the people I love. You like that?" She nodded toward the jar Nikki held, sat down next to her and scooped cream into her palm. "Here, turn around and I'll do your back. When did your tits get so big?"

Nikki gasped and turned to stare at Pam over her shoulder. "Aunt Pam! I keep telling you I'm seventeen now. I'm supposed to have tits. And mine are only a little bigger than yours."

"Must get those from Chad's side of the family," Pam murmured, referring to the fact that her own breasts were a conservative 34C and Nikki's were at least two sizes larger. She brought a mental picture of Chad's mother to the front of her mind and nodded at what she saw. Nikki would probably have breasts like Angela Greene; plump and juicy, the way most men liked them. She smoothed the last of the cream into Nikki's skin and gave her back a light pat. "Seems like just yesterday you had braces on your teeth and ponytails hanging down your back. God, you had the wildest, tangliest hair I've ever seen in my life."

"You know what you gotta do, don't you, Aunt Pam?"

"Oh no, not the comb." Pam hopped off the bed and backed away from the comb Nikki held out to her. She darted a glance at the tangled mess on Nikki's head and cringed, which made Nikki burst out laughing. "You're tender-headed Nikki, and you know how you used to scream and holler when it was time to get your hair combed."

"At least I already shampooed it. Come on, Aunt Pam. I just need you to moisturize my scalp and then comb it out for me. Do me one of those French buns you always wear." She saw the tortured look on Pam's face and stuck out her bottom lip pitifully. *"Pleeeeeease?"*

Nikki refrained from screaming and hollering, but still over an hour had passed when they finally walked into the dining room, ready to sit down to lunch. Chad came to pick up Nikki just as they finished the caramel cheesecake they were sharing for dessert.

He approached the table, hands in his pockets and looking from one to the other expectantly. "If any crimes have been committed tell me now," he said.

"You just missed the police, Dad," Nikki said. "And you're late."

He spread his hands wide in surrender. "Some of us do work, you know. I wish I could've spent the day lounging around the pool like you, but them's the breaks. Where's your stuff?"

"I left it in Aunt Pam's room. If you'd let me drive we wouldn't have these kinds of issues. You know that, right?" She gave him the evil eye as she pushed her chair back and stood up slowly.

"Maybe after I forget about those three tickets you got, I'll give you back your keys."

"That's not fair."

"That's fair as hell, especially since Harper just made it his business to inform me that you and Kelly were out past two o'clock in the morning last Saturday. You want to talk about that?"

"Old Man Harper has the biggest mouth in town," Nikki complained dramatically.

"Yes, he does," Pam agreed quietly and looked away when Chad grimaced in her direction.

"I just want you to know that I'm feeling really mistreated right now."

"Duly noted. Go get your stuff." Chad stepped back and pointed a finger toward the staircase, eyebrows raised. Pam remained silent, handing Nikki her room key as she passed.

"She's a spoiled brat." He dropped into the chair Nikki had vacated, picked up her water glass, and downed the rest of it in one gulp. He locked eyes with Pam over the rim of the glass. "It's a damn shame she has me wrapped around her finger and she knows it." He set the glass down and folded his hands on the table.

"She's a good kid," Pam said, but her next thought wrinkled her forehead prettily. "She's also nosy as hell, too. That damn diary could bring up a lot of questions that I don't have answers for. She's circling around like a vulture as we speak."

"I was thinking the same thing. I thought about sneaking in her room and making it disappear, but I'm sure she'd notice it was gone."

"She asked me if we dated and I couldn't think of anything to say, except that it was ancient history and that Paris probably embellished a little bit."

He grinned and shook his head. "That sounds like the same thing I told her when she approached me, which undoubtedly makes us both look guilty as hell."

"And here I thought we were being so careful back then. Keeping secrets and sneaking around, and all the time Paris *knew*?"

"From what I understand she *suspected*," Chad clarified. "After we were married the conversation came up and I got around to admitting that you and I were lovers for much longer than she knew, but I had no idea she'd write it down in that damn diary of hers."

"Oh, for the . . ." Pam lifted a hand and let it drop back to the table disgustedly. "Thanks a lot, Chad. That was a really smart thing to do. And why were you discussing my business with Paris, anyway?"

"It was my business too, remember?" He leaned across the table slightly. "Plus, it helped explain why things were the way they were between Paris and me. How was I supposed to know she'd write the shit down? And what is this obsession women have with keeping diaries any damn way?"

"For your information, Moira gave us those diaries when we were twelve," Pam hissed. They didn't make journals like them anymore. They were heavy, hard bound and covered with floral printed cloth, both of them at least five hundred pages thick. The pages were lined with midnight blue ink, the lines set close together for elegantly tiny entries, and the edges of the pages rimmed in gold. She and Paris's arms had been sore after lugging them all the way back to the home after Moira had surprised them with the books. She'd probably be seventy years old before a replacement was necessary. The cloth had since taken somewhat of a beating, but she had just recently reached the halfway point in her own 8X10 diary. Even journaling daily, Paris couldn't have been that much further along.

"And?"

"And nothing, I'm just saying. You shouldn't have said anything to Paris about us. What if she wrote that down, too?"

"So what if she did? Look, forget about the diary for a minute." Chad sat back and ran a hand around the nape of his neck. "Nate called the other night."

"I thought he was still in the Middle East somewhere?"

"He is, but he's ready to come home."

Happiness about Nate returning to the States safe and sound had a smile turning up the corners of Pam's mouth. Then, just as quickly, she was frowning. "She could ask Nate about us."

Chad dismissed the possibility with a flap of his hand. "Don't even go there. He won't tell her shit. She's too damn nosy for her own good, though."

She reached across the table and laid a hand on top of his. "Does he know about Paris?"

"He does now. That's why he called, said he'd just gotten the message. I called his publicist right after it happened, but apparently he's been out of contact for a while. You know he would've been here otherwise. He took it pretty hard." Nate had cried for ten minutes straight, and all Chad could do was hold the phone helplessly and listen to his friend's grief. "He was shocked when I told him you were still here."

"Well if he wants to see me, he'd better hurry home. I guess Nikki told you about the tour I've got coming up next month?" Pam took her hand back and lifted her water glass to her lips.

"She mentioned it, but I was waiting for you to bring it up."

"I would've . . . eventually."

He looked up and saw Nikki coming down the stairs. "There are some things I need to discuss with you, Pam. Can you come by the house tonight?"

"Can't. I have an appointment with Miss Verna in a few hours and then I'm going to see Moira."

"What about later?"

"I told David I'd meet him for dinner. What is this about, Chad? Is it something to do with Nikki?"

"I don't want to get into it right now, not with Nikki around."

Nikki approached Pam from behind and surprised her with a smacking kiss on the cheek. She smiled at her niece and leaned sideways for another kiss on the lips. "Thanks for today, Aunt Pam. I had fun," Nikki said.

Pam nodded that she was welcome. "Did you take the cream you like?"

"You mind?"

"Of course not, you little thief. I'll see you soon." She looked up at Chad, who was now standing over the table and sighed. "I guess I'm coming to the house."

Dear Diary,

Aunt Pam said that my mom embellished things in her diary, but I have proof positive that she didn't. I did a horrible thing today. When I went to Aunt Pam's room to get my bag I looked in her diary. I thought with her being older, she'd have a really so-phisticated hiding place for her diary, but she didn't. I stood there, looking around her room, wondering where I would hide my diary if I was her and then I found it at the bottom of her suitcase under the bed.

I didn't get too deep into it, just flipped through the pages near the front. I just wanted to see if Aunt Pam had written anything about my dad. And if so, what? So I could compare stories and know the truth for once and for all. I know the truth now, all right.

My dad was Aunt Pam's first and she was his. How crazy is that? Some really screwed up shit must've been going on back then. Had to be and that's why everybody's so secretive when I ask about stuff now. One thing I know for sure, I'm not ask-ing my dad or Aunt Pam about what I read. They'd know I was snooping big time then. But I'm going to start paying closer attention to what's going on around me from now on.

This is like a mystery or something. Now I have

*even more questions than I started out with. I feel a
little sick to my stomach, thinking about Aunt Pam
and my dad being together like that. God, I wish I
could go back in time and be a fly on the wall.*

Nikki

Scalp still tingling from Miss Verna's magic fingers,
Pam pushed through the restaurant door and spotted David sitting in a booth near the back of the room.
She sent him a short wave of acknowledgment and
then let herself be waylaid by the hostess and two wait
staff. She'd been talking all day and a few more minutes wouldn't make too much of a difference. She
signed her autograph across the bottom of a menu
and helped select the spot on the wall where it would
hang, then went to join David.

"Sorry I'm late." She slid into the booth and smiled
across the table at him. "It got a little crazy in the
beauty shop and then again in the A&P."

"Crowds of adoring fans?" Miles wanted to know.
He lifted a hand to signal the waiter, a little irritated at
having been kept waiting for twenty minutes.

"Not exactly the kind you're thinking about. More
like crowds of old folks, anxious to remind me of all
my dirty deeds and laugh about them. Seems like I
was public enemy number one back then, but now the
shit is just plain hilarious. What are you having?" She
picked up a menu and perused the selections.

"I thought I'd have the enchilada platter. Have you
decided what you're having?" She told him and he
gave their orders to the waiter. Then he sat back and
studied her intently. "Your hair looks nice."

"Thanks. I swear Miss Verna has voodoo in her
hands. I almost fell asleep over the bowl."

"So she's not part of the reason you stayed away so long then?"

Pam caught his eyes and held them. "I never said she was. How was your trip to New York?"

"How did you know that's where I was?"

"Moira mentioned it." She noticed the look on his face. "Was it a secret?"

"Why should it be? What else did Moira say?"

The waiter returned with their drinks and she took a sip of wine before responding. "Nothing much, just that you were in New York on business. We spent the rest of the day looking through old photos and drinking tea. You're the spitting image of your father, by the way."

"If you'd seen him just before he died you wouldn't think that's a compliment," Miles said offhandedly. "You looked at pictures of Moira's dead relatives?"

"Grandmothers, grandfathers, parents, the whole bit. I wonder why Moira never had any kids."

"For one thing, she never stayed married long enough to make any."

A shocked laugh escaped Pam's mouth before she could stop it. She shook her head at him and tsk-tsked as the waiter arranged their plates in front of them. After he moved away she said, "That wasn't nice, David. She was married to the last one for quite a while, I think. I remember that he was there sometimes when I visited Moira. He was nice enough." She picked up her knife and fork and cut into her steak.

"Do you ever think about your birth parents, Pam?" The question caught her off guard, just as he'd intended and she stared at him wide-eyed as she chewed slowly.

"Where did that come from?"

"I'm just curious. Most adopted people go looking

for their birth parents at some point in their lives. I wondered if you ever had." He remembered his beer and swallowed a mouthful, completely at ease with the direction of the conversation.

"We weren't adopted, remember?"

"The principle's still the same."

She shook her head and speared a broccoli floret. "No, it's not. I had and have no desire to look for people who dumped me in a children's home and left me there all those years. No one ever came looking for us, so why would I go looking for them?"

"Simple curiosity? Maybe to rub it in a little?"

"I wasn't curious and, that I know of, neither was Paris. But of course, we can't ask her now, can we?"

"You never wondered where your green eyes came from or who gave you your hair? The color of your skin?" He bit into his enchilada and watched her face suffuse with red heat.

"No, I didn't. Where is all this coming from, David?"

"I told you, I'm just curious."

"Well don't be. Do I give you the third degree about your life? I've never once asked where you live or what you do, have I? I don't even know if you have a wife and kids at home or a criminal history as long as my arm, for that matter."

"Ask me whatever you want to know."

Her silverware clattered to her plate and a frustrated groan filled the space between them. "That's just the thing, David. I don't care. I came back to this dreary little town to bury my sister and to make peace with her death. Then I met you and you seemed harmless enough, so I figured, what's the problem with a couple of meals and some easy conversation? But you keep poking at me and asking questions that are really none of your business, which is starting to be suspect. Now if you want a few tidbits of juicy gossip to sell to the tabloids for some quick cash, just say so and I might oblige you. I mean, hey, we've all got bills to pay and you might have a sick kid at home or something. But if you're just one of those people who didn't learn in kindergarten when to back off, then I'm telling you right now, *back off.*"

"I've upset you," Miles said unnecessarily. He knew damn well that he had upset her. "I didn't mean to do that."

"I don't know if I believe that." She pushed her half-eaten food away and reached for her wine.

"You can't blame me for being curious, Pam. Hell, you said yourself that you hate this town, but you never say why."

"Leave it alone, David."

"Why? What are you afraid I'll find out if I don't?"

"I'm not afraid of you finding out anything." She snatched her purse from the seat and slung it over her shoulder. *I have to get out of here,* she thought with something like panic rolling around in her gut. She slid along the seat until she was free to stand, then looked down at him. "I'm not afraid of you at all, and I don't owe you any explanations for the way I live my life."

"Pam, please sit down. I'm sorry if I've offended you. I guess I forgot my manners for a minute. Let's—"

She cut him off with a trembling hand. "No, let's not. Come to think of it, I don't think you should contact me again, David. It was nice meeting you and thanks for everything, but seeing each other again doesn't seem like such a good idea right now. This isn't really working for me."

"Pam," Miles called after her as she darted through the restaurant toward the exit.

He looked out the window and saw her drive off the

lot erratically, then slid back down in the booth wearily. "You really fucked that up, Miles," he mumbled behind the hand over his mouth.

"Excuse me?"

He glanced at the hovering waiter and massaged the bridge of his nose. "I said, could I have another beer, please?"

FOURTEEN

Pam gripped the steering wheel and tried to regulate her breathing as she drove. The restaurant was only a little over ten minutes away from Paris's house, but the minutes seemed to creep by. She could literally hear a clock ticking in her head, and she felt herself becoming more and more agitated in response.

Near the exploding point, she turned into the driveway and shut the car off. She was in such a hurry to be indoors that she left the keys in the ignition and her purse on the seat, and raced across the grass to the porch. Chad and Nikki were in the sitting room when Pam came crashing through the front door and fell against the wall.

"Purse . . . and . . . keys," Pam wheezed as Nikki came running toward her. She pointed out the door frantically. She sounded like she was having an asthma attack, felt like her throat was closing in on itself. Invisible needles pricked at her skin, all over her body, and the ringing in her ears was getting louder and louder. Nikki bolted out the door.

"What the hell?" Chad took long strides in her direction and all but carried her down the hallway to the kitchen. There, he pulled a chair away from the table and pushed Pam into it. She felt his palm against her neck seconds before he urged her head between her knees. "Take deep breaths, Pam. That's right baby, just like that." He didn't notice Nikki standing in the doorway clutching Pam's purse and looking sick with worry.

"Bag . . . paper . . . bag," Pam huffed. She sucked in air like she was drowning and lifted her head to stare at him. Her hands wouldn't stop shaking and now her legs were trembling. Chad slammed through drawers and cabinets until he found a small paper bag filled with individual tea bags. He dumped them on the counter and brought the bag over to her. She snatched it from him, shook it out, and clamped it over her mouth.

He stood over her, looking on in silence as the bag ballooned and collapsed rhythmically. After what seemed like forever, her breathing regulated and quieted and she took the bag from her mouth. She slumped back against the chair and closed her eyes in relief. Chad knelt in front of her and placed his hands on her knees, willing her to open her eyes and look at him. Finally she did and then she leaned forward and pressed her forehead to his.

Nikki watched her father's hands slide back and forth over Pam's thighs in stunned silence. They stared at each other and she stared at them, feeling like she was seeing something personal and private, but she was unwilling to look away or to leave them alone. She was worried about Pam, but she was more worried about what might happen next if she didn't do something quick.

"Aunt Pam, are you all right?" She stepped into the kitchen and stopped beside Pam's chair.

Pam sat back and smiled reassuringly at Nikki. There were unshed tears in her eyes and she swiped them away with ice cold fingers. "I am now. Thanks for getting my purse and keys." She took her purse and set it on the table, dropped her keys next to it, and ran her fingers through her hair. "It was just an anxiety attack. Every now and again they sneak up on me. Sorry I scared you."

"Are they always bad like that?"

"I've had worse," she told Nikki. "Usually by now I'm drenched with sweat and damn near speaking in tongues, so this one was about a five on the Richter scale." The concerned look on Nikki's face wasn't going away, and she reached up and flicked a finger down her cheek softly. "I promise I'm fine."

"Would you leave us alone for a minute, Nikki?" Chad took his eyes from Pam's face long enough to shoot Nikki a meaningful look. He rolled to his feet and leaned a hip against the counter, waiting.

"But Dad, I—"

"Nikki," Chad cut her off, his tone no-nonsense and brisk. "A minute, please?" He tracked Nikki's progress as she reluctantly retreated down the hallway, then he motioned for Pam to follow him out onto the back porch. "How long have you been having anxiety attacks?" he asked the minute the back door was closed and they were alone.

"I don't know, Chad. They just started one day, that's all I remember."

She was pacing around him and wouldn't look him in the eye. He cuffed her arm and brought her up short. She stood in front of him and he used a finger to tip her face up to his. "You could never look me in the face and lie very well, you know that?"

"I'm embarrassed enough without having to talk about it."

"Since when? We used to talk about all kinds of shit and you didn't know the meaning of the word. Hell, sometimes *I* was embarrassed by some of the things that came out of your mouth, but *you* never were. Tell me when the attacks started, Pam."

"I started having them before I left Mercy, but I didn't know what was happening back then. I was fine for a while, for a long time as a matter of fact, and then Paris . . ."

"She never mentioned you having anxiety attacks."

"She didn't know. I never told her."

"Why didn't you ever tell me? Particularly if you started having them before you left?"

"I didn't want you to think I was losing my mind. I really thought I was and the last thing I wanted was for you to think I was flipping out, mentally. My reputation wasn't the best to start with, anyway. Add in me flipping out and the old folks would've really had a field day. You were at school during the week so you never saw, and I didn't want you to see."

"That's why you spend so much time in your room, isn't it?"

"The attacks are part of the reason, yes."

"What the hell happened to you, Pam?" Chad moved closer to her and held her face in his hands. He pushed his fingers into the hair at the nape of her neck and searched her eyes. "One minute we were talking about moving away together, getting married, and having kids. I proposed to you and you accepted, do you remember that? And the next thing I knew you were getting on a bus and leaving me behind."

"You still hate me for that."

"How can I still hate you and still love you at the same time?"

"Chad . . ."

"I mean, yeah, I tried to hate you, and for a while it worked. I couldn't understand how you could do what you did. Still don't. But I had Nikki, so I tried to let you go. I accepted that you didn't want me. Is that what brought on the attacks in the first place, you feeling smothered by me, by us, and needing to get away?"

"I told you once before that you had nothing to do with me leaving. You won't get me to change my answer because it's still the same."

"I must've played a part in it because you didn't ask me to go with you." He released her and went to stand at the storm door, staring out at the backyard. "And I would've. I would've packed my shit and gotten on that bus with you and Paris. I was in love with you. I would've gone anywhere if it meant we would be together. I could've gone to school anywhere. Hell, I *wanted* to go somewhere else, but I stayed close for you, Pam. I was waiting for you to graduate and then it was going to be whatever we wanted it to be."

"You married Paris," she whispered at his back. "I was in love with you and you married Paris. That hurt me."

"*Hurt?*" He spun around and gaped at her, incredulous. "How do you think I felt when I found out about Nikki? I can't even begin to describe the hurt I felt then. She was two when I discovered that we'd made a child together, and I swear to God I could've killed you with my bare hands. If nothing else, you could've given her to me but no, you gave her to Paris and there was no way in hell I was going to pretend like she wasn't mine. I couldn't do that, especially knowing that she was yours, too."

Pam trudged over to a chair and dropped into it list-lessly. In the encroaching darkness she leaned an elbow on the table and pressed stiff fingers to her lips. After a time, she shook her head and squeezed her eyes shut against the memories floating around in her mind. "She told me you had some classes together and that you didn't know about Nikki. Everything was under control, she said. And then one day she calls me, telling me that you'd gone to the justice of the peace and gotten married. I didn't speak to her for six months after that. I was frozen, in shock, I think. The day . . ." she trailed off and worked to get her throat under control. She felt like screaming. "The day you called, yelling and screaming at me, saying that you hated me, was the first time we spoke after she told me."

"I remember that day. I snapped, completely lost it, and I needed you to know how I felt."

"You didn't leave any room for doubt, that's for sure. After that, I figured you had what you wanted, so I stayed out of it as much as I could and still maintain a relationship with Nikki."

"I wanted you and you weren't here."

"And I wanted you, but I couldn't be here. Then you had Paris and I thought, well that's it then. There's no reason for me to ever go back to Mercy again. I had nothing here and no one."

"You had Nikki and Paris."

"Portable, both of them. Seeing you again wasn't an option I gave myself."

"Please don't tell me it's my fault you never came back."

"I keep telling you, you had nothing to do with me

leaving this damn town, Chad. What part of that are you not getting?"

Chad crossed the porch and hovered over her. "Why don't you tell me about the part I'm not getting? If it wasn't me, then what the hell was it?"

"I had . . . things . . ."

"*Things*," he spat out. "You said that before. What *things*?"

"Things I'm too tired to get into right now. Can we drop it, please?"

"Drop it?" he shuffled back unsteadily, running his hands over his face. "You want to drop it? I'm standing here with my dick as hard as a fucking rock from just *looking* at you and you want to *drop it*? I'm sorry, baby, but I need some answers."

"And I need you to let it go. Please." She stood and ran her hands up his arms and over his shoulders. She pulled his face down to hers and pressed a soft kiss to his lips. "I loved you with everything I had, okay? I still love you, but I need you to let it go right now." He reared back, resisting her hold, intending to step away and force the issue, but she wouldn't release him. "Come on, Chad. Do this for me, please. Just for now, all right? Just for now. Tell me what you wanted to talk to me about. We haven't gotten around to that yet. Tell me now."

"I think maybe you did lose your mind way back when, Pam. You must have because you forgot that I was there for you. We could've dealt with whatever you were going through together and still *been* together in the process."

It was Pam's turn to resist. She tried to step back and take her hands away, but Chad slid his arms around her waist and kept her close. He took in the confused look on her face, the tears in her eyes and let out a long breath. "Okay, okay. We'll drop it. Aw, Pam, don't cry. Don't do that . . ." His hands slid down to cup her butt and pull her in closer, against his erection. She moaned low in her throat and opened her mouth for his kiss.

They were still standing close and breathing hard when the doorknob turned. Chad took a quick step back from Pam and looked at Nikki over his shoulder just as she pulled the door open. She stuck her head out and zeroed in on Pam. "I just wanted to check on Aunt Pam," she said.

"I'm fine, Nikki. Good as new." Pam sucked her swollen bottom lip into her mouth and tasted Chad. "I appreciate you looking out for me. It helps."

"Is the minute up, Dad?"

"No," Chad chirped. "Could I have like, two *more* minutes, please?"

"I guess, but after that you have to share," Nikki replied and closed the door.

He waited until he heard the click that told him the door was completely shut, then turned his attention back to Pam. "What are we going to do about her?"

"You think she was eavesdropping on us?" The idea was just now occurring to Pam and it scared her.

"She would've interrupted long before now if she was. I wasn't talking about right now, Pam. I mean what are we going to *do* about her?" He pulled a chair away from the table and straddled it, draping his arms across the back and resting his chin on top of them to stare at her.

"You mean . . . ?" Pam trailed off, comprehension dawning by degrees. As his question settled in her mind her eyes grew wide and alarmed. Her mouth opened, then closed, then finally fell open again. "Chad, I don't know . . ."

"Paris was her mother Pam, we both know that. I just wondered if you ever intended to tell her the truth about her biological parents? About you? Us?"

"Do you?"

"Some would argue that she has a right to know."

"What would you argue?"

"I don't know," he admitted, sounding conflicted. "I think if it were me I'd want to know the truth. But then again what purpose would it serve at this point?"

"Then why bring it up? Did you think I'd want to do something like that because Paris isn't here or what?"

"It's been known to happen."

"You know me better than that. Telling her now would kill her and she'd probably hate my guts for the rest of her life. Maybe when she was three or four, hell, even ten, we could've sugarcoated the situation and explained it away, but not now. Nothing I could say to her would excuse what I did."

"So we just go on the way we have been? Leave her with me?"

"You're her father, Chad. Where else would I leave her?" She searched his face, trying to uncover what it was he was getting at with little success. His eyes were clear and focused, but utterly blank. She was trying to read him and he was reading her. "Are you working your way around to telling me that you don't want her anymore?"

"I'm working my way around to telling you that I want to take Nikki with me when I leave Mercy, Pam. For good. I want to know how you feel about that."

She said the first thing that came to her mind. "Paris will be here all alone."

"Paris isn't here, Pam. She's in my heart and yours and Nikki's, but she isn't here. She'll go wherever any of us goes and we could always come visit. You could too."

A strangled sound clogged her throat. She dropped into a chair, leaned forward and laid her head on her folded arms. "Where would you go?"

"Seattle."

Her head popped up. "With Nate." Chad nodded slowly. "You've been thinking about this for a while."

"I have. I've gone there a few times, and Nate and I have talked about it off and on over the years. Don't look so put out about it. You've been to Seattle to visit Nate plenty of times, and at least it's not a place you mind visiting. This could be a good thing for you and Nikki. It's closer to California too."

"Can you do this, though? Just pack everything up and move across the country? Can you afford this?"

"Easily. I have some IRAs and stocks that have done extremely well over the years. There's also the savings accounts we had, though that's mostly for Nikki's college expenses . . ."

"Use it if you need to," Pam said quickly. "I've saved for Nikki's college since the day she was born. There's no problem there, believe me."

"All right," he said carefully. "Then there's the money from Paris's life insurance to be factored in, some of which she left to you. We need to—"

"I don't want it." She jumped up from her chair and paced the length of the porch anxiously. "Put it away for Nikki, use it however you think is best, but I won't take it." She had a thought and glanced at him sharply. "Donate it to the children's home. I don't think she'd mind that."

"She'd like that idea a lot."

"She would." Pam stopped abruptly and bent over at

the waist. She braced her hands on her knees and took deep breaths, stayed like that for a long time. When she straightened, tears rushed to her eyes and filled her throat. She laid her head back, studied the ceiling and let herself cry.

"She was a special person," Chad said softly. He came up behind Pam and turned her in his arms, pressed her head into his chest as his arms slid around her waist. He dropped a kiss on the side of her face. "She was the kind of person God puts on Earth to remind the rest of us that good does exist. You remember how she would follow us around when we were up to no good, harping about you, me, and Nate growing up to be career criminals?" Pam laughed and sobbed at the same time, nodding. "And the time we smoked a joint and convinced her to smoke it with us? She threw up all over Miss Merlene's new couch and got us run out of the house . . ."

"With a broomstick," Pam finished and cracked up.

June 27th

Dear Diary,

I think maybe Jasper was right and I'm glad I listened to him. I never stopped to think about how the old folks would see my leaving Mercy. I figured they would be happy to have me gone, since I did my best to create as much havoc as I could back then. I had a ball doing it too. You remember, don't you? I wasn't trying to punish them when I left; I just needed to get away. I didn't know they would want me to remember them.

Apparently, I did forget where I came from, though,

because the old folks in Mercy are a trip and a half. How could I forget my duty as a Mercy youngun? I was supposed to acknowledge them in all my ways, right after God, and I forgot to do that. I'm sorry about that now.

I went by the funeral home today and let Jasper put me to work. He has a woman who works there part-time, but he says she doesn't "do like I did." I think he just wanted somebody to drink beer and talk shit with. I stayed anyway and ended up helping him organize his files. They were bad back in the day but now? Oh my God. I hope he remembers the system I set up for him. Hell, I hope he doesn't ask me to explain it again because by the time I finished I'd had four beers and I couldn't tell you what I did, really.

I wanted to go and sit a while with Moira, but I didn't want to take the chance of running into David. I definitely don't want to see him again just yet. He really pissed me off and you know why, so I won't get into all that again. Suffice it to say, I'm done trying to make friends for the next little while.

Now if I could just get Nikki to stop asking all her ridiculous questions, I'd be all right. She keeps pressing me about me and her dad, wanting to know if we were really serious or not. I guess it's a foregone conclusion that we had a thing for each other and she wants to know exactly what kind of thing it was. (Thanks a lot, Paris!) I didn't know Paris was keeping close tabs on what Chad and I were doing the way she obviously was. Sneaky little heifer. Good thing she didn't know the absolute truth, huh? At least not until the very end, when it was obvious that I'd been with someone and I had to tell her who.

The in-between, before my life went to hell, was my secret. Mine and Chad's. As small as Mercy is, we managed to keep our relationship between the two of us. And it's a good thing too, isn't it? Paris would've blabbed that too, and Nikki would really be on the scent. Not that she isn't on the scent now, mind you. I see the way she looks at me and Chad when all of us are together, like she suspects something. Thank God she doesn't know what we've done. I wouldn't know where to begin explaining the complexities of what is happening to her. What would I say? That I can't control myself and that he can't, either? All she will see is that her father and her aunt are fucking. But we've never simply fucked. There was always love there, even in the very beginning. I think we both knew that we'd stumbled across something precious all those years ago.

Nikki wouldn't understand that, though. She's not old enough to fully comprehend all that happened and why. Shit, I'm still a little shaky on the whole deal myself, to tell you the truth. But I do know one thing. It's so good being with him again, feeling his touch and experiencing his intensity. Doesn't matter that it's wrong, I can't make myself turn him away when he comes to me. Even more reason for me to get the hell out of Mercy and soon. That and the anxiety attacks. Four since I've been here, and that's not good.

It might be harder to leave this place again, but I have to do it. I won't say that I'll never come back this time, though. Paris is here and she will surely draw me back, whether I want to come or not.

I feel so guilty about loving her husband, but then you know that. You know that I have always loved him, and I think it's my curse that I always will.

Pam

"**P**am," Chad barked. She didn't move, didn't even hear him, she was sleeping so hard. He pulled the covers back and tipped the can of soda he was holding over just far enough to send a stream of liquid splashing down onto her back. She jumped like she'd been shot, then gasped as his mouth slurped at her skin, cleaning up the mess he'd made. He caught the last drop and sucked it up along with a mouthful of skin, then sank his teeth into one of her ass cheeks. "I know you ain't sleep now, girl. Wake up. You been sleeping all day."

Pam cracked one eye open and peered at the alarm clock on the bedside table. "It's just now one o'clock. That's not all day." She had climbed in his bed around eleven, after he'd left to go to his last two classes for the day.

She was supposed to be in school, but instead, she'd skipped out and hopped on the early morning bus headed to Atlanta. It dropped her off right down the street from GSU, where Chad was waiting to bring her back to his dorm room. She came at least twice a month on Fridays and they had it down to a science now. He could sneak her into the dorm and into his room without being caught, with his eyes closed. She stayed all day and then returned to Mercy with him later in the evening.

"I brought food and if you want some you better wake up and stake your claim because I'm hungry as hell." He laughed and shook his head when she bolted upright in bed, pushing her hair out of her face and sniffing as she looked around the room.

"What did you bring and where is it?"

Chad sat on the side of the bed and looked into her eyes long and hard. She was buck-naked underneath the covers and sitting up, so he had a lovely unobstructed view of her breasts. They were high and tight, begging to be kissed, but he'd skipped his first two classes making love to her, so he refrained from indulging himself. Besides that, he had other things on his mind, and he needed to see her face to look into her eyes rather than stare at the body he damn near worshipped.

"What Chad? Where's the food?" Lines of confusion creased Pam's forehead. There was no food in sight and he was looking at her like he didn't know who she was. She reached out and tugged on his arm playfully.

"I just wanted you to wake up, girl. I didn't bring food because I'm taking you out. You thought I forgot today's your birthday?"

She scratched her arm, thinking. "Damn, I forgot myself. How old am I today?"

"Eighteen," he said.

"Shit." She glanced at the clock again and mentally calculated. "Paris should be off from the work-study thingamajig by now. I better call her and tell her happy birthday." She went to climb over him and only made it to the point where she was straddling his lap before he stopped her with a hand on her waist.

"Call her later. Talk to me now."

Pam reared back and searched his face, surprised by his tone. "What's up with you?"

"I love you," Chad said softly.

"And you're mad about that?"

"What do you think?"

"I think you better love me or else I'm going to jail today." He laid his head back and shot deep laughter toward the ceiling. Pam linked her hands around his neck and shook him. "You think I'm playing?" He fell back on the bed and took her with him, still laughing.

"Girl, if you're playing with me, I'm the one who's going to jail," he said, when he could talk. "You love me?" He watched her eyes close and listened to her purr like a contented kitten as his hands massaged a path from her waist to her shoulders. Finally, she looked down at him through slits, sucked her bottom lip into her mouth and nodded. "Say it to me, Pam. Tell me."

"I love you," Pam whispered. Suddenly shy, she pushed against his chest and sat up. "You know I do. What are you doing?"

Chad bounced her around on his lap as he pushed his hand in his front jean pocket. He sat a small box in the middle of his chest and folded his hands under his head, watching her watch the box. "You gonna stare at it all day or are you gonna open it? It's for you. Happy birthday, Pam."

"What is it?" She reached for it, then snatched her hand back, reached for it again.

"Open it and see."

"Chad . . ."

"Open it, Pam."

She cried out and covered her face when she saw the pretty gold ring nestled inside the box, with the perfect round diamond perched on top.

Thinking that she didn't like it, Chad rose to his elbows and used one hand to touch her neck. "I know it's not much, but..."

"It's perfect. Put it on, put it on," Pam chanted, bouncing on his lap impatiently. She looked away from the ring long enough to give him a beautiful smile, then she was transfixed by the ring again.

She held her hand out for him to slip the ring on her finger, but it was the wrong hand. Chad brought her right hand to his mouth and kissed her palm, then gently lifted her left hand. "Marry me, Pam."

She gasped and gave him another beautiful smile. She didn't need to think about her answer. "Today. Right now. When?" Pam asked him, meaning every word.

"You gotta get dressed first," Chad laughed and sat up to kiss her lips. Not satisfied with a simple peck, he pulled her face close and buried his tongue in her mouth. "Then you gotta graduate from high school. The day after that, though, okay?"

"Okay."

FIFTEEN

Miles was lying on his hotel bed, letting the television watch him while he thought about his remaining options when his fax machine came to life and began spitting out papers. Three, to be exact.

He rolled off the bed and padded across the room to retrieve them. He took note of the sender, nodded absently, and perused the second page. He wasn't aware that he'd stopped breathing until his throat tightened and he coughed to open it back up. He felt his heartbeat accelerate, felt the familiar rush of adrenaline zing through his veins, and sank into a chair to absorb it. He stared at the application for a marriage license until his eyes damn near crossed. There at the bottom of the page were two signatures: Pam's and Chad's.

Miles did the math. Chad would've been around twenty years old and Pam eighteen, when the form was completed and filed. He scanned the month again, just to be sure, and hissed in anticipation. The application had been submitted in March, just a few months prior to the day Pam had scurried out of Mercy, Georgia and never looked back. He felt vindicated. If nothing else, certain that his innate hunches were right on the money.

Chad and Pam had obviously been involved once upon a time. So involved that they had planned to marry. And then something happened, either to Pam or to Chad or to the both of them, and they hadn't gone through with it. Chad had married the other sister Paris, instead.

Why? Miles wondered.

He paced the floor in his room like a dog on a fresh scent. Chad and Pam. And then Chad and Paris. Those kinds of situations only happened in a man's wildest dreams or his sexiest fantasies. *Or his darkest nightmares*, Miles thought. He recalled everything he'd learned about Pam from the people of Mercy and realized with a start that he'd heard nothing about a relationship between Pam and Chad. Either very few people had known about it, or the town was better at keeping secrets than he'd given it credit for. Surely Paris would've known about her sister's relationship with Chad. So why had she married him?

Miles stalked over to the bed and pulled his briefcase from underneath. He found his notepad and began scribbling furiously, adding the questions that were now running through his mind to the growing list already there. Several at the top of the list had been marked off with red ink, reminding him that he'd already acquired satisfactory answers for those, but there were still more remaining than he was comfortable with. He wasn't used to working at a snail's pace when it came to gathering information and compiling his manuscripts. Most of the celebrities he went after were long past futile attempts to hide their pasts, and they secretly wanted to be written about and gossiped over.

Not Pamela Mayes, though. Since beginning her career as a commercial jingle singer she'd moved on from singing background vocals for established artists to putting out solo albums that consistently went double platinum. Her concerts sold out, her voice mesmerized men, women and teenagers alike, and there was even talk of movie scripts being tossed her way. Yet she lived like a virtual hermit, and no one really knew a damn thing about her. She didn't want to be gossiped over or written about, that much was clear. Why that was so, wasn't.

Miles experienced a moment of genuine regret. He'd actually grown to like Pam as a person. She was down to earth and laid back. She didn't priss and preen like so many prima donnas he had encountered. Much of the time she didn't even seem to be aware that people stopped to stare at her. She tossed around four thousand dollar Gucci bags like she had no idea how much she'd paid for them, dropped thousand dollar sunglasses on a table without wincing, and sat in the grass in Vera Wang like she was wearing burlap. Yes, he liked her. He really did. And he almost hated himself for what he planned to do to her. Almost.

He already had a top-notch editor lined up to take possession of his manuscript after he was done with it, and it would be a literary masterpiece. Tongues would be wagging for a long time to come, and his would be the name everyone remembered. The man who had finally cracked the legendary Pamela Mayes's seemingly indestructible shell. Perhaps some day she would forgive him, maybe even thank him for boosting her career even further. He reasoned that he wasn't the only one who stood to benefit from the book.

He smiled as he sat down in front of his laptop and accessed his personal email account. He sent two messages marked urgent, signed off the Internet, then slid the disk containing his partially completed manuscript into the drive.

There really is no rest for the weary, he thought as his fingers began flying over the keys.

Chad caught sight of Nate coming down the walkway toward him hoisting a camouflage knapsack almost as tall as he was, and rose to meet him. He was relieved to see his best friend whole and healthy looking after several months of sporadic contact. His smile grew wide and mocking as he took in Nate's bushy beard, which was new, and the overgrowth of curly hair on his head. The Nate he knew was always dapper and well groomed. With the hair on his face he resembled a travel weary truck driver or a shepherd running away from his flock.

Nate dropped his bag at his feet and Chad stepped forward to grip him in a bear hug. They stayed that way for several seconds before pulling apart and inspecting each other for obvious changes.

"This all you got?" Chad nodded toward the bag that looked big enough to hold a human body.

Nate shrugged and retrieved it from the floor.

"Should I even ask what's in it?"

"You could, but then I'd have to kill you," Nate chuckled. "Where's Peachy?" He was referring to Nikki.

"Off somewhere with Pam. Who knows where." They walked outside and weaved through standing traffic to reach the parking lot on the other side of the driveway. Chad opened the trunk and helped Nate toss his bag inside.

"You told her Uncle Nate was coming home and she chose Pam over me?"

Chad grinned at the phony look of shock on Nate's face and shook his head. "She doesn't know you're here yet. Feel better?"

"A little." He folded his tall frame into the passenger seat and sighed as the car started and ice cold air shot out of the vents into his face. "Does Pam know I'm here?"

"If she did, she'd probably be sitting in your lap right now."

"And I wouldn't be complaining one bit," Nate quipped. "How's she holding up?"

"Better than I expected. Both she and Nikki are. Nikki keeps Pam from hiding in her room at the B&B all the time, and Pam keeps Nikki from moping around the house."

"And you."

Chad cruised onto the interstate and accelerated smoothly. He glanced in the rearview mirror, merged with oncoming traffic, and looked at Nate sharply. "And me what?"

"Pam keeps you from moping around the house, too."

"Are you making your way around to a point?"

Nate rested his head against the seat and laughed. "You've got the same expression on your face you used to get whenever I asked if something was going on between you and Pam, when we were kids. Back then I didn't know any better, but I do now, so spit it out. You and Pam been seeing each other?"

"Not exactly," Chad hedged. He leaned forward and switched on the radio, filling the car with upbeat jazz music.

Nate leaned forward and switched the radio off, filling the car with easy silence. "What is it . . . exactly?"

"It's complicated, Nate. The only reason Pam came back is because Paris died and because of Nikki. I'm not kidding myself about that. Whatever it is we're doing doesn't fit into any category that I can think of right now. Maybe I'm being selfish and greedy, maybe I need to let the past go, I don't know."

"What does Pam say?"

"Pam's not saying too much of anything. We've talked about some of what happened, but I still have more questions than answers at this point. We've hashed the shit out as much as we can and still nothing. I'm pretty much just soaking up as much of her as I can, so I'll at least have that after she's gone. I told her about Seattle."

"Did she go ballistic?" Nate pressed the buttons on the base of his seat and situated himself so he was fully reclined. He spread his knees and laced his fingers low on his belly. Fatigue was creeping up on him slowly but surely, and the lulling rhythm of the car ride threatened to take him under.

"She was worried about Paris being here alone, but other than that she basically told me to do what I felt was best. I don't know why I thought she'd have more of an opinion where Nikki is concerned," Chad said. The exit ramp for Mercy was just ahead, and he maneuvered the car so he could get on it, then settled back in his seat for the remainder of the ride home. They were still at least forty minutes away.

"You've had Nikki all this time and you thought Pam would suddenly demand parental rights?" Nate studied Chad's profile for several seconds and then he began to understand what his friend was alluding to. "You want to tell Nikki the truth."

Chad released a long, tense breath. "I don't know what I want to do. It just seems wrong for her to go through the rest of her life believing a lie."

"Paris isn't here to defend herself, Chad."

"Paris had no defense for the part she played in all this shit when she *was* here, Nate."

"She did what Pam asked her to do."

"But why did Pam ask her to do it? That's the million-dollar question, and she had plenty of opportunities to answer it, but she didn't. Either way, Nikki deserves to know the truth. Hell, maybe she can get some answers out of Pam where no one else can."

"Would it help any for me to say that things have a way of working out the way they're supposed to in the end?" Nate ventured carefully. He scratched his beard and considered Chad. Secretly, he agreed with him. Nikki had been wronged all those years ago, and she did have a right to the truth, just as Chad was and did. They were both unwitting victims of circumstance, and as much as it hurt Nate to continue feigning innocence, he had been sworn to secrecy. He and Chad had been best friends since high school, but he and Pam had been best friends damn near since birth. He rationalized that he was doing everyone a favor by staying out of it.

"No, it wouldn't," Chad snapped, irritated. "There is no way I'll ever completely accept that I was meant to marry a woman I wasn't in love with just so I could have access to my child. I did it and I do accept that, but that's where I draw the line."

"God moves in mysterious ways."

Chad took his eyes from the road long enough to give Nate a hair-curling look. "What, did you join a religious cult while you were in Iraq?"

"I'm just saying . . ."

"And I'm just saying, if this is some bullshit God thought up, he certainly has a fucked-up sense of humor, don't you think? Shut up and ride, Nate."

Instead of shutting up, Nate chuckled and tapped Chad on the arm. "You remember how Paris was always the one running behind us preaching about the consequences of doing whatever it was we were doing at the time? Sounding like a little old lady?"

Chad had to laugh too. "Yeah, I remember that. Funny how she didn't do that when it might've made the most difference, huh?"

Nate had no response, and a little while later, Chad pulled to a stop in his driveway and shut the car off. Pam's car was nowhere in sight, which meant that she and Nikki were still missing in action. He hauled Nate's bag from the trunk and opened the passenger door to poke at Nate's still form until he woke up. Nate followed Chad inside the house, mumbling under his breath about his internal clock being way off.

"You got my setup ready?" he asked Chad as he trudged down the hallway toward the alcove just off the kitchen. It took him to the lower level, where he usually stayed when he was in town. Situated like a small efficiency apartment, there was a combination sitting area and bedroom down there and a full bathroom, which he planned to make use of immediately.

Chad grunted out an affirmative response while carefully bringing the bag down the steps behind Nate. He set it next to a sectional sofa and propped his hands on his hips to catch his breath. Across the room, Nate turned on a table lamp and looked around with satisfaction. "Perfect," he declared, eyeing the neatly made bed longingly. "You know how long it's been since I slept in a real bed? I'm about to ejaculate just looking at it."

"Were things that bad over there?"

"Badder than bad, but don't get me started. Let's just say the first thing I did after the plane landed was kiss the fucking ground. I got some priceless footage and interviews, though."

"You should've gone home first and gotten some rest." Chad could see the weariness in Nate's shoulders and knew he was exhausted.

"I did go home first. Long enough to dump out my dirty clothes and pack clean ones, call my mama and then my publicist, and then you. And then I hopped on a plane coming here. A couple of hours of uninterrupted sleep and I'll be ready to roll, I promise you."

"You got a good excuse for why you're staying here ready for Miss Merlene?"

Nate threw Chad a charming smile as he laid his bag on the couch and unzipped it. He pulled out his camera equipment and set it on the coffee table gently, then dug around for clean underwear, jeans and a T-shirt. "Just the same ones I had the last time and the time before that and the time before that. The gospel music is *too* loud, I'm *too* old to have a curfew and she *doesn't* have the porn channel. Need I say more?"

Nate spent a long time in the shower, scrubbing his skin with good smelling soap instead of the utility soap he'd been forced to use over the last several months. He shampooed his hair and beard, then punished his mouth with Colgate until every crevice tingled. His hair was long past the point where a simple trim was needed, and he gathered it in a loose ponytail at the nape of his neck, thinking he'd sweet-talk Pam into trimming it for him later.

He laid his shaving kit open on the vanity and went to work removing the fur from his face. In Iraq, the facial hair had helped him blend in with the other men and maintain a low profile, but here in the States it only aggravated the hell out of him. He bid it a fond farewell.

He'd been gone seven months, and too many things to count had occurred in his absence. One of his oldest and dearest friends was dead and he hadn't even had the opportunity to say goodbye to her. The last time he'd seen Paris was the last time he'd been in Mercy, the year before for the Christmas holiday. He'd sat at her table, eaten the delicious dinner she had prepared, and teased her nonstop until she was laughing so hard tears were running down her cheeks. The night before he left they had taken a long walk around Mercy and then sat in his mother's living room like they'd done so many times as kids. On the way back to her house, as they were crossing Truman Field, he'd pulled out a joint and lit it, held it out to her like he really expected her to take it from him and slip it between her lips. She had slapped at his hand and fanned away the smoke he blew in her direction comically, the same way she'd always done when they were kids. He'd had no idea then that, as he pecked her lips and hugged her tight at the airport, it would be the last time he'd get to do so in this lifetime.

Thinking about it now brought stinging tears to his eyes and he held his straight razor still until he could see clearly again. He took a deep breath and started in on the left side of his face carefully. He was in the second grade when he met Pam and then Paris. They were in kindergarten and Pam was removed from her class because she'd said something mean to another kid, something about the other kid's mother, he thought. Her teacher had washed her little razor sharp mouth out with soap and then brought her to Nate's class, where she was to sit in the corner for the rest of the day as punishment.

At some point, his teacher had felt sorry for Pam and let her out of the corner while his class was having art time. Finger paint, he remembered and shook his head sadly. She was seated next to him and given a sheet of construction paper to paint on. She made different colored handprints all over the paper, while he spent most of his time poking her in her side with his elbow. He was trying to make her mad, and the more she ignored him, the harder he poked her. Finally, she'd turned to him, smiled sweetly, and then dumped a whole bottle of red paint right in his lap, all over his brand new Levi's. She went back to the corner happily and he fell in love.

Discovering that there were two of them was an added benefit to Nate. It meant that he had two girls he could pick on and two sets of long silky ponytails to yank on when he didn't get the responses he thought he should. Two sets of cat-shaped green eyes to challenge him into taking silly dares. Paris was always the quiet, passive one. The one who would put up with his shit and then cry when she was tired of it. Pam was the one who damn near whipped his ass when he gave Paris shit and made her cry. They were like alter egos, one shy and prissy, and the other bold and unpredictable. He had wriggled his way into their world, gotten comfortable and never considered leaving it.

Somewhere along the way Nate had developed an adolescent crush on both Pam and Paris, because they looked just alike and because they were so different. It was like having two girlfriends, but still having only one, if that made any sense. Then, as they'd grown older, the dynamics had shifted and they'd settled into

the roles they occupied up until this very day. Pam and
Paris were the sisters Nate had never had, and he was
the big brother they hadn't asked for, but had wel-
comed, because they hadn't really had a choice in the
matter. Despite the relationships he'd had with other
women over the years, no one had ever come close to
touching the part of his heart that was reserved for his
sisters.

Once when he was drunk, Nate had grabbed Pam
and kissed her senseless. By then Chad was the fourth
person in their little group. The four of them were in
the woods out past Mercy town limits, drinking and
smoking weed one Sunday afternoon and Pam was
high. She was giggling like crazy, making fun of the
girl he was dating at the time and saying that she was
cross-eyed and pigeon-toed. The girl was neither of
those things, but Pam wasn't willing to be dissuaded
from her opinion and Nate had accused her of being
jealous.

"Jealous of what?" Pam chirped, flopping her hands
on her hips and leaning her weight to one side.

He decided to show her rather than try to explain it
to her. He grabbed her face and mashed her lips
against his. She didn't protest and he took it a step further, pushing his tongue between her lips and coaxing
hers out to play. She kissed him back, there was no
question about that, and several seconds of humming
silence passed before she pushed against his chest and
swiped his spit from under her bottom lip with a shaky
finger.

"Damn, Nate," she drawled sarcastically. They stared
at each other and then she said, "I didn't know you
had it going on like that. Shit, no wonder Janetta's always mooning over you."

"And don't you forget it," he shot back. A lazy grin took over his face and they'd all burst out laughing. But, he hadn't laughed so hard that he missed the fire in Chad's eyes. Pam had sensed it too, and Nate thought he'd detected a slight shift in her demeanor throughout the rest of the afternoon. He'd silently wondered about it, but back then, he hadn't known that she and Chad were lovers.

The day he and Paris had sneaked into Chad's house and seen Chad and Pam rolling around on the bed together was an eye-opener for Nate. Suddenly his and Paris's suspicions were confirmed and he wasn't quite sure how he felt about it. Chad was his best friend, but Pam was like his little sister and he felt protective of her. A little jealous, too.

He felt it his duty to find out where Chad's head was and then to bash it in, if he decided that was called for. Pam's reputation around Mercy was bad enough without Chad potentially doing more damage. The rumors were all lies, but Nate knew that if something got around about Pam and Chad, there would be nothing but truth to it, coming straight from Chad's lips.

He and Chad were walking home from school after basketball practice one afternoon when he finally broached the subject. A group of girls had come running up to them as they crossed the parking lot and, player that he was, he'd spent several minutes enjoying the attention while Chad stood off to the side, politely deflecting it. Hadn't taken Nate long to realize that Chad was always deflecting female attention and he thought he finally knew why.

"What's up with you and Pam?" Nate asked as soon as they were alone again.

Chad's step faltered slightly, so that you had to be

watching closely to notice it and Nate noticed. "You trying to ask me something?"

"I'm trying to find out if you're just trying to get some ass or if you really like her?"

When Chad might've mentioned that he'd lost count of the number of times he had gotten some ass from Pam, his lips remained closed. They were almost to his house when he spoke again. "I'm not just trying to get some ass," he said.

"So you really like her?"

"I love her." He skipped up the steps to his front porch. "See you later."

Hearing the *L* word had thrown Nate for a loop. He never told Paris what he'd learned, but he did pay closer attention when the four of them were together. The looks that passed between Chad and Pam took on new meaning, as did the touches that passed between them. Their unexplained absences were no longer unexplained, and he wondered just how far they'd gone together.

Nate didn't think he would ever forget the fateful night he slept over Chad's house and finally learned the truth. He remembered it as the night he'd smoked so much weed and drank so much cheap wine that he knew better than to go stumbling into his mother's house. Chad's house was closer and his parents wouldn't be standing guard the way he knew Merlene would be, so he'd crept into Chad's room, called his mother, and then fallen into a deep sleep across the foot of the bed.

It was also the night he witnessed his two best friends making love and knew that they were *in* love. He'd rolled over in the middle of the night and decided to tiptoe down to the kitchen, looking for a snack to settle his upset stomach. He wolfed down three bananas and gulped down two handfuls of chocolate chip cookies, standing barefoot in the dark kitchen, and then he heard them.

They were on the sun porch at the side of the house in the dark, going at it and completely oblivious to Nate's presence. He debated throwing the lights on and demanding to know what they were thinking. It could've just as easily been one or both of Chad's parents who'd walked in on them, and Nate couldn't believe they hadn't chosen a better place to make out. Surely they were smarter than that.

Apparently not, he thought as he stood in the shadows and watched them. They were in the far corner naked on the floor. Chad's mouth was open and greedily roaming over Pam's neck and shoulders, as if he was starving, and Pam's legs were wrapped around Chad's waist. They thought they were being quiet, but Nate could hear the hoarse moans rising in Chad's throat just before he caught them and swallowed them back down. Chad turned his head, tongued the skin along her arm, went back to her neck and shoulders and then stretched her mouth wide for his tongue. Nate could hear Chad whimpering, sucking in air through nostrils that were pressed against Pam's cheek as he rolled his hips rhythmically. His fingers stretched wide and tense on her thighs and gripped tightly as he stroked Pam steadily and carried her through her orgasm. Her nails dug into the skin across Chad's shoulders and he threw his head back to release a defiant gasp toward the ceiling. Then he lifted her thigh, draped it over his arm and rolled them sideways, cupping her ass like it belonged solely to him. The force of his strokes had Pam burying her face in his neck and holding on tight. A few seconds later, Chad snatched himself from inside her and drew her breast deep in his mouth as he suffered through a noisy orgasm of his own.

They were kissing wildly, loudly, when Nate withdrew and crept back up the stairs to Chad's room. He fell across the foot of the bed and worked to get his own breathing under control. Watching them had aroused him to the point that he was fully erect and straining toward release himself. An hour later, Chad had slipped into the room, curled up at the head of the bed and immediately drifted into a peaceful sleep. Nate had stared at his back for a long time, wanting to wake him up and question him nonstop. They'd both just turned seventeen and he was dying to know where Chad had learned to make love so expertly. Not that he was a lightweight, Nate thought. Both Janetta and Desiree could attest to that. But, still.

Nate blinked and focused on his image in the mirror over the vanity. That was another memory he'd never shared with Paris because he had somehow known that what he'd seen was more than what it appeared to be. It was more than sex, and it was either Chad's or Pam's to share. Neither of them ever had, so he'd kept his mouth shut.

He wished Paris were here now so he could talk with her, make her laugh, and hear her voice. Between the four of them, they had collected enough memories to carry them into old age, reminiscing and reliving them, but she would never have that luxury. It was just the three of them now. He was saddened when he had finally accepted that Pam wasn't coming back to Mercy and he'd have to settle for never roaming the streets with her here again. But the sadness he felt just then, as he accepted that Paris was never coming back to

Mercy and he'd never roam the streets with her again anywhere, was staggering.

Nate stepped into clean jeans and pulled a T-shirt over his head. Then he lay across the end of the bed and fell into much-needed sleep. When he woke up he had places to go and people to see, starting with his mama and ending with Miles Dixon.

SIXTEEN

Dear Diary,

I don't know why I didn't tell Chad when I had the chance, before everything got so mixed up and out of control. I could look at him and see that he was hurting. He pretended to be okay with what happened and he never talked about it, but I've known him long enough to know when something is bothering him. He would've gone to her and maybe they would've been able to get past Pam's issues. Before Pam left they were in love. She didn't have to tell me that because I saw the light in her eyes and the ring on her finger. Knowing all that, I should've told him what I knew and helped them to heal.

But I didn't.

I'm not a bad person. I know that too. Can I help it if I was tired of everything always being about Pam? She's my sister and I love her with everything that I am, but she was always in the spotlight, *while I stood on the sidelines and let life happen to me. Even today she goes after what she wants and I just take what I can get. I was never jealous of her (I wasn't!) and many times I feared for her safety because she never seemed to look before she leaped, but I did always wonder what she had that I didn't that made her so spirited and tough. I wished I could stand toe-to-toe with someone and scream into their face, even as they screamed into mine, and then throw my head back and howl with laughter in the next breath. I wished I had the guts to fall in love with someone and then do whatever love told me to do, without regret.*

She had that with Chad, that no-holds-barred love. They were just kids, but it didn't matter to them. They were making love and carrying on long before what happened, happened and it became obvious that's what they'd been doing. She always did think she was grown and the thing with Chad was no different. She put herself in it all the way—soul, mind, and body.

Chad was always so intense, so strong-willed and possessive of her, in that quietly reserved way he has. His face was never expressionless when he looked at her. Even on the day we met him he was intent on Pam, focused on her in a way that he was never focused on me. We look just alike, I remember thinking then, so why doesn't he look at me the way he looks at Pam?

I guess I never had whatever it was he saw in Pam. I accept that and I don't envy Pam her liveliness and vibrancy. I love her for being who she is. She balances me out; the same way she tells me that I am the voice of reason for her. She talks me into wearing bright pink and showing a little cleav-

age, and I remind her not to get herself arrested when she is angry with someone. That's the way it has always been and it works.

So I should've remembered what Pastor Young always says during sermon, "What God has joined, no man can put asunder." He makes that saying applicable to all kinds of situations and he is right. I should've told Chad.

At first I think it was like a game to me. I wanted to see if I could make him love me the way he loved Pam. After all, I had something that was priceless to him and I looked like his precious Pam. Maybe I could make him look at me with those big eyes of his and see Pam. Like that silly movie with the twins who were separated at birth and then tricked their parents into getting back together. It was an experiment that went horribly wrong. He never looked at me with anything other than sorrow and guilt because we both knew he didn't really love me, not like that anyway. Still, I held out hope that something would grow between us. Then he called out for Pam in the dark, in the middle of the night and I knew . . .

Twice before that he called out for her, and once he opened his eyes and looked at me and started crying. We were married almost a year by then and he could only bring himself to touch me in the black of night, when he couldn't see my face and know that I wasn't her and only after he'd been drinking. I know it's not normal to be married all these years and only have your husband touch you a handful of times. It sickens me to think that he had to be drunk and hallucinating to touch me. Not because I'm angry with him, but because I'm angry with myself. I am a liar and a thief, and I feel so guilty about it that sometimes I can hardly stand to look at myself. All of this started with me wanting to have something that was never meant for me.

No . . . that's not quite true. It all started with Pam running from Mercy. But regardless of that, I should've told him and let him run after her. He's been waiting for her to come back to him all these years anyway.

I hope God can find it in his heart to forgive me when my time comes. Pam too.

Paris

Pam and Nikki didn't pull into the driveway behind Chad's car until well after eight that evening. At the last minute, Pam decided to take Nikki school shopping and they had driven to Atlanta to scour the malls there. Afterward, they'd had lunch and then taken in a movie. Pam shut the car off and elbowed Nikki, who was in the passenger seat with Pam's cell phone glued to her ear, talking a mile a minute to Gillian. Nikki reluctantly turned the phone over to Pam.

"Are your jaws even a little bit sore?" Pam asked as they climbed out of the car and headed to the trunk. Nikki stuck her tongue out and grabbed an armful of bags. Pam grabbed the rest and they made their way to the porch. "Okay, Gil, I better go now," she said into the cell phone. "What? Hell no, I'm not helping Nikki put away all this crap. My duty is done. I'm hungry and I'm tired. She can handle the rest."

"Bye, Gillian," Nikki loud-talked so Gillian would

hear her and then pushed the front door open with her
elbow. She staggered into the house juggling bags and
with Pam on her heels.

"Nikki, get the molasses *out of your ass*," Pam grum-
bled, pushing Nikki farther into the house none too
gently. "My feet hurt and I'm hungry again. Hurry up."

"I'm going, Aunt Pam," Nikki snapped back. One of
the bags slipped out of her hands and landed at her
feet. Colorful bras and matching panties were draped
across the tops of her sandals and she was trying not
to step on them as she walked. "Wait a minute, don't
step on my pink panties. I'm putting those bad boys on
after I get out of the shower tonight. Dang, Aunt Pam!"

Pam looked down at the pink panties wedged under
the sole of her Manolo's and cringed. "Shit, sorry. If
you weren't such a butterfingers this wouldn't be a
problem. And I thought I said no to the pink panties
anyway?" They were little more than thongs and she
distinctly remembered vetoing them outright.

"You left me your credit card when you went to the
restroom."

"Ah," Pam said expansively, narrowing her eyes.
"Why don't we let Chad have a look at them and see
what he thinks?"

"Aunt Pam, please, they're just panties," Nikki
protested. The last thing she needed was to have her
father inspecting her underwear.

"Yeah, underwear grown women wear. What's that
little four-eyed boy's name, the one who was drooling
after you like a little puppy the other day?"

"Alan," Nikki supplied with a long-suffering sigh.

"Well, Alan won't be seeing these panties anytime
soon. Make sure they're in my hands when I leave, will
you?" Nikki huffed and gathered up the garments.
Pam huffed to mock her and helped her set the bags at

the base of the staircase, out of the way. They made their way down the hallway to the kitchen, snipping back and forth at each other.

Nate rose from his seat in the sitting room and walked into the kitchen just as they crossed the threshold and they both froze, their mouths dropping open in surprised shock. They stood there, staring at Nate and his face split into a wide smile as he stared back, thinking that the daughter was more and more the spitting image of her mother everyday. Pam cried out and catapulted across the kitchen to throw herself into Nate's open arms.

She wrapped her arms around his neck, her legs around his waist and pressed her lips to his in a smacking kiss that lasted five long seconds. Nikki had never seen her aunt swinging from a man's arms the way she was swinging from Uncle Nate's and she was almost scandalized. Nate's big hands cupped Pam's butt and held her close as she took her mouth from his and turned it loose all over his face.

"Nate, they told you . . . Paris . . ." Pam's voice trailed off as she swallowed the lump in her throat and pushed her face into the side of his neck to breathe in his scent. "Where *were* you?" she asked a few minutes later, pulling back to look in his eyes.

"You don't want to know where I was, Pam. You know I would've been here if I had known. I almost died myself when I found out."

"I know, Nate. She knows, too." She leaned forward and touched her nose to his briefly before grinning lightning quick. "Did you bring me something from Iraq?"

Nate was tall like a tree and as solid and steady as one, too. She couldn't recall a time when she hadn't swung around on him like a monkey and loved every minute of it. His skin was a perfect shade of chocolate brown, soft where it should be soft and hard where it should be hard and he had a head full of curly black hair. It was pulled back into a ponytail now and she slid the rubber band off and pushed her fingers deep into the midst of it, scrubbing her fingers through it wildly. Because she couldn't help herself, she pulled his face back to hers and kissed him on the lips again.

"No, I didn't bring you anything, you heathen. Now get down, you're too old to be hanging off of me like this." He slapped her on the butt sharply and laughed out loud as she slid to her feet with a pout on her lips. "I still love you," he said, pinching her chin and stealing one last kiss before he stepped around her to get to Nikki.

"Hey, Peachy." He hugged his niece tightly to his chest and breathed in the floral scent in her hair. The top of her head fit under his chin and he dropped a kiss there. "You doing all right?"

"I'm okay, Uncle Nate. I'm glad you're here though," Nikki said. She reached up to kiss his cheek and blushed when he gave her one of his lady-killer smiles. She thought her Uncle Nate was fine, even if he was pretty old. She liked the way his hazel eyes crinkled at the corners when he laughed and made you laugh with him. He had thick black eyebrows and a dimple in his chin, which made him look like a pirate when his lips parted and he gave you a glimpse of all those sparkling white teeth. The fact that he traveled all over the world, taking pictures and writing about the things he saw, only added to his mystique, as far as she was concerned.

"All right," Pam piped up. "Back off, Nikki. He's mine." She latched onto Nate's arm and grinned up into his face. He rolled his eyes and shook his head.

"Still possessive, I see," he teased her.

"That's not true. I share with the people I love. Most of the time anyway. Were you careful over there, Nate?"

"I'm standing here right now, am I not?"

"Yeah, but don't go back over there. I don't like not knowing where you are or if you're safe. I saw that story on television, where they had that one man and they..."

"Shhh," Nate said, pressing a finger to her lips. "I called you from over there all the time, so you'd know I was safe. Plus, I came out to see you before I left."

"I know, but still. Paris is gone and I still can't believe it. And then you were over there in that crazy place and . . ." Tears stood in Pam's eyes. She ran her hands over her hair and pushed out a sharp breath. "God Nate, if something had happened to you over there I would've lost it. I swear to God, I would've. You know I'm not lying either."

He did know. That was why he wrapped his arms around Pam's waist and lifted her high into the circle of his arms, and let her hold on as long as she needed to. The trembling in her shoulders told him she was crying and he spent a few minutes rubbing her back soothingly. Then he shifted her weight and opened an arm for Nikki.

Nikki's mind was clicking as she hugged her uncle. She wondered if there was any truth to the old rumor that Aunt Pam and Uncle Nate had messed around back in the day. She knew they'd grown up together and were best friends, but they seemed totally comfortable kissing each other on the mouth and holding each other close. She wondered if they had secrets between them that no one else knew. Her friend Kelli swore up and down that men and women couldn't just be friends without wanting to screw each other at some point in time. And, as Nikki thought about her friend Alan, she had to admit that she wanted to do more with him than just talk. Had Aunt Pam and Uncle Nate ever felt that way about each other?

"Did I miss something?" Chad spoke into the silence in the kitchen. He came through the back door and looked at the scene before him curiously.

"Peachy and Pam are feeling me up and I'm letting them," Nate said over Pam's head.

"Uncle Nate," Nikki chastised softly and stepped away guiltily. She *had* been appreciating the hardness of his back. She felt her face glowing bright red as Nate's knowing chuckle reached her ears.

Nate slapped Pam's butt again. "Pam get down, damn. Isn't this what she was doing when you first met her and Paris, Chad?"

"Something like that, as I recall. We were on our way over to what's her face's house to swim and she was wearing these super short shorts and a red bikini top, hair hanging down her back, hips switching from side to side and mouth going a mile a minute. I decided right then and there that I couldn't stand her."

Pam crawled down from Nate's arms and shot Chad a baleful look. Nate and Chad burst out laughing, giving each other knowing looks over her head. Nikki thought about the entry she'd read in her mom's diary that morning and felt her face heat up from embarrassment. She saw the look her mom had written about on her dad's face and shrank away from it. The air in the room seemed to evaporate and she felt a little queasy in the absence of it, wanted to be away from it and them.

"I'm going to unpack my stuff," she said to no one in particular. Three pairs of eyes turned in her direction and she hoped the expression on her face didn't betray her thoughts.

"You got stuff today?" Chad asked.

"We got a head start on school shopping," Pam said. "And my shorts weren't super short."

"Is that a nice way of saying you went crazy in the mall? And yes, they were."

"No, it's a nice way of saying we got an early start on school shopping. One less thing for you to worry about, so get that look off your face and thank me. Your credit card was saved from major damage."

"Must be nice having a rich auntie." Nate winked at Nikki and went to the refrigerator. "Peachy, I got some raw footage I want to show you later on, so don't let me forget, okay? And Pam, the shorts *were* a little risqué."

"Okay, Uncle Nate," Nikki said and left the kitchen.

He watched her go, then turned his attention to Pam. "What are you about to get into?"

She shrugged and pushed her hands in her back pockets. "Nothing much. I was planning on running by to holler at Jasper and then going back to the B&B."

"You got time for me later on?"

"Yeah." Pam noticed the creases in Nate's forehead and frowned. "What's going on, Nate?"

"Nothing too serious. I have to go make nice with Merlene, but I should be done by midnight, at the latest. How about you meet me at the spot around half after?" He pulled a canned soda from the refrigerator and popped the tab, took a long swallow. "You still remember how to get there, don't you?"

"That's a joke, right?"

He dropped a kiss on her forehead and moved past her, calling out that he'd see her and Chad later.

Nate took his soda with him as he jogged down the

porch steps and set off down the sidewalk. It was a nice, breezy night, and the air felt good against his skin. He sucked in a mouthful and released it slowly, wondering at the luxury of being able to walk down the street and not worry about snipers and random gunfights breaking out at any minute. He'd learned a long time ago not to take freedom for granted, but there was nothing like having firsthand knowledge of what it meant to be held captive to jog his memory.

He reached the end of the block and turned left, headed toward the center of town and his mother's house. As he crossed Juniper Street, he fished his cell phone from his pocket, flipped it open and scrolled through the numbers saved in its memory. He came to the one he was looking for and pressed *send*.

"This is Nathaniel Woodberry," he said when the phone was answered on the other end. "I understand you've been trying to get in touch with me for some time." He listened for several seconds as Miles Dixon introduced himself and heaped compliments on Nate's head. Swatting them away like worrisome gnats, Nate cleared his throat. "Why don't you tell me what I can do for you, Mr. Dixon?"

He agreed to meet Miles in the small bar on the first floor of his hotel and disconnected the call. Then he dialed his mother's number. Merlene was not very happy to learn that her only son had been in Mercy all day and hadn't gotten by her house to see her. He listened to her rant and rave for long minutes, inserting soothing sounds and platitudes when he could get a word in and then he promised to be on her doorstep first thing in the morning. Tomorrow was Sunday, she reminded him tartly and she would be in church first thing in the morning. He reluctantly promised to escort her to church and sit through the whole, endless service without falling asleep as recompense.

Nate dropped the phone in his pocket, wondering what the hell he'd just agreed to and why he would, being of sound mind and body, willingly offer to subject himself to one of Pastor Young's fire and brimstone sermons without first considering the repercussions. When the answer finally came to him, he shook his head and chuckled ruefully. He was a sucker for the women he loved, and he loved Merlene Woodberry like he loved breathing.

He also loved Pamela Mayes, which was why he was going to meet the man who was intent on hurting her. One way or another, Miles Dixon would be stopped.

At half after midnight, Pam appeared in the clearing and spotted Nate sitting on the creek bank with his feet submerged in the water. She dropped down next to him, toed off her slides and found his feet with hers underwater. Their spot was Valley Creek, and it was on the northern edge of town, not far from the children's home where she and Paris had grown up. She leaned her head on his shoulder and reached to lace her fingers with his. Sighed as he turned his head and his breath fanned her face softly.

"How are you, P?" His voice was low and intimate, for her ears only.

"I'm way better than I thought I would be. I thought I'd be having anxiety attacks every day that I had to be here. I haven't, though, and it's been good to be back, see some of the old folks." She giggled quietly. "I let your mama run me out of her front room with a broomstick the other day too."

"She always had a soft spot for you. One of the biggest

gossips in town, but she never told anybody about the day she caught us together, going at it in the basement. I think that's why I kiss her ass the way I do right today."

"The day after you kissed me out in the woods," Pam whispered, remembering. She was glad it was dark and he couldn't see her skin turning a deep shade of red. "Chad went to Atlanta with his mother and we were supposed to be playing video games."

"Uhmmhmm. Felt guilty about that shit for the longest. Couldn't look Chad in the face for a month afterward. I knew you were his."

"It was one time and nobody got hurt. I think we had to get the curiosity out of our systems."

Nate caught her eyes in the darkness. "What about those three months we spent undercover together in Barcelona? Was that curiosity?"

"No, I think that was pure and simple lust. You were back from Korea and neither of us was thinking straight. We were supposed to be sightseeing and relaxing together for old time's sake."

Neither of them had expected to cross the line from friends to lovers in Barcelona, but they had. Their coupling was almost like a bad cliché or a late-night television movie. She had stepped out of the shower just as Nate had come into the bathroom. She'd reached for a towel to cover herself and then somehow, his mouth was on hers and she was kissing him back. The decision to minimize expenses and lease an adjoining suite was suddenly not such a smart thing to do, but the damage was done. They had spent most of their vacation in bed, having hot, mind-blowing, anything-goes sex.

"That month together in Athens was relaxing as hell

too, now that you mention it. You never said anything to Paris?"

"Hell no," Pam gasped. "Did you?"

"Hell no," Nate mimicked her playfully. "To Chad either. How would I have been able to explain what happened between us and still keep my best friend? Some things aren't negotiable, and I have a feeling that where Chad is concerned, you're one of them. I'm just glad we didn't ruin *our* friendship in the process." He brought their clasped hands to his lips and kissed the back of hers gently.

"It was good."

"Damn good. Still is. You ever regret it?"

She looked at him, surprised. "Regret what? Having the chance to know all of you? Never. Why, do you?"

Nate released her hand and laid it over the sleeping semi-erection resting against his thigh inside his jeans. "That answer your question?"

Pam allowed herself a gentle squeeze before slipping her hand away. "Don't tempt me, Nate."

"Are you tempted?" She rolled her head around on her shoulders and ran her tongue along the skin just below his sleeve. A chuckle rumbled low in his chest and worked its way up and out of his throat. "You're bad, Pam. You make it hard for me to remember that you're still his. How do you suppose it's so easy for us to fall in bed together, then hop back out and carry on like nothing happened?"

"A true sign of friendship?"

"Or treachery," he replied smoothly. "Idle minds are the devil's playground. Speaking of which . . ." He reached around and stuck a finger in his back pocket, came out with a half-smoked joint and put it between his lips. The rest of the world had moved on to smoking blunts, but he still preferred smoking his weed the old fashioned way.

"You lured me all the way out here to get me high and relive the past, Nate?" She laughed and watched him light the joint with a disposable lighter.

"Don't think the idea didn't cross my mind. Think anybody would notice if I conveniently left town the same day you did? This is premium Jamaican shit here, P. Pace yourself." He took one, then two drags off the joint and passed it to Pam.

"Now who's bad? How'd you smuggle this shit past customs?"

"Did you hear me a few minutes ago, talking about treachery?"

They were quiet as they passed the joint back and forth between them. When Nate was satisfied that Pam was good and high, he tossed the roach in the creek and shifted in the grass until they were facing each other. Her eyes were tight and the silly grin on her face matched the one on his.

"You are fucked-up," he said and burst out laughing.

Pam thought the sight of him laughing was funny and she joined in, laughing so hard her stomach hurt and tears ran down her cheeks. "Where was this weed when we were kids?"

"The grown folks had it all," Nate predicted. "Keeping it a secret and shit. Tell me what you know about Miles Dixon, Pam."

Pam's brows met in the middle of her forehead. Genuine confusion was on her face as she locked eyes with Nate. "Whoever he is, I don't know him. Did he say I knew him?"

"I think he might've introduced himself to you as David. David Dixon. Sound familiar?"

"Oh, yeah. He's Moira's stepson. You know him?"

"I know of him," Nate said carefully. He was fucked-up too and concentrating on keeping his thoughts in logical order. "He's the dude that owns all those news-papers and gossip magazines, P. He writes those tell-all books about celebrities."

Pam was shocked. She leaned forward and put her face close to his. "Who do you think he's going to write about next?"

For a second, Nate was speechless. He stared into her tight eyes and caught his breath. Then he threw his head back and laughed hard. "Pam listen to me," he said, still giggling. "That motherfucker followed you here to gather information about you for his next book. It's about you, baby."

"*What?*"

"Yeah. You remember Humpy?" He was referring to James Humphries, a boy they'd hung around with a few times in high school. It took Pam a few seconds to connect the dots in her head, but she finally nodded. "Apparently, he dropped a dime on you about some of the shit we did back in high school and from what I understand, Dixon's been going around town asking folks what you were like back then."

She was silent a long time, soaking in the ramifica-tions of what Nate was telling her. Then she dropped her head in her hands and moaned disgustedly. "I met him for lunch a few times. I thought he was nice and he's Moira's stepson, so I didn't see the harm in it. What the fuck was I thinking? I should've known bet-ter than to think he didn't want something from me."

"What did you tell him?"

"Nothing much. He already knew about Jose, but that's about it. I guess now he knows whatever fat-ass Humpy told him. I told you that cocksucker was no good," she snapped and punched Nate in his thigh. She had never particularly cared for Humpy.

"You did and we cut him loose before he could get too comfortable, so fuck him. How do you want to handle Dixon?"

"Wait a minute, let me see if I have this straight. David, I mean *Miles*, followed me here and pretended to be friendly with me so he could pump me for information. Is that what you're telling me, Nate? That he intends to write one of those cheesy-ass books about me?"

"That's the understanding I got."

"And how do you know all this?"

"He called my publicist several times while I was away and left messages for me to get in touch with him. Your name came up, and I got on the first plane here to see what was up. This is what's up, and he needs to be dealt with."

Pam hopped to her feet, snatched up her slides and took off toward the woods. "I'm going to fucking kill him," she spat out as she stomped past Nate. "And then I'm going after Moira because she had to know what he was up to."

Nate rolled to his feet and caught up with Pam before she could disappear into the woods. "Hold up, P. You can't go storming over to his hotel tonight."

"Why the hell not?"

"Because you're high as a kite, for one thing. I didn't come all the way to Mercy just to get hauled off to jail, and you know I would, right? You'd go over there throwing shit and clowning, and I'd have to come with you because that's just how we do it. He'd probably fuck around and do something stupid and I'd have to kick his ass, and then we'd both go to jail. I told Merlene I'd go to church with her in the morning, so I *can-*

not go there with you tonight, okay? You know I wouldn't hear the end of it if they had to drag her ass out of the sanctuary right when the choir was getting down on 'Amazing Grace' to come and bail me out."

Pam had a thought. "Chad could come bail us out. He wouldn't hesitate to spring you and then you could talk him into springing me, too."

"Pam . . ."

"Come on, Nate. We've done shit like this before. I'll just knock on his door and when he comes out, I'll punch him a few times and then we'll tear his room up looking for the evidence. By the time the police get there, we could be back at home, damn near asleep. No witnesses, nice and quick. And Paris isn't here to harp about consequences and shit, either."

He had to admit the idea did sound tempting. "Listen to me, forget Dixon for now. I want you to let me handle him. If I need some backup, I'll let you know, okay?"

"But what if he—"

"Hey," Nate cut her off. He lifted her chin with his finger and made her look into his eyes. They were cold and hard. "I said to let me handle Dixon. You trust me?"

"With my life Nate, you know that." She stepped into his arms when he opened them and burrowed in, hugging him tightly. "Oh . . . Nate, I'm so glad you're here. I missed you so much."

"I love you too, Pam." He laughed as she spun away from him, grabbed his hand and dragged him along behind her through the woods. Just before they reached the road where her car was parked, he cuffed her arm and brought her around to face him. She slammed into his chest breathlessly and opened her eyes wide as his head dipped toward hers. Their lips pressed together, stayed that way for long seconds, and then slowly opened against each other's. The kiss was long, wet, and deep.

"Damn, Nate," Pam drawled as they climbed in her car. "I didn't know you had it going on like that."

The line had a ring of familiarity to it and it brought that day so long ago back to his mind, fresh and vivid. He reclined his seat and got comfortable as Pam shifted into drive and shot off down the road.

"Yeah, you did," he responded and let his eyes slide closed for the remainder of the drive back to Chad's house.

Chad and Nikki were in the kitchen when Nate and Pam came stumbling through the doorway and trudged down the hall. Chad's water glass stopped midair, halfway to his mouth, as he surveyed the silly grins on their faces. He shot a careful glance toward where Nikki was seated at the table flipping through a fashion magazine and doing her damndest to stay awake, then wriggled his eyebrows at Nate. Pam paused in the hallway long enough to dig around in her purse and slip her sunglasses over her eyes. Chad thought he'd told Nikki to go to bed an hour ago and now he wished she'd listened. Pam and Nate were high as hell.

"What are you still doing up?" Pam studied Nikki's face through the black lenses.

Nikki turned flat eyes on her aunt and then on her uncle. "I was just going to bed," she mumbled. "Good night everybody."

Chad watched his daughter disappear down the hallway, thinking that she'd been acting strange lately, then he divided an expectant look between Pam and Nate. "What's up?"

"Tell him what's up, Nate." Pam nudged Nate in his side. Her tone implied that she was too disgusted by the recent developments to be bothered with repeating them.

"Well . . ." Nate began in a reasonable tone of voice.

Pam rolled right over his words clumsily. "What's up is that David Dixon is a *spy* and he's been playing up to me hoping I'll tell him *all* my little dirty secrets. He wants to write one of those *unauthorized* biographies about me and my life in this *hideous* little town." She whipped the glasses off her face and propped a hand on her hip. Her head rotated back and forth between Chad and Nate. "Can you *believe* that shit? I mean, doesn't that just take the damn cake?"

"You are *so* fucked-up," Nate murmured, shaking his head and pinching the bridge of his nose. He took two steps backward, bent over at the waist, and roared with laughter. Pam dropped into the nearest chair and joined him. Chad shook his head at both of them.

SEVENTEEN

Dear Diary,

    Pam and I got on the bus that night knowing where we were going and what we were going to do. We had it all planned out, right down to the last detail. Pam saved her money from working at the funeral home and I had mine from my work-study job, and that's what we lived on during those last seven months in California. We got off the bus in a little town called Orange and stayed in a claustrophobic little hotel room. Pam wasn't famous then, so nobody took any notice of the two of us walking around town getting exercise and waiting for Pam to go into labor.

    Her water broke in the middle of the night and we took a cab to the hospital. They tried to separate us there in the emergency room. Tried to make me wait in the waiting area until after Pam gave birth, but Pam told them she would get off the stretcher and go out into the middle of the street to give birth be-

fore she let them separate us. What could they do? She was scared, hurting like she'd never hurt before, sweating like a pig, and screaming these blood-curdling screams. I thought she was dying, her face was so red. I started crying right along with her.

Nikki made us wait for her for fourteen long hours and then she finally made her appearance. Oh, she was the most beautiful baby. Brown and perfect. She looked like Chad from the very beginning. And Pam, too. She has Pam's eyes and her mouth, my eyes and mouth. We held her and just stared at her for the longest time. Then the nurse came to take her away for the night. Pam had to have stitches and the Demerol they gave her made her sluggish and tired. She decided to get a good night's sleep while she could.

"What are we calling her?" I asked Pam.

"Nicole," Pam told me. "Nicole Angela Greene." Her middle name is for Chad's mother, since we never had one, and Pam wanted her to have a connection to someone, to have a history.

That was the name Pam wrote down when the woman came around to collect the information for Nikki's birth certificate. The woman wrote down the time of birth, the city and state, the sex of the baby and then turned to Pam, pen poised. "Father's name?" she asked. Pam told her that Chad Anthony Greene was Nikki's father. The lady asked Pam to please spell her name, so that no errors were made and me and Pam looked at each other one last time before we did what we did.

Right from the start we called our baby Nikki. And we told the woman that her mother's name was Paris Marie Mayes. We had no idea what we were doing. We didn't know that by switching places *we'd be casting our lives in stone. Pam had no reason to believe that I would betray her and do what I did. It never occurred to her that I would marry Chad and steal what was hers. Why should it? She trusted me to keep my word to her.*

The second part of our plan was over before it even began. Pam was supposed to come back for Nikki, but two years passed before she was ready to come, and by then it was too late. We fought bitterly. She called me names that I can't bear to write down here, but I know I deserved them, just as I deserved the six months of silence I suffered through. I robbed my sister of the ability to come home again. But two years is a long time, and in all that time she would never give me a date. She never said when she was coming...

This loveless marriage has got to be my punishment. That and the occasional look that comes over Pam's face when she is looking at me and thinks I'm unaware of her eyes. She doesn't love me the same, I feel it in my bones. When we were kids we always said, "We come first," and we meant it. It was our solemn oath. Nothing and no one would ever come between us. Yet, this has. There are no words to describe what I feel. I wonder what might've happened if I had gone out with one or two of the guys who asked me out in college. Would I have gotten married and had a couple of kids of my own? Would I have made a life for myself, instead of stepping in where Pam's left off and failing miserably at filling her shoes? I don't know and I suppose I never will.

Nikki is a wonderful child, bright and curious, lively and so loving that it hurts my heart sometimes when she looks at me with those big, trusting eyes. I love her so much. Too much, I know. Enough to want to make her mine. Chad says nothing, but I can see in his eyes that he wishes I was Pam and that the two of them were raising their child together.

I promised Pam and told myself that I'd never write about it, never tell a soul. And I haven't ever told anyone, but I have to get it out somewhere. Chad is not an option and every time I bring the subject up to Pam she says she doesn't want to talk about it. I have made it so that Nikki can never know that Pam is her mother. So where does that leave me? Some things are too big, too consuming to keep inside forever, don't you think?

Paris

Nikki closed the diary and stared into space. She wasn't aware of the exact moment the anger she tried to swallow bubbled to the surface and twisted her face into a rigid mask of outrage. She didn't hear her own ragged breathing as she swept everything from the surface of her bureau and sent bottles and jars crashing to the hardwood floor. Mingled scents floated up in the air, reached her nose, and turned her stomach. She stumbled away from the bureau, gasping for air, and vomited down the front of her pajamas.

The wall at her back kept Nikki from losing her balance and falling to the floor. She collided with it, with a loud thud and slid down to her butt. The scent of vomit was thick in her nostrils, and she sucked in air through her mouth to escape it. She wondered if this was what Aunt Pam felt when she was having an anxiety attack, like her heart was going to jump out of her chest and land with a splatter on the floor, like needles were jabbing into her skin all over, like she couldn't catch her breath. Then she remembered who and what Aunt Pam was, and the tears came.

In the kitchen, Nate's eyebrows shot toward the ceiling as the noise upstairs grew louder and louder. It was still early, way earlier than he would normally be up and about if he was home in Seattle. It took him several minutes to remember that Chad wasn't home and that Nikki was the only other person in the house. He sipped his coffee slowly, unconsciously listening for the sound of footfalls on the stairs, hushed voices and doors creaking open. If Nikki thought she was about to sneak some little peanut-headed boy past him and out of the house, she had another think coming. It wouldn't hurt his feelings one bit to start the day off with a little ass kicking.

Why wait? Nate thought. If he moved fast enough he might just be able to catch the little thug with his pants still around his ankles.

Nate took the stairs two at a time, knocked once on Nikki's closed door and then stuck his head inside. His eyes darted around the messy room, taking in the clothes strewn everywhere, the bottles and jars scattered on the floor, and finally, the pool of vomit in the middle of the floor. The smell slapped him in the face at the same time that he noticed Nikki curled in a ball against the wall. He left the doorway and went to kneel beside her.

"I thought I was about to catch you sneaking a boy out of the house," he said, hoping to get her to lift her head and look at him. He pushed her hair away from her face and felt her forehead. She was sobbing uncontrollably and he was, for once, at a loss for words. Crying women made him nervous, so he said the only thing he knew to say. "Peachy, what's wrong?" It was enough to have her crawling into his arms and crying on his shoulder.

Chad was called out of an administrative meeting to take the call from Nate. He went to his office and closed the door so he'd have some privacy. Nate wasn't one to call during a workday just to shoot the breeze or to ask where Chad kept the sugar. He was more the type to tear the house apart looking for the sugar and to hold whatever news he needed to share until work was done and it was time to play. Chad punched the button for line two and put the receiver to his ear, already knowing something was wrong.

"Nate?"

"Thank God," Nate breathed a sigh of relief. "I thought I was going to have to come through the phone on that damn secretary of yours. Listen, you might need to come home, Chad. Nikki's flipping out. I stopped her from doing too much damage to her room, but she isn't all that rational right now. I could use another pair of hands."

"Flipping out? What the hell happened?"

"What the hell *didn't* happen? Whose bright idea was it to give her Paris's diary?"

"Pam thought Nikki would want it since it was her mother's." Chad's heart was racing.

He ran a shaky hand over his head and turned to look out the window at his back. He swallowed twice before speaking again. "Why, Nate?"

"I think you should come home. And call Pam and tell her to get her ass over here, too. Paris isn't here to defend herself, but I have a feeling Pam might have some questions to answer before the day is over. You understand what I'm saying?"

"She wrote it down?" He sank down into the chair behind his desk and pressed stiff fingers to his eyelids.

"She wrote it down," Nate confirmed gravely. "I don't know what the fuck she was thinking, but she wrote it down and now Nikki knows."

"*Shit*," Chad growled. "I'm on my way." He slammed the receiver into the cradle and hit the floor running. He drove with one hand on the wheel and the other working his cell phone. He called Pam's cell phone three times and got her voice mail each time. *Where the fuck is she?*

He waited impatiently for the beep. "Pam, this is Chad. All hell is breaking loose at the house, and I need some help with damage control," Chad snapped into the phone. He started folding it closed, then thought better of it and brought it back to his ear. "*Damage control, Pam. Get over here.*"

Pam slept off the Jamaican high and woke up with a clear head. She got dressed, slipped her feet into high-heel mules, and pulled her hair into a ball at the crown of her head. She was pushing large silver hoops in her ears when her cell phone rang the first time. She glanced at the screen, saw Chad's home number and continued on with what she was doing. She figured it was Nikki, wanting to chat, and she was strung too tight for chatting at the moment. She'd call her back when she wasn't feeling quite so wound up.

The second time her cell phone rang, she was putting the finishing touches on her makeup. This time it was Chad's cell number. She caught herself reaching for the phone and forced herself to ignore it. He too, was a distraction she didn't need right now. His voice would invade her senses and cause her thoughts to scatter in too many different directions. She needed to stay focused. She waited until it stopped ringing and set it to vibrate, then dropped it in her bag on her way out the door.

Nate had said he'd take care of David or *Miles* Dixon, whoever the hell he was, but he'd said nothing about Moira and that was just fine with Pam because Moira was hers to deal with. Of all the people in the world, Pam had considered Moira a friend, and the idea that she could know what Miles was up to and not warn her infuriated her. As she drove to Moira's house, Pam thought about how very sick and tired she was of people thinking it was their right to be in her life, to know all of her business, every move she made and every feeling she had.

Once some psycho had even gone through her trash, looking for information about her to sell to the tabloids. Her birth control pill prescription information was front-page tabloid news for weeks. As if anybody really gave a shit about estrogen levels and little blue pills. She was photographed coming out of her doctor's office, buying gum and cigarettes at the filling station, standing in line at the grocery store. Everyone knew that she had kicked the habit four years ago, but when she did slip and smoke she preferred a certain brand of menthol cigarettes. They knew that she was five-six and one-hundred-thirty-five pounds. If she gained so much as an extra pound rumors started circulating about her being pregnant. And who was the father, they all wanted to know?

Oh, she was so sick of it. Then there was David, no *Miles*, with his phony smiles and casual questions, all the time trying to con her out of information, so he could put it in a fucking book about her that she hadn't even given him permission to write. She wanted to light a cigarette and toss it on his gasoline-soaked body. Moira she just wanted to strangle.

Who had made the law that just because she sang a few songs and people liked her music she had to open her private life up to public scrutiny, Pam wondered as she parked her car in Moira's driveway. She ignored the cobblestone walkway in favor of stalking across the exquisitely manicured grass. She pushed the dark glasses higher on her nose and raised her hand to press the lighted doorbell.

EIGHTEEN

Moira was inside, she knew that much because she could hear her talking through the closed door. Pam didn't think she'd ever heard Moira speak in anything other than soft tones and, as she realized that Moira's voice was raised far beyond that, she frowned. She hadn't bothered to call before coming, and it was obvious that this was a bad time to have it out with Moira. She seemed to already be having it out with someone. Pam took two steps back and turned toward the steps, intending to return to her car and leave, but halfway down the steps, she heard her name. She froze and stared at the door curiously. At least she thought she'd heard her name. She went back to the door and listened.

"I mean it, Miles. Go back to New York and forget about this crazy plan of yours," Moira was saying. Her voice was strained and high-pitched, as if she was on the verge of losing the ability to talk completely.

Hearing Miles's name and knowing that he was on the other side of the door revived Pam's anger. She heard Nate's voice in her head, telling her to let him handle Miles Dixon, but she wasn't listening. Without thinking, she opened the storm door and touched the brass knob softly. Enough to show her that the door wasn't completely closed. It eased open silently and she stepped inside the foyer, drawn by the strength of Moira's tone and the ferocity of Miles's response, when it came.

"I can't do that, Moira," Miles barked. "And why are you so upset about this anyway? It's not really about you, it's about Pamela Mayes. If you would just calm down and think about this rationally you'd see that this really has nothing to do with you at all."

"This has everything to do with me, you idiot. You were in my home, rifling through my personal papers and violating my privacy. You had no right to do that and you have no right to take what you saw and use it to destroy people's lives."

"Destroy people's lives?" Miles's tone was incredulous. Pam could almost see his head snapping back on his neck. She heard his feet shuffling on the carpet in the great room where they were. "You've kept the secret all these years because you were too cowardly to own up to what you did. You were going to wait until after you were dead to tell the world about the cruel thing you did and *I'm* destroying people's lives? Come on, Moira. You know as well as I do that's bullshit."

"I had no choice!"

"You had choices. Hell, it was the seventies. Free love and sex and all that shit. Even in Georgia you could've gotten away with keeping those girls. You didn't even have to stay here. You could've taken them somewhere more liberal and raised them yourself."

"I was afraid, Miles. Don't you understand that? Georgia in 1970 was not the place you obviously think it was. Everyone knew that Jasper Holmes was doing some work on my stables. Do you think they weren't paying attention to his comings and goings, waiting for the slightest sign of impropriety? The Klan might not have been marching up and down the street in full view, but they were still here lurking around. And suddenly I pop up with brown babies? *God*, Miles. Innocent people would've been hurt."

Miles stopped pacing and looked at Moira. He ran a hand around the back of his neck and hissed through his teeth. A few minutes ago, she had been standing tall, confronting him with fire and fight in her, but now she was slumped in a ridiculously fluffy chair, clutching her trembling hands in her lap and fighting back tears. She suddenly looked every bit of her seventy-five years and pitiful with it. He felt like shit for being the cause of her distress.

His head rolled back on his neck and he studied the domed ceiling at length. In the silence, Moira began crying softly and the sound squeezed his heart. She had been more like a mother to him than his own mother and all of his stepmothers combined and he truly did love her. "Tell me what happened, Moira," he said a long time later. "Tell me how you could give up your daughters and let them grow up in an orphanage, thinking no one wanted them. Do you know that's what Pam said to me once? That no one wanted them?"

"I stayed here, Miles. Even though it killed me to look at those beautiful girls, to face them knowing who and what I was, I stayed." Moira's voice was low and injured sounding. "I fixed it so they would always be here and I made sure they had everything they wanted and needed. We did that, Jasper and me. We talked about it once, when they were still babies,

about how we'd do things. I'd go there and take things."
She waved her hands negligently, then let them drop
back in her lap noisily. There, they shook as if currents
of electricity were flowing through her body. "Clothes
and things for the other children and toys. I'd play
with the other children and hold them in my arms for
a while, but I'd sit with my girls for hours, just watching them together. They were always so close and so
good to each other. Jasper went too, and he looked out
for them when they were running around town." Her
next thought widened her eyes and staggered her breath.
She sat up in the chair and pinned Miles with her eyes,
intent on making him understand. "When they were
older, I made sure they weren't kept locked up in that
home all the time. I wanted them to be free to run and
play . . . and to come to me whenever they wanted to.
They came, Miles . . . I had my babies and they had
me."

Moira's face crumbled right before Miles's eyes, and
it was a humbling thing to see. This woman who was
always so strong and independent, crying like a baby
and wiping her face with the sleeves of her shirt. I did
this to her, he thought and sighed tiredly. He went to
her and kneeled beside her chair, squeezed her hands.

"You never got the chance to meet Paris," she said in
a dreamy voice, lost in thought. "You would have really
liked her, Miles. She was sweet and soft and shy. She
had this way about her that people were drawn to, this
light in her eyes. I always said she got her personality
from Jasper." She chuckled ruefully and took her
hands from Miles to rub her face. "Oh, but Pamela,
she's all me, but even bolder and brassier than I was at
that age. She doesn't have light, Miles, she has fire,
and people are drawn to her because they can't help
wanting to be burned. She was fifteen and keeping

company with all those boys, and I could see that every one of them was half in love with her, so I pulled her aside one day. And I told her, I said . . ."

"Pamela," Pam mocked Moira's tone as she came forward and stood in the great room doorway. Moira gasped and Miles came to his feet slowly, both of them wearing mirroring expressions of shock and remorse. Pam ignored them and continued with the memory. "That's what you said Moira. Pamela, you have a gift and you have to be careful how you use it. Men will either love you to distraction, desire you unreasonably, or loathe you intensely. Many times it might be all three at the same time, so you have to be careful. Please always remember to be kind, no matter what you do."

Pam watched Moira come to her feet and start across the room in her direction. She locked eyes with her and shrank away, though she hadn't yet been touched. "Please don't come any closer, Moira. I might have to kill you if you do. I might start remembering all those years we lived in that fucking home, while you knew, *you knew*, and you never came for us. All the holidays we had no one and you were here all the time, embarrassed because you had a black man between your thighs and got yourself knocked up." Her head jerked toward Miles as if someone had snatched it. "And you, you lying son-of-a-bitch."

"Pam." Miles stepped toward her with his hands out in surrender.

"Fuck you," Pam spat. "Go back and write your *unauthorized* book, you bastard. I'll see you in court about that underhanded shit, by the way. How *dare* you follow me here and pretend to care that my sister is dead just so you can get a story. Moira, I swear to God, don't fucking come near me. *I mean it.*"

"Pamela, please," Moira begged. She came forward

anyway and reached for Pam's hands. "Come in and let's talk about this. There's so much I want to say, so much I need to say to you. I didn't want you to find out like this. *Please*."

Pam felt Moira's hands brush hers and jumped. She held her hands out of reach and backed into the foyer. "There's nothing you could say that I want to hear right now, Moira. And whatever you were planning to reveal after you died, don't. I'm just as embarrassed as you are at the idea of people knowing who gave birth to me. So don't do it, okay?"

Pam almost tripped in her high heels, racing out the door and down the steps. She moved like the hounds of hell were on her heels when it was really Miles who was behind her, calling for her to please wait. She locked herself inside her car and fumbled with the key until it was in the ignition and the engine roared to life. Miles ran around the perimeter of the car, checking the doors, hoping to find one unlocked. He slapped at the windows and yanked at the doors uselessly. Pam shot him a venomous look as the car shifted into reverse and she pressed down hard on the accelerator. He stepped back just in time to avoid being dragged alongside the car.

"I will *not* have an attack," Pam chanted to herself as she drove. "I will *not* have an attack. I am in control of myself *and* my feelings. I *know* that what is happening to me is not real. I *am* strong enough to fight it."

She repeated the affirmation to herself over and over, taking deep breaths in between, and cursed herself when she faltered. "*Dammit*, Pam. You *know* this shit. Say it without *fucking up*," she told herself. "For *once* in your life do *something* right."

Fifteen minutes later, she pulled into Chad's driveway and shut the car off. She climbed out of the car on shaky legs and counted the number of steps she needed to take to reach the door. Nineteen, she told herself as she went inside. Nineteen steps to sanity.

Chad was pacing back and forth in the living room when Pam came through the door. He did a double take, then whirled around to face her angrily. "Where in the hell have you been?"

"What?" Her forehead wrinkled in confusion. She stared up at him and blinked rapidly. She was cold, frozen, really, but starting to perspire like she was at the boiling point.

Chad recognized the signs of an impending attack and gripped her shoulders, shook her so hard her teeth rattled. "Snap out of it, Pam. This is not the time for one of your performances. Did you get any of the messages we left?"

Numb, she shook her head. Her hands flew to her ears and covered them, but the ringing grew louder and louder. She shook her head and tried to sink to the floor at Chad's feet, but his grip was strong. He held her up even as her legs buckled.

"What the hell is the matter with you, Pam?" She said nothing, just stared at him like she didn't know who he was. He shook her again. "Talk to me!"

"Moira . . ."

"Moira? What about Moira? Is she sick, did something happen to her?"

"No, Chad. I'm trying to tell you . . . it's Moira . . . all this time it was Moira and we didn't even know. I heard them talking . . . David . . . his real name is Miles . . . he was there and she admitted it. I can't . . . please . . . I need to sit down." Nate walked into the room and Pam reached out blindly for him. "Nate! It was Moira. She put us there. Me and Paris. She left us there. Her and Jasper, they're the ones."

Nate soaked in the brief sentences and understood completely. He was sure the expression on his face conveyed the shock and disbelief he felt, but there wasn't time to get into it right now. Nikki was on a rampage and he needed to . . .

The diary flew across the room and rapped Nate between his shoulder blades. He jerked and spun around to intercept Nikki as she stormed into the living room from the kitchen. Chad stepped in front of where Pam sat on the couch and caught Nikki's eyes.

"Nikki . . . could you give us a minute . . ."

"She doesn't need a minute, Dad," Nikki shouted. She was busy trying to get past Nate. "She's had eighteen years worth of minutes. Now I need a minute, okay? That's all it'll take for her to explain to me why she gave me away. Why didn't you want me? What did I ever do to you that you had to give me away?"

"*Oh God . . . oh God . . . oh God . . .*" Pam covered her face with her hands and sang childishly.

She rocked back and forth, powerless to stop her voice from steadily rising, until hers was the only sound in the room. They were all staring at her, silently wondering if she was losing her mind and asking themselves if they should call someone to come for her and take her away.

Chad knelt by her legs and rubbed her thighs soothingly. He'd never seen Pam so upset, and he struggled with wanting to cradle her in his arms and not being able to. He smoothed strands of hair away from her face and traced his thumb along her cheek to catch her tears. He had never loved another woman the way he loved Pam. Never loved another woman, period. "Baby, please . . . come on . . . what can I do for you? Anything . . . tell me and I'll do it . . . you know I will." He eased her hands away from her face gently.

"You have *got* to be kidding me," Nikki exploded. Pam jumped in her seat and squeezed her eyes shut. "What *is* this shit?" Nate spoke to her in low, sharp tones, but she wouldn't be calmed. "I don't care, Uncle Nate!" She caught him off guard and pushed past him. She loomed over Pam and pointed a shaking finger in her face. "I want to hear what you have to say for yourself, *Mother*."

"Nikki . . . please. It's not what you think. There were things . . . ."

"Things like what? Look at you, you can't even look me in my face when you lie to me. You're pitiful, Pam. I feel sick just looking at you. And you know what else? My mom was ten times the woman you are. She loved me even if you didn't."

Pam swallowed the rage Nikki's words called forth and took a breath for patience. "You don't know the whole story, Nikki. I wasn't well. For a long time . . . I was sick."

"Whatever, Pam," Nikki snapped.

"No, it's not whatever. It's the truth. Just like it's the truth that I gave birth to you and I loved you enough to do what I had to do to keep you safe. I knew Paris would take care of you until I could come for you, but . . ."

"You never came back!" Nikki skidded across the room and scooped up the diary from the floor. She advanced on Pam, holding the book out and flipping through the pages. "She wrote about it right here, how you were supposed to come back, but you never did! Be honest for once, Aunt Pam! Tell the truth. You didn't want me. Just say it!"

"I will not say that," Pam hissed, jumping to her feet. She slapped the diary out of Nikki's hands and watched it fly across the room. She wrestled with control and finally claimed it. Calm now, she said, "It's not the truth."

"I think that's enough." Chad stepped between Pam and Nikki like a referee and sent Nate a meaningful look. "We need to calm down and discuss this rationally."

Nate came away from the wall where he was leaning and reluctantly ventured into the fray. He had been paying close attention to the scene, content to let it play out however it would and thinking that it was long overdue. Instead of heeding Chad's call for assistance with coming between the two women, he wanted nothing more than to drag Chad to safety, so they could have it out. One or the both of them might come away bloodied and scarred, but they would both be better for it. He only wished Paris were there to accept her part in the chaos that was unfolding.

"Nikki." Nate touched Nikki's arm softly and motioned for her to come away. As he did so he shot Pam a veiled look, one that she intercepted so beautifully he could've kissed her.

"I carried you in my belly for nine months, Nikki," Pam informed her daughter. The shock had lessened, then moved aside completely to make room for the anger she'd buried years ago. "I was in labor with you for fourteen long hours and mine was the first face you saw when you finally decided to grace us with your presence. I named you Angela, for your grandmother and I nursed you at my breasts for the first six weeks of your life. I loved you so strong and so hard that I cried for weeks after you were gone. I woke up in the middle of the night, hearing you crying for me. I thought I would die from missing you. But I was sick and I wanted you safe, so I sent you back here with Paris. She was supposed to take care of you while I got

well, while I got my head on straight. She was supposed to be ready when I came back for you. She wasn't
supposed to take what I had, what I loved and needed,
from me. She wasn't supposed to do that, Nikki."

"You should've come back," Nikki bit out from between clenched teeth.

"You're right." Pam glanced around for her purse,
saw it on the far end of the sofa and reached for it. She
slipped it over her shoulder and looked at Nikki. "You're
absolutely right. I should've come back. I should've
come back and fought for what was mine, but I didn't
know how to do that, what with the man I was in love
with married to Paris and you thinking that she was
your mother. That train left me standing at the station,
honey, and it was too late for me to hop on. I told you
before that I share with the people I love and I shared
you and Chad with Paris because I loved her and I figured that if she would go to the extremes she went to,
to have you, she must've wanted you *awfully* bad. How
could I fight against a mind that diabolical?"

"Don't talk about my mom like that," Nikki snapped.
"She was better than you any day."

"A better actress, anyway." Pam moved away from
them and headed for the door. She extended a parting
hand toward Nate and gasped in shock when Nikki
reached out to slap it down.

"Get out," Nikki said. "And don't come back."

Pam's hand flew through the air before she thought
about what she was doing. The back of her hand met
Nikki's cheek with a loud crack and sent the girl stumbling sideways. Nate caught her and then swung her
away when she would've charged toward Pam with
her claws bared.

"I hate you, you bitch!" Nikki was livid. She wrestled
against Nate's hold with a ferocity that neither Pam or

Chad had known she possessed. Her feet kicked at the air, arms flailed wildly. "Get out, get out, get out, get out!"

The slap shocked Chad out of his stupefied trance. But rather than go to his daughter, he went to Pam. "We need to talk," he whispered heatedly.

"Talk to Nikki, Chad. She needs you right now." She pulled at his wrists, trying to loosen the hands he'd clamped around her face.

"What about what I need?"

"What do you need, Chad?" She was anxious to be off and away, shifting from one foot to the other impatiently.

"I need you to tell me what the hell happened, Pam. Finally put me out of my misery and tell me what happened."

"Get your hands off of her!" Nikki screamed. "Don't touch that lying bitch!"

Chad lost it. "Nikki, shut up!" His voice boomed through the room and Nikki's mouth dropped open. Nate pinned her against the wall by her arms and she struggled against his iron hold uselessly.

"Nothing happened, Chad. And then everything happened. Please . . . just . . . I need to go."

Chad released her slowly, searching her eyes for answers and finding none. He stepped away from her and let his hands fall to his sides. "I don't understand."

"I'm sorry." She left him standing there and went to the door. Before pulling it open, she pressed her forehead to the wood and let her eyes slide closed. Nikki was damn near hysterical and the sound of her rage cut through Pam like knives through butter, threatening to break her. She debated returning to the living room and offering the only explanation she had to offer, but everything inside her rejected the idea. The thought of revisiting the past dampened her armpits and caused sweat to soak her scalp. Not even Nikki's fury could make her turn around. Pam's fear was much stronger.

She pulled the door open and swooned. Locked gazes with the man standing on the other side of the storm door and opened her mouth to speak, then she gave up the fight and crumbled to the floor like a sack of bricks. Hearing the noise, both Chad and Nate raced to the door and came up short. Chad looked from Pam's still body to Jasper's worried face and sighed wearily. Then he bent to scoop Pam from the floor and carried her back into the living room.

"Will somebody please tell me what *the fuck* is going on around here?" Nikki came toward him and he stopped her with a look.

Nate ushered Jasper inside the house and motioned for him to go on into the living room. He closed the door soundlessly, turned the lock and walked up behind Jasper. "We're having a good old time here at the Greene house, Jasper," he drawled close to the man's ear. "As you can see, Nikki's out of sorts and Pam's out cold. She's not much help to us now, so maybe you could help us out in her stead?"

Pam was sprawled on the sofa and Jasper stood over her, looking down into her face. He glanced over his shoulder at Nate distractedly. "Excuse me?"

Chad looked up from his perch beside Pam's head. "Family business, Jasper."

"Oh but Jasper *is* family," Nate said. "That being the case, why don't you take a look over here at your granddaughter and while you're at it, explain to her why her mother left Mercy eighteen years ago. I think it would really mean a lot."

"I don't like your tone, boy."

"And I don't like *you*, so that makes us just about even. Start talking."

"Nate, what is this?" Chad was confused. He recalled Pam's words when she had first arrived. Something about Moira and then David, who was really Miles, and then something about Jasper. Realization dawned slowly and with it came shock. He took a seat on the sofa, in the narrow space Pam wasn't occupying and stared at Jasper. "I'm starting to think Pam has the right idea. Is everybody in this fucking town crazy?"

"I'm going to my room," Nikki announced on her way out of the room.

"I don't think so," Nate told her. "First, you're going to the kitchen to wet a towel with cold water and bring it back to me. And then you're going to sit down and listen." She hesitated a second too long and his patience dissolved. "*Do it!*"

"Do you know something, Jasper?" Chad asked. *Pam has his forehead*, he thought, *and his mouth. How could I have missed that?* Nikki came back with the towel and he laid it across Pam's forehead.

Jasper hadn't come here to get into the mess from years ago. He really hadn't. Moira had called and begged him to find Pamela, to make sure she was safe. She was sobbing and screaming into the phone and Jasper could hardly understand a word she was saying. Finally, Miles had taken the phone from her and explained to him what Moira was having such a hard time explaining.

"Moira and I were talking, Mr. Holmes," Miles said and Moira could be heard screaming frantically in the background. "Pam came in and we didn't hear her. She knows that . . . well, that you and Moira . . ." He took a deep breath. "Moira would like for you to find Pam and see that she's okay. She was rather upset when she left here earlier."

"I see," Jasper had replied and then hung up the phone.

But he didn't see at all. He didn't see how, in the space of a few days, his life had been turned upside down. He didn't see how he could've thought, all those years ago, that he and Moira would never be found out. And he didn't see how he could've gone along with everything that happened in the first place. He'd buried one child, never having told her who he was and that he loved her, and now Pam would probably never speak to him again. When she left this time there wouldn't be any cards and short notes to tell him that she was thinking of him. She would lock him out of her life forever. He'd lost her all over again, just when he was beginning to believe that she had come back to him.

He had come hoping to catch her before she disappeared and praying she gave him a chance to explain. To Chad, he said, "You remember the day I came home and caught you and Pam messing around?" There was an empty chair nearby and he sank into it gratefully.

"I do."

"She ran off embarrassed, the way women do, but you, you came and faced me like a man." Chad grinned despite himself and Jasper allowed himself a brief chuckle. "I don't mean to say that I didn't want to take your head off, because I did. But you faced me. Couldn't do nothing but respect you for that, even if your fly was standing open and your shirt was on backwards."

"Oh *God*," Nikki groaned from across the room. Nate quelled anything else she might've said with a look that told her she was skating on thin ice.

Jasper glanced at his granddaughter and cleared his throat. "Anyway, I knew you two was planning on getting married and I could see that you was in love, so I was happy. Threw me for a loop when she ran off and then when Paris came back you married her instead. I wasn't so happy about that. Looked to me like you was messing around with both my girls."

"Nikki is Pam's daughter, Jasper," Chad supplied lest there be any confusion. "I know this looks screwed up to hell and back and that's because it is, but I don't want to get into that right now. I'd rather hear what you have to say, if you don't mind. And if you could say it before Pam comes to and starts talking about *things* again, I'd greatly appreciate it."

"I would too," Nikki chirped sarcastically. "This ought to be good."

Nate did a double take and glared at her, letting his eyes speak to her. She snapped her mouth shut and fell into mutinous silence. He had no idea why she felt the need to test his limits the way she was, but he was on the verge of taking off his belt and wearing her ass out. He hadn't had to spank her since she was seven years old, but looking at her, he was thinking that now might be the time to offer her a refresher course.

Jasper took his eyes to Pam's face and left them there. He sat back in his chair and propped his elbow on the arm, covered his mouth with tense fingers. "She didn't want nobody to know what happened to her here and she made me promise I wouldn't tell a soul. Course I told Moira anyway, but nobody else. She wouldn't even let me call the police or take her to the hospital. We fought about that something terrible, but

you know how she could be." His eyes skipped up to
Chad's briefly, then over to Nate's. "You do too, I
think." Nate was the first to look away from the knowledge in Jasper's eyes.

"The police . . . the hospital . . . ?" Chad's voice trailed
off as he began to understand. He dropped his head in
his hands. "Damn . . . what the . . . what are you saying?"

"He hurt her bad. Caught her walking back to the
home after she got off work and grabbed her. She said
he choked her until she blacked out and when she
came to he had her tied up someplace. It was dark and
she couldn't see where she was. She couldn't see who
he was and we never found out, but wasn't no question
about what he did to her. She left work on a Thursday
evening and she showed up on my doorstep that Friday night," Jasper sobbed. "That's how long that bastard kept her, doing things to her before he let her go.

"She wouldn't let me do nothing for her," he pleaded
with Chad to understand. "She told me if I called the
police she would run off and never come back and I
didn't want her to do that. She took so many baths and
scrubbed herself so hard, she made herself bleed. And
I couldn't do nothing for her."

"I came home from school and I was looking for
her," Chad said, remembering. "She was supposed to
skip out on school and come up to the university to be
with me, like she always did on Fridays, but she didn't
show up. I was jealous because I knew Nate was supposed to be coming home from school that weekend
and I thought she blew me off to be with him." He
scooted around on the sofa and looked down into her
face. "She let me think that's what she did and we ar-
gued about it. I thought she didn't want to make love
with me because she was angry with me. *God.*"

"She was already pregnant with Nikki when it happened, Chad," Nate put in. "About eight weeks, if I recall."

"You *knew*?" Chad was stunned. He gaped at Nate for long seconds. "You knew that some bastard had put his hands on my woman and you didn't *tell* me?"

"She wouldn't let me tell you, Chad. Hell, we fought about it, too. She wanted to forget it happened. Told me she'd kill herself if I told you. If you'd seen what she was like back then you would've believed her, too. Trust me. I had to call Nathaniel and make him come and help me with Pam," Jasper confided softly. "She was going crazy, screaming and crying, threatening to hurt herself and I couldn't stand to watch it anymore. Nathaniel, he's like a brother to her, and I knew he could get through to her. You, you wasn't nothing like a brother to her and she didn't want you to see what that bastard did to her. She thought she was ruined."

"Somewhere in this town a rapist is running loose and nobody knows *who he is*?"

Three heads turned in Nikki's direction. "Somebody hurt her like that and got away with it?"

"She couldn't say who it was, Nikki." Nate's tone was gentle as he reached for her hand and squeezed it tightly. "In her mind it was the mailman or the man at the grocery store or her third period teacher, any man she looked at. Not knowing is what made her leave Mercy. Knowing he was possibly still here is what kept her away."

"But, why didn't she take me with her? Why, Uncle Nate?"

"She said she was sick and she was. Do you know what clinical depression is, Nikki?" She covered her face and exploded into tears. Nate brought her hand to his lips and kissed it. He'd been by Pam's side as much as he could be during that time and he could attest to the fact that Nikki's tears weren't wasted. "The two years she spent in therapy saved her life. You had to be here with Paris so she could heal. You didn't know Pam when she was younger, but you can ask your dad and he'll tell you that she was a hundred times more alive than she is even today. She was something else and that's the truth."

"She was," Chad seconded. A sad smile curved his lips. "I took one look at her and decided I couldn't stand her. Then I took a breath and realized that I wanted her like I'd never wanted anything in my life. She drove me crazy with her smart mouth and those switching hips. I couldn't think straight when she was around."

"He broke her . . . whoever he was, he broke her," Jasper hissed angrily.

Nate rolled to his feet, just as angry. "I don't know about anybody else, but I need a drink." Unable to listen to any more, he escaped to the kitchen without a backward glance.

"Mom wasn't like Aunt Pam," Nikki caught her father's eyes and said.

"No baby, she wasn't."

"Then why did you marry her?"

"Because you were someone else I realized I wanted like I never wanted anything in my life."

In the kitchen, Nate tossed back a shot of cognac and grit his teeth as the liquid burned a path down his throat. He looked at the ceiling. "All right, Paris. If your scheming ass is in heaven, start working some miracles, would you?" He slammed the glass down on the counter and went back into the living room with a purpose. He didn't stop walking until he was standing by the sofa, looking down at Pam's inert form. "All right, sleeping beauty, it's time for you to wake the hell up." He dropped down on his haunches and eased Pam into a sitting position, held her up with one hand and used the other to slap at her face. "Come on, P. Snap out of it. Open those big eyes and look at me, baby. Come on."

"Uncle Nate, stop hitting her *so hard*." Nate shot Nikki a look over his shoulder and kept right on slapping Pam's cheeks.

Pam's arms came awake before her eyes opened. She moaned sleepily and then swatted at Nate's hands, irritated. Her eyes came open slowly and darted around the room. When they landed on Jasper she jumped up from the sofa and almost fell over Nate.

"What the hell is he doing here? Who called him? Did you, Nate? Chad, did you?" Both men shook their heads wearily. Unlike Nikki, if Pam suddenly decided to go wild and start swinging it would take both of them to restrain her, and barely at that. Neither of them had the energy or the inclination to tangle with Pam right now.

"I came to talk to you, Pam. Moira called me and . . ."

"That bitch," Pam gasped. "Tell her I said to stay the fuck out of my life. And you too, Jasper, you stay out. I trusted you, I believed in you. I thought of you as a father figure and all the time you really *were* my father. I hate you for that, and I never want to see you again." She looked around wildly for her purse, couldn't find it and heard the ringing start back up in her ears. "Both of you, feeding me cookies and patting me on the head. If Paris wasn't already gone this would kill her for sure. Stay back!"

"Pam, please let me talk to you. I'm still the same Jasper you used to love. That ain't changed. We used to talk about everything and we can talk about this."

"Still the same? That's a joke, right?" Pam backed

away from Jasper's outstretched hands and walked in a wide circle around him. "I thought I knew a man who would never lie to me, who was my friend, but you are a liar, Jasper. A liar and a coward. How did you sleep at night, knowing you had children down the road in a fucking home, standing in line waiting for dinner like slaves?"

"Pam . . ."

"Fuck you. Where is my goddamn purse?"

"Here it is, Aunt Pam." Nikki came up behind Pam and held her purse and sunglasses out to her. Pam whirled around and reached for them at the same time that Nikki went to push them into her hands. Their hands collided and they both froze. Pam's eyes flickered up to Nikki's face and darted away from what she saw there. She looked at the wall for several seconds and then swallowed audibly.

"I have to go," she said.

Chad caught up to her at the door. "Pam, you shouldn't drive. Let me get my keys . . ."

"I'm fine, Chad. I learned a long time ago to roll with the punches and get back up swinging, so don't worry about me."

"If you won't let me drive you, then I'm coming with you."

"Unless you're coming to California, no you're not." She spared him one last look and touched her palm to his chest over his heart. "I'll be in touch." She slipped out the door before he could think to stop her.

Chad returned to the living room looking like he was returning from a trip through the depths of hell. He sat next to Jasper on the sofa and covered his face. Nikki called out to him and he shook his head tiredly, telling her not to bother. He wasn't listening, couldn't listen to another thing. After a few minutes, he got to his feet and climbed the stairs to his room. The sound of his bedroom door slamming shut shook the house.

Pam fished her cell phone from her purse as she sped down the road toward the B&B. "Gil, it's me. I need you to make me a reservation on the first thing smoking out of Atlanta. *Yes, tonight.*" She listened for a moment. "I could care less. Coach, first class, the baggage hold, I don't give a shit. Just get me the hell out of here."

Dear Diary,

Aunt Pam is gone. She must've left in the middle of the night because Uncle Nate said that when he went to the B&B the next morning she was gone. I've never seen my dad so sad looking. It's like Aunt Pam died, instead of my mom. He barely sleeps or eats and he's drinking too much. Uncle Nate keeps saying not to worry, but I can't help it. What if he's not just sad, but so mad at me that he hates me now? What if he thinks I drove Aunt Pam away?

I don't know what to think or what to say. I see now that my dad and Aunt Pam were in love and I'm confused about why my mom would marry him if she knew that. Even if he asked her she should've said no. I asked Uncle Nate why my dad asked my mom to marry him in the first place and he said that it was because I was already two-years-old when my dad found out about me and he didn't want to miss anymore time with me. He knew my mom wouldn't just give me to him.

I don't know if I'm mad with my mom or not. She loved me and took care of me all these years, but I'm not sure it was because Aunt Pam didn't want me, like I first thought. Part of me believes that my mom's reasons were selfish and that Aunt Pam was cheated. I feel guilty for thinking bad things about my mom, but I can't help it.

And, oh my God, what happened to Aunt Pam was terrible! It's like something out of a horror movie, something I can only think of in my worst nightmares. Now I will look at every man in town, wondering if he is the one who did that to her. If he is the one who killed her spirit and made her run away.

Everything is so mixed up in my head. I love Aunt Pam and I miss her, but I don't want to see her again, yet. Does that make sense? I love my mom and I miss her, but I'm angry with her, too. Some of the things she wrote in her diary are starting to make sense to me now, and I don't like how they make me feel about her. I love my dad and I hate that he is so sad, but I don't know if I'll be able to accept seeing him and Aunt Pam together like that if he decides to go after her. It would be weird. Would I go with him, if he went? I don't know.

Dad took the diary in his room with him and he hasn't given it back. Nothing makes sense.

Nikki

PS: How can Aunt Pam expect me to understand what she did if she won't even listen to Moira's and Jasper's side of the story? She said some mean things to Jasper . . . and I said some mean things to her, too, didn't I? I don't know what to do or what will happen next.

NINETEEN

Miles was emotionally wrung out by the time he'd settled Moira down and returned to his hotel room to pack his things. He assumed Pam would be headed back to California the first chance she got, and he was itching to get the hell away from Mercy too. He planned to spend a few more days with Moira at her house before leaving to make sure she was really all right, and then he would go.

He slid his room key card in the slot, saw the light turn green, and heard the automatic lock click. He knew something was different the instant he stepped inside his room and switched on the floor lamp. Nothing was visibly out of place and everything appeared to be just as he'd left it, but something was different.

He went over to the bed and lifted the bedspread, looking underneath for his briefcase. He couldn't really say he was surprised to find it gone. Nor was he surprised, after he turned on his laptop and booted it up, to find that the entire memory had been erased, programs and all. It would have to be professionally re-built to even be useful again.

Miles crossed the room and pulled the nightstand drawer open. The standard issue Bible was still there, as was the box of tissues he'd dropped inside the drawer days ago. But the backup disk he'd slipped between the pages of the good book was gone and so was the one he'd pushed down inside the tissue box. He knew without having to look that the information he'd taped to the bottom of a dresser drawer was gone too, but he still checked to be sure.

Cocky idiot that he was, he had brought all the information and notes he'd made on Pamela to Mercy with him. He hadn't bothered to make copies and ship them back to New York for safekeeping, which was his usual modus operandi. Backup, then backup again. Save and separate. He had always meant to, but he hadn't quite gotten around to it.

Miles's shoes were still lined up neatly along the bottom of the compact closet, but they were now pointed toward the door rather than the wall, the way he'd left them, a sign to him that every nook and cranny of his room had been swept clean. He pushed a hand inside a blazer pocket and breathed a sigh of relief as his fingers wrapped around the wad of bills stashed there. He counted the money carefully, decided that all three thousand of it was present and accounted for, then headed to the bathroom.

He came up short in the doorway and stared at the mirror. His visitor had left a calling card. *Back off* was written in red lipstick across the glass. An involuntary smile took his lips.

Miles would bet all three thousand of his spare change money on the fact that Nate Woodberry hadn't

left a single fingerprint in his wake. He didn't bother
with calling the police to report the fact that someone
had stolen from him that which he'd stolen from
someone else.

It took Chad two weeks to work his way through
Paris's diary. He read late at night, before he rolled
over and drifted into restless sleep. He was unable to
talk about the things he read, not even with Nikki,
who'd already read them. He walked through the endless days thinking about Paris's words, processing
them and trying to assimilate them into the image of
the woman he thought he'd known.

Paris wrote about his parents, about when his father
died years ago, and about Chad's inconsolable grief
when he'd had to place his mother in a nursing home
after she had suffered from the stroke that ultimately
killed her, in such a way that endeared her to him. In
her words he recognized his best friend, the gentle and
giving person she was. Yet, when she wrote about Pam
he thought he could feel hostility propelling her words
onto the pages. Almost like she was fighting a battle
with herself, like she loved her sister, but couldn't quite
figure out why.

He couldn't fathom the closeness and intensity of
the relationship Pam and Paris had shared. He was an
only child and the closest he'd ever come to being obsessed with someone was with Pam. She had spun a
web around him and held him captive for half his life,
but he quickly came to the realization that Paris
must've been captivated by her long before he had ever
come onto the scene. She must've wondered at her sister's electrifying energy, fearless personality, and animal-
like sexuality, and craved it for herself.

Chad brought an image of Paris to the front of his

mind and looked at it long and hard. She could've been anything she wanted to be, could've done anything she wanted to do. There were times during their years together when he had glimpsed different aspects of her personality, sharp contrasts to the demure, dignified persona she'd always portrayed and he knew that she'd had more than she realized inside of her waiting to blossom. Only she had never accessed it. He was sorry he hadn't cared enough to point those aspects out to her, so she would know they were there. And then he was sorry he was never able to love her the way she had imagined he would.

Paris might've looked like Pam, but he could, to this day, close his eyes and pick his lover out of a room full of clones. It was simple for him and it always had been. He had claimed Pam for his own the moment he set eyes on her. Anything and anyone else had simply been a diversion; temporary pacifiers who, in his mind, were incapable of holding a candle to the real thing.

Paris would have known she wasn't even any of those things to him, she must have. She was a smart woman, and she had to have known that he had never seen what she wanted him to see in her eyes. She had used other things to hold him though. Nikki, for one, and her silence, for another. She could've set him free, but she had chosen not to.

Chad thought he could hate her for that alone. And then for the way she had wronged Pam, he thought he could quite cheerfully murder her. But she was already gone. He remembered and recalled his nasty thoughts. If for nothing else than the fact that Paris had helped him to raise a beautiful, confident, and talented daughter, he wished her a speedy crossing over.

He read the entry immediately following Pam's attack and put his face between the pages to cry. Then he took the book down to the kitchen and out the back door with him. He stood over the incinerator and watched it burn until he could no longer recognize it. He took a step back from the smoke and squinted at Nikki. He hadn't noticed her until just then.

"I burned it," he told her.

She stepped up next to him and looked where he was looking, nodding slowly. Her fingers closed around his and she rested her head against his arm. "Good," she said.

"She was crazy about you, you know."

"I know. You too, Dad. She was crazy about you, too. That's why she did what she did."

"I know," Chad said softly.

TWENTY

Gillian stuck her head inside Pam's dressing room, saw Pam sitting at the make-up table, and came all the way into the room, closing the door softly at her back. "Hey, hey," she sing-songed as she sashayed over to the table. "One more set and you're out of here. You ready to go home to your own bed?"

"Like nobody's business," Pam sighed. Gillian massaged her shoulders expertly and she purred like a kitten. "I feel like I've been to a hundred cities instead of nineteen."

"You sang better than I've ever heard you sing, though."

"Nobody sings sad songs better than a sad person, Gil. You know that."

"Speaking of which, I was a little sad to see that luscious Nate Woodberry get on a plane this morning." Gillian met Pam's eyes in the mirror and they grinned at each other. "You sure know how to pick them, I'll give you that."

"Nate is the quintessential playboy. The day he finally decides he's ready to limit himself to one woman will be the day hell truly freezes over." Pam picked up a pot of lip gloss and swirled a brush across the surface. She leaned forward and began applying the color to her lips. Gillian pulled up a stool and plopped down next to her at the table. "You ever been in love with two men at the same time, Gil? One you want and the other you need?"

She considered the question carefully. "Once I was. Couldn't figure out what the hell to do about it either. Which one is the one you want and which is the one you need?"

"I don't want to answer that," Pam decided. She shuffled tubes and bottles around on the vanity and slid an envelope from under her makeup case. "Look, I want to show you something."

Gillian studied the photos Pam handed her for several seconds. "This is your mom?"

"I never had a mother, but yes, that's the woman who gave birth to me. Moira."

"And the old dude with your mouth? This is your father?"

Pam caught her breath and nodded hesitantly. She couldn't say she'd never had a father, just not one she had officially recognized as such. "Yeah," she breathed.

Gillian flipped back to the photo of Moira and divided looks between it and Pam's face. She tsk-tsked and shook her head knowingly, a wide grin on her face.

"What?"

"Nothing." She handed the photos back to Pam, stood and pushed the stool under the table with her foot. "It's just . . . I always told you, you had some white girl in you. Now I know why you can't dance."

Pam laid her head back and roared with laughter.

There was a knock at the door and Gillian went to

answer it. She talked in hushed tones to a stage assistant and then eased the door closed. "Freckles says we have ten minutes."

"Okay." Pam moved around the room gathering her things and dropping them carelessly in the duffel lying open on the floor. She tossed Jimmy Choos in with Manolos and topped them off with DKNY blouses and Kenneth Cole skirts. As an afterthought, she stuffed the photos back in the envelope and zipped them in a side compartment.

"Woodberry brought you those pictures?" Gillian asked from the doorway.

"Yeah." Pam swished a makeup brush loaded with face powder across her nose, forehead, and cheeks, then stepped back to survey her handiwork in the mirror. She thought she looked like a circus clown. Stage lighting was harsh, though. "Nate always knows when I need him." She missed Gillian's knowing look.

The tour wrapped up in Oakland, a little over three hours away from where Pam lived in Los Angeles. Just past two in the morning, she and Gillian boarded a private plane headed home. A limousine was waiting for them at Los Angeles International and they both slept stretched out on the backseats until the driver buzzed them awake after they pulled to a stop in Pam's circular driveway. She shook herself awake and said her goodbyes to Gillian, then went inside to reacquaint herself with her house and her bed. Too many nights in hotel beds had made her neck stiff and her back cranky as hell. She walked from room to room, making sure that all the windows were closed and latched and that she was the only person in the house.

It wasn't a large house by celebrity standards, but it was enough for Pam. When she was shopping for houses, this one was the fourth on the list, and as soon as she had walked in and felt its aura, she knew it was the one for her. There were five bedrooms, each with private baths, a formal dining room, an exercise room, and a den with a fireplace. She had converted the attic into an all-purpose studio, where she indulged in whatever pastime that currently struck her fancy. Some years back it was yoga, then painting and then it was dancing. These days she wiled away her free time curled up on a chaise, reading or simply staring at the sky through the skylight. It was her tranquility room and the only one she barred the interior decorator she'd hired from transforming.

Off the eat-in kitchen at the back of the house was a sunroom, which looked out over the pool and modest backyard. She took a long bubble bath, dropped a floor length caftan over her head, and took her mail there to read. She switched on a small lamp and began flipping through the envelopes methodically. There was the usual credit card offers and those she tossed into a rattan trash can. A leather bustier in one of the mail order catalogs caught her eye and she considered it at length before deciding against it and tossing all the catalogs, too. Her bank statement she perused carefully, noting each debit and credit and checking that the balance was in the vicinity of where she thought it should be. She employed an accountant to handle all the pesky details surrounding the money she made and she had an excellent portfolio, but she still paid careful attention to where her money went and on whose authority.

The next envelope in the stack gave Pam pause. It was postmarked a week ago from Georgia. She recognized the flowing script and the faintly floral scent clinging to the envelope. There was a dried flower inside, somewhere between the folded pages, she knew. The first letter Moira sent had come along with a handful of pressed rose petals. The second, a daisy. This one would have something different. Maybe a lily, Pam mused as she slid her finger along the fold and opened the envelope.

She had been home two days when the first letter arrived by overnight delivery. In it, Moira had begged and pleaded for Pam to call her and tell her that she was safe. Pam never called and the second letter had come by Federal Express three days later. She sat in the same chair she was sitting in now and read it. This one was more of the same. Wanting her to get in touch, wanting the three of them to get together, so that they could talk, get everything out in the open. A pressed tulip tumbled from the pages into Pam's lap and she held it to her nose to inhale the fading scent. She had no intention of answering any of the letters.

She flipped the next item up to the light and froze. Jasper's scratchy, grumpy looking handwriting jumped out at her from the back of a postcard and snatched her breath. *Thinking of You,* he'd written. Just as she had written to him many times over the years. Short, simple lines to let him know that he meant the world to her and that she could never go far enough away from him to forget that. He had to know that she would get it, the wily old bastard. She cracked a smile despite herself.

After that, the letters and postcards stopped coming and Pam was relieved. Another month passed before a large padded manila envelope appeared. Pam nearly tripped over it as she came through the door. She had just finished in the studio, recording the final version of the song she had titled "Have Mercy On Me," to be included on an upcoming motion picture soundtrack, and returned home. She cursed her housekeeper as she kicked the envelope out of the doorway with one foot and closed the door with the other. Her hands were full of clothes she'd picked up from the dry cleaners and the mail was hanging from between her lips.

Time to have a serious talk with the help, she thought as she laid the clothes across an armchair and scooped up the envelope. She figured it was a script that had somehow slipped past Gillian's eagle eye, so she brought it with her to the kitchen. Knowing that she had no real acting talent whatsoever and knowing that whoever sent the script probably knew it too, she didn't rush to open the package. She was constantly being courted for roles as promiscuous sex goddesses or ones that required her to be at least partially nude, and she wasn't particularly interested in either.

The envelope sat undisturbed on the kitchen counter for the rest of the day and halfway through the next. Then Pam finally decided to open the flap and peek inside. She took a seat at the breakfast bar and opened the cardstock folder. Miles Dixon's name caught her eye immediately. He'd given himself credit as the author of the manuscript she held in her hands. There was no title but there was a note paperclipped to the first page. She unfolded it slowly.

Pam,

I'd like you to be my first advance reader. As you know, I was extremely interested in writing the story of your life, the story of your rise to fame, if you will. I still am and this is what I have conjured up so far. Please do me the honor of reading it and letting me know what you think.

Rather than rely on various sources, who may or may not be credible, I collaborated with a most knowledgeable source. I hope that you will find this manuscript to be written with integrity and sensitivity. That was my intent, as it should have always been.

Truly,

Miles

Pam's first instinct was to toss the manuscript in the trash and then to call her attorney, but curiosity won out over common sense. If she was going to be laid bare for the public to pick the meat off of her bones, then she might as well be prepared. Forewarned is forearmed. She took the manuscript with her to her attic sanctuary and spread out on the chaise to find out just how much damage Miles Dixon was planning to do.

She read straight through the night, only pausing to use the bathroom and to unearth her emergency stash of "I don't smoke anymore, but just in case I'm going crazy" cigarettes from the butter compartment inside the refrigerator door. She dragged the manuscript all over the house with her as she read. She took it with her to the sun porch to keep her company while she soaked up some rays, to the kitchen to entertain her while she ate, and then to bed with her.

Her bedside clock read 9:20AM when she rolled across the mattress, stifled a yawn, and plucked the cordless phone from the base on the nightstand. Miles answered on the second ring.

"You've read it?" he asked by way of greeting.

"How did you know it was me?"

"Caller ID. What do you think?"

She took a deep breath and eyed the papers spread across the bed. "I think I hate you for being so persistent. Why is it so hard for you to leave well enough alone?"

"It's a great story, Pam."

"It's my story, David, I mean Miles. Whatever your damn name is."

"David is my middle name and Miles is my first name. Sorry about that, by the way."

"Kiss my ass. It's good, I'll give you that. One thing, though. Your source got a few minor details wrong. It has to be absolutely accurate."

"Tell me what they are and I'll double-check them with Moira."

"Moira?"

"Yeah, I thought you would pick up on the fact that she narrated most of the text. She insisted on accuracy, too."

"You didn't use the stuff Humpy told you and Clive Parker." Nate had given her the rundown on the notes he'd found in Miles's hotel room.

"It's all hearsay anyway and not really relevant to the story. Who's Humpy?"

"James Humphries," she clarified for him. "Where's the shit he said about me?"

"It's not included in the manuscript."

"Duh. Why not? I thought you wanted a bestseller, a titillator?"

"That manuscript is not a titillator, Pam. It has strong literary merit, and titillator is not a word," Miles said, sounding offended.

"That's why you get paid to write trash about people and I don't. You don't need my permission to publish this manuscript, so why send it to me?"

"You're right, I don't need your permission, but I'd like to have it anyway. I thought maybe you could write the foreword."

"I'm not a writer."

"You could be. What do you say? Give the manuscript your stamp of approval, and I'll share the advance and the royalties with you, fifty-fifty. That's fair, isn't it?"

She ignored his question in favor of one of her own. "It goes to the press just like it's written?"

"Except for the changes you mentioned and anything else you might want to add."

"I don't have anything to add." The rape hadn't been included in the manuscript, and neither had any mention of her connection to Chad and Nikki. If it had to be published, it was perfect the way it was.

"Does that mean I can send you a contract?"

"The money," Pam hedged. "I don't want it."

"Neither does Moira, and I wouldn't feel right keeping all of it. You know this book is going to be a national bestseller, don't you? The profits will be significant, too much money to just ignore."

She had a thought. "The home."

"What?"

"I'm donating my portion to the Angels of Mercy Children's Home."

"Include that in the foreword and the profits just doubled."

"It's not about the money, Miles."

"I never thought it was. I'm just stating facts. So can I send the contract?"

"Send it to my agent slash publicist," Pam decided and gave him Gillian's contact information. "She'll go over it with a fine tooth comb and make sure I'm not getting screwed. I don't trust you, David, or Miles or whoever the hell you are."

He chuckled into the phone. "I guess I deserved that."

"Damn right you did. I need sleep now. Goodbye." She hung up and rolled over, pulled a pillow under her head and fell asleep.

She opened her eyes seven hours later and settled them on Nate. He was sitting on the side of the bed, flipping through the pages of the manuscript rapidly. She remembered that he was a speed-reader and sat up to rake her nails down his back. "He wrote it anyway," she said unnecessarily.

"It's good. Clean and fair." He looked over his shoulder at her and smiled. Then he leaned sideways and met her halfway for a kiss. "You ready to come into the world again, P?"

"It might be time."

"It is. You planning on putting Chad out of his misery while you're at it?"

"Is he still angry with me?" Nate would tell her the truth.

"For not telling him about what happened to you?" He shook his head. "I don't think so. More hurt that you didn't feel you could come to him for what you needed."

"Instead of going to you."

"Something like that." Nate dropped the manuscript on the floor, crawled across the bed, and lay down next to Pam. He bent an elbow under his head and looked at her. "I wouldn't have it any other way though."

Pam slid down on the mattress and scooted close to him so that her back was pressed into his chest and the length of their bodies were touching. Nate moved closer and fit his knee into the space she made be-

tween her legs. They spooned, as they had done so
many times before, for so many years.

"What am I going to do with you, P?"

"You could marry me and put me out of my misery,"
she suggested, playfully.

"And live with having to share you with my best
friend? I don't think so. I like it better this way. I had
first dibs so he's sharing with me. You couldn't choose
between us if your life depended on it anyway and you
know it."

"You couldn't either and you'd probably cheat on me
anyway."

"Probably so," he admitted with an uneasy chuckle.
"Too many women, too little time. But you never can
tell about these things and I always come back though.
Chad won't cheat."

"He had other women when he was married to Paris."

"I knew that. But alas, Paris wasn't you. They'll erect
a monument when you go, P. You're a dangerous
woman. You make a man forget all kinds of shit he
should be remembering."

"Moira told me that once."

"Moira was right." Nate's hand slid around her waist
and untied her caftan. He eased the material off her
shoulder and replaced it with his open mouth. "You
had Jose Marillo so mixed up in the head he forgot he
had a wife and kids. Then you had that old Greek dude
trying to buy you an island and shit." He flicked his
tongue over her shoulder, up the side of her neck and
bit in. "And you had me. Quiet as it's kept, you still
do."

Pam laughed. "What do I have you doing, you fool?"

"Whatever you need me to do. Whenever, wherever.
It goes both ways. You do the same for me."

She took his hand from her breast and lifted it into the air with her own, watched their fingers thread together and clasp tightly. "You won't ever go away, will you, Nate?"

"Where the hell would I go and why? I share with the people I love, too."

Pam shifted her head on the pillow and locked eyes with him. "I thought you went back to Seattle?"

He grinned sneakily and dipped his head to catch her lips between his. He eased his tongue between her lips and took his hand back to her breasts. She moaned and kissed him back and he pushed deeper. "I heard you calling me. You need me right now, P?"

TWENTY-ONE

Chad was just settling into bed when he heard the first ping. He thought nothing of it and leaned back against the headboard with a pillow at his back. The television was on, more for the constant noise and light it provided than anything else, and he glanced at it every few minutes, in between reading pages of the high school's faculty handbook revision proposals. He had put the chore off until the last possible minute, and he was expected to give feedback on the proposed changes first thing in the morning. It was after one now.

The second ping caught him off guard. In the brief seconds between commercials, the noise crackled in the silence and drew his eyes to the window. He set the stack of papers aside, lifted the remote from the bed, and lowered the volume of the television, counting now and tracking the seconds between pings. He estimated that thirty seconds had passed between the first and second pings, and when the third one finally came, he realized that yet another thirty had gone by.

The next three pings came one right behind the other, separated only by the length of time it took to select a pebble of appropriate size and then swing back to aim precisely. He waited, frozen in his reclined position on the bed, to see if, thirty seconds later, the second round of pings would begin, if the pattern was still the one they had decided on decades ago as being their signal.

He went to the window and pulled the curtain back just as a pebble struck the glass somewhere in the vicinity of his naked chest. She was in the midst of swinging back to launch another one and everything about her froze when he appeared in the window. From the safety of his room he spread his hands wide and shrugged. *What do you want me to do?* She stamped her foot and pointed a finger to the ground. *Come outside*. He backed away from the window and let the curtain fall back in place. He lay back on his bed, folded his hands under his head, and looked at the ceiling. There was a time when he would've heard the pings on his window and damn near broken his neck creeping out of the house to meet her. But not tonight. The pings kept coming and he ignored them.

Though the lights were off and she was snuggled under the covers in bed, Nikki was far from asleep. She heard the doorbell and sat up to listen. She was certain that her dad would be treading down the hallway and then down the stairs to see who was at the door in just a few seconds. All she had to do was wait. If it was nobody, she'd give up on trying to stay awake and get some sleep, but if it was somebody important she was ready.

Seconds turned into minutes and the doorbell kept ringing. Nikki climbed out of bed and went to stand in the hallway, looking toward her dad's open doorway curiously. His lamp was on and she could hear papers shuffling around, but his feet never hit the floor. She hesitated, then tipped down to his room.

"Dad, did you hear the door?" Her eyes darted around his room before coming to rest on him. He looked relaxed and at ease, like it was any other night and someone wasn't ringing the doorbell at after one in the morning. He was wearing striped pajama pants and his long bare feet were crossed at the ankles.

Chad's eyes slowly rose from the page he was pretending to read and locked on Nikki's.

"Did *you* hear it?"

"Yeah, but . . ."

"Then why don't you go and see who it is?"

Heart pounding and eyes wide, she glanced down the hallway as if she expected whoever was at the door to suddenly be inside the house, bearing down on her. "I don't know if I want to."

"Why not?"

"I'm scared," she admitted softly. "What if she doesn't want to see me or talk to me? What if she's just here because she forgot something?"

"You won't know that until you answer the door, Nikki. Are you going to stand there playing *what if* the rest of the night?"

"Why don't you go and answer the door?"

"Because I think she might've forgotten something too, but you'll have to be okay with her claiming it. You should decide if you want to let her in or not. Do you understand what I'm saying to you?" His gaze was intent on hers and he knew the exact moment that she really did understand what he was saying.

"Can I ask you a question?"

"Anything."

"What happens if I don't let her in?"

He considered his response carefully, wanting to be gentle, but still truthful. "Then I go outside where she is." Nikki would be an adult in a few short years. She would make a life for herself, which was no more than he hoped for her, and he wanted to finally be able to do the same for himself.

"You really love her, don't you?"

"Yeah, I do, Nikki."

"You want to be with her, like *together* together?"

He nodded seriously. "I do. How do you feel about that?"

Nikki slumped against the doorjamb and hugged herself tightly. A multitude of expressions raced across her face, revealing her thoughts. She was angry about what she'd learned, sad about what happened to Pam, hurt that she was lied to, and afraid of her dad's feelings for Pam. The thought of Pam being close enough to touch made her happy, but still sad because she didn't know if Pam *wanted* to be touched or even if she wanted *her*.

"I'm still a little angry with her," she finally said.

"Why aren't you angry with me or Nate or with Paris? We all knew that Paris wasn't your biological mother, too." He felt that was an important point to make. He had expected to be on the receiving end of some of Nikki's anger, but it had never come. She seemed to be focusing the whole of it on Pam and he wondered about that.

"I don't know . . . it's like, you and Uncle Nate were always here, you know? She wasn't and I remember always wanting her to be, but she never was."

"You saw her a lot, when you and Paris visited her in California."

"I know, Dad," her tone was slightly irritated. "I know all that, but I still wanted more of her. I'm angry because now I know I could've had more of her and I didn't."

"That's a lot like I've felt all these years. Angry because I wanted her and I couldn't have her. Here lately, I've been angry because none of what happened had to happen."

"But you still want her now?"

"But I still want her now."

"Did you ever love Mom?" She watched his face closely, trying to read his mind. That was another reason she was angry, though she would never admit it to him. The idea that he had never loved her mom. No kid wanted to think that, no matter how weird the circumstances were.

"She was one of my best friends, so yes, I did love her, but in a very different way. Don't get me wrong," he put up a hand, "I'm still confused by what she did but even that doesn't make me want to take back the love I felt for her. I have some great memories of the times we spent together when we were kids."

The doorbell rang again and she looked in the direction of the sound. Goosebumps rose on her arms and she got the same feeling in her stomach that she always got when the gun finally went off, signaling that it was okay for her to take off running and leave her opponents in the dust. The decision to open the door rushed at her and she trembled from the force of it. But first, there was something else she wanted to know.

"Dad?"

"Yes, Nikki?" At last count, the doorbell had rang seven distinct times. He worked to keep impatience out of his voice.

"What about Uncle Nate?"

"What about him?"

"Does it bother you that he and Pam are so close? They kiss a lot."

"They grew up together," was all he said. It hadn't escaped his attention that Nikki now referred to Pam as simply *Pam*, without any particular familial classification. He thought of it as a step, but he had no idea in which direction. "Have you decided what you want to do about the door?"

Chad watched his daughter shift around a few seconds longer before she disappeared from the doorway. He heard her footfalls on the stairs and held his breath until he picked up on the sound of locks twisting and the door creaking open. Their voices were low and he couldn't hear what they were saying to one another, but he wasn't really trying to overhear. At this point, their words were for each other's ears only. He'd have his time with Pam soon enough.

He dragged a hand down his face, sucked in a deep breath and thought, *What about Nate?* He was almost ashamed to admit that as he read Paris's diary, he'd looked for references to Pam and Nate, entries that might've given him answers to a few of the questions he'd pondered over the years. Nate had always been his source for information about Pam. Where she was, what she was doing and who she was seeing, if anyone, at the time. Over the years, he had casually volunteered the information to Chad, expertly slipping in tidbits here and there during the course of a normal conversation, knowing that Chad would want to know, but that he would never come right out and ask.

He'd always known that Nate and Pam had remained in close contact. There were photos of Pam in the photo albums downstairs in the living room that Nate had taken with all that expensive photography equipment he never left home without. Candid shots, posed shots, ones of her in her home, and a few in exotic looking locales. And it never occurred to Chad until after Nate was long gone and he was sitting up in the middle of the night with images of the photos stampeding across his mind, that Nate would've been wherever Pam was at the times they were taken.

He remembered one photo in particular, perhaps because it had snagged his attention and held it exclusively for a long time after he'd seen it. It was a head and shoulders shot of Pam, asleep with her lips slightly parted and her face partially hidden in the depths of a fluffy pillow, her shoulders bare. He'd held the photo in his hands for long seconds, staring at it. Then he'd stared at Nate for just as long, while he bustled around with his cell phone clamped to his ear, dictating the particulars of his upcoming itinerary to his publicist and oblivious to Chad's intense scrutiny. Chad didn't think he was meant to have seen the photo, since Nate hadn't given it to him as part of the selection he had originally shown him. In fact he knew he wasn't. He'd come across it on his own, while looking for something completely unrelated and by accident. But he'd found it and he had pondered.

He and Paris had been married four years, with him in the middle of his second affair and her regularly seeing Ben, when he first began to wonder about Pam and Nate. But all he'd ever done was wonder. He had no claims on Pam and he'd had relationships with other women, so he wasn't really in a position to hurl accusations and demand answers, particularly in light of his marriage to Pam's sister. When he reminded himself of that fact, most of the wondering ceased and the inevitability of his life had come into sharp focus.

Chad accepted that he would probably never know if Nate and Pam had crossed the line. He knew them both well enough to know that neither of them would ever speak of it, if they had. And it was for the best that he didn't know because he thought of Nate as the brother he'd never had and he simply thought of Pam all the time. Truth be told, he really didn't *want* to know. He avoided digging too deeply for fear of uncovering something he was better off not knowing.

What he wanted was for Pam to come to him and say the things he needed to hear her say. That she was ready for him, ready for what he wanted to give her and to have with her. Ready to pick up where they had left off and get it right this time. He stayed where he was, pretending to read over the papers in his lap and waited to see if the prayers he'd been whispering under his breath for the past eighteen years had finally been answered.

"I like your shirt." Nikki stepped back from the door to make room for Pam to come inside the house. Her eyes traveled over the silky material, admiring the way the bright colors swirled together and crossed her eyes.

"You can't have it," Pam told her. That was coming next, she knew.

"I wasn't going to ask for it."

"Oh. Well, what were you going to ask then? There has to be something you want to know."

They stared at each other, neither of them willing to be the first to look away. Nikki's eyes filled with tears she tried to blink away. "I want to know . . ." she began, then stopped to swallow the lump in her throat and take a deep breath. She couldn't talk around it. "I mean, I know why you left, but I want to know if you really wanted me?"

"*Nikki*," Pam sighed heavily. "I always wanted you. *Always*. There's never been a day that I didn't want you. It sounds stupid now, but that's part of the reason I stayed away, because I didn't want to suddenly show up and confuse you. I didn't want you to think that, at first I didn't want you and then I suddenly decided that I did." She moved closer to Nikki and reached out to smooth away a tear with the tip of her finger. "The other reason I stayed away is because it killed me to see you and hold you and smell you, and know that I couldn't have you. I died a little every time I had to hear you call someone else *Mom* because I knew I'd done it to myself."

"You were sick," Nikki whispered.

"I was stupid and weak. Too weak to come back here and fight for you . . . and your dad."

"It was that good between you two?"

Pam's eyes slid closed on a low moan. Her arms crossed over her chest and her hands wrapped around her shoulders and squeezed. She tried to put her memories into words. "It was like the first rain shower of spring, the first snow of winter, the last day of school, and the first day of summer all rolled into one. It was perfect." She took her hands down to her abdomen and flattened her palms there, caught Nikki's eyes. "And then I had this . . . this person inside of me and he put it there. He put *you* there and I felt like I was given the most precious gift. I knew you would be the best of both of us, the best of what we brought to each other, so yes, it was *that* good. It was *so* good. Then . . . the rest happened and I . . . I couldn't deal."

"What happened to you...I'm sorry it did. It was bad. Mr. Jasper told us about it and he said it was *so bad* for you. Dad was upset and I was trying to be mad at you but . . . *God* . . . he said that whoever did that to you wouldn't let you go for a long time and . . . Why would somebody *do* that to you?" Nikki burst into tears and covered her face. Pam rubbed her arms as she cried and then, unable to resist any longer, she pulled Nikki into the circle of her arms and held her.

"I don't know why, baby, I don't know," she pressed kisses to the side of Nikki's face between words. "I do know that I made the biggest mistake of my life when I sent you away. I love you so much."

Nikki breathed Pam's scent deep into her nostrils and sighed as Pam's fingers threaded through her hair and caressed her scalp. She could feel Pam's heartbeat against her cheek and the steady rhythm of it soothed her. Hesitant at first and then possessively, her arms slid around Pam's waist. She fisted the back of Pam's shirt in her hands and clung as if her life depended on it.

"Please forgive me, Nikki," Pam said a long time later.

Chad heard her heels on the stairs, tracked the sound of them down the hallway and looked up just as she appeared in the doorway. He stalled for time by fiddling with the remote and carefully stacking papers before setting them aside.

"You look like you've got something you want to say," he remarked evenly.

"Do I?" He gave her a completely blank expression; one that he knew from experience would drive her nuts. The effect of it was no different now and she smiled. "You're not going to make this easy for me, are you?"

"Should I?"

"You wouldn't come outside."

"No, I wouldn't."

"You always used to come outside."

"We always *used* to talk, Pam. And we always *used* to trust each other."

"I trusted you, Chad."

"Not when it counted," he snapped. Silence stretched out and filled the room as they considered each other. "You should've told me."

"I was too ashamed to tell you. I was hurt and embarrassed and I thought I had done something to bring the rape on myself, to make someone feel like they could do that to me. The last thing I wanted to happen was for you to find out and feel the same way."

"But you told Nate."

"I wasn't wearing Nate's ring or carrying Nate's child. I didn't want you to have that image of me in your head. I wanted to be perfect for you."

"I knew the first time I saw you that you weren't perfect," he drawled.

Pam leaned against the doorjamb and crossed her arms under her breasts. "Well, maybe I didn't know you knew that. I was trying to be."

"You weren't perfect, Pam, but you were perfect for me. You didn't have to try. I fell in love with you without the slightest problem."

"Do you still love me, Chad?" Her eyebrows met in the middle of her forehead. "You said you *fell* in love with me back then, but do you still love me now?"

"What do you think?"

"You have a smart mouth, you know that?"

His eyebrows shot up. "Kiss my ass, Pam."

"I'll do that if that's what it takes," she said.

"Depends on what you want out of the deal."

"I want you to look at me the way you used to and I want you to touch me the way you used to."

"I never stopped looking or wanting to touch. You were just too far away from me to see or feel it." He swung his legs over the side of the bed and braced his elbows on his knees. Looked at the floor between his bare feet. "You left me here."

"I've regretted that decision every day since."

"So have I."

"Is it too late to ask you to come with me now?" Her eyes pleaded with him. "Is it too late for us?"

"You expect me to just pack up and run off with you?"

"Yes."

"Leave my job and take Nikki out of school, away from her friends?"

"Nikki might not mind."

"But I might."

She caught her breath, speechless. Two full minutes passed before she spoke. "I'm tired of living without you and without my daughter."

"Then come back, Pam. Go back to California, get all your shit and come back here. Will you do that?"

The question ricocheted through her mind and froze her where she stood. Come back to Mercy to live? She wanted to give in and let herself glide into an anxiety attack, fall to the floor and let it take her wherever it would. But he was watching her, waiting for an answer and there was no running from the situation this time. He was telling her that if she wanted him she'd have to come back to Mercy to have him.

"Damn you, Chad. Okay." She fought the shakiness in her voice and met his gaze. It would probably mean her final and complete undoing, living in Mercy again, but for him she would try.

"*What?*" He looked at her like she was crazy.

"I said okay. I love you, so . . . okay."

"Just like that, okay? You'll move back here to be with me?"

"As long as I get to say I told you so when you have

to have me committed." She smiled, expecting to see him smile in return, but he didn't. Instead, he scrubbed a hand across his face and released a harsh breath.

"It's too late for you to move back here, Pam," Chad informed her briskly. "I wouldn't expect you to do that anyway. I love you too much to put you through that." He sat back and ran a hand around his neck. "Tell me something, though. If I was to come to California with you, would you marry me? Have my babies?"

Pam took slow steps in his direction. She dropped to her knees between his legs and pressed her face to his chest, wrapped her arms around his waist. "Today," she said, her lips moving on his skin. "Right now. When?"

Chad raked his fingers through the hair that flowed down her back and tugged on the strands to tip her head back. He stared into her eyes for long seconds, rested his forehead against hers and kept on staring.

"Will you come with me, Chad?"

"Yeah, I'll come," he whispered into her mouth and took a soft kiss. "Damn, Pam. What took you so long?"

She was never known for being especially considerate of other people's feelings, Pam wasn't. Legend had it that she was unpredictable in both action and deed, and a few of the case examples used to fuel the legend were actually true. She had never fallen into the habit of glancing at a clock before picking up the phone to call someone, and she'd hardly ever given consideration to conventional schedules when she got it in her mind to knock on someone's door.

Feeling bad about waking Jasper from a restless sleep didn't even cross her mind as she stood on the small porch in front of his apartment door and rapped her knuckles against the wood. He came to the door looking frazzled and grumpier than usual because it was almost three o'clock in the morning.

They stood on opposite sides of the threshold, staring at each other. Now that she was here and confronted with the sight of him, Pam was speechless. Finally, he caught the ball she had thrown in his court by coming and parted his lips.

"It's late," he tried to complain. He searched her eyes and silently sent up a prayer of thanks that she was whole and safe and here. He'd nearly worried what little hair he still had left out thinking about her being so far away and dealing with everything that happened on her own.

"I know what time it is," Pam said. "Seems like to me it might be thirty-five years too late."

"You ain't the only one who's got a say in this, Pam." Anxiety and fear caused Jasper's voice to be sharper than he wanted it to be. He left the doorway and went to stand behind the sofa, bracing his hands on the back and leaning his weight on them. His head dropped to his chest and stayed there, while he collected his scattered thoughts. "You think it was easy doing what we did and having to live with it all these years?" He grabbed her eyes with his own and refused to let her look away from him.

"Apparently it was easy enough," she decided right then and there. "You never took back what you did. You didn't come for us, Jasper. Hell, you didn't keep us and you could've."

"Moira . . ."

She cut him off, slicing a trembling hand through the air. "I don't want to hear about Moira right now. I came here to talk about you."

"No you didn't, Pam. You came here to scream and

holler some more and to cuss me to hell and back. That's what you came here for, so why don't you go ahead and do it and get it over with? You don't want to hear nothing I got to say anyway."

"Yes, I do. I want to hear why you did it. At least give me that much to take with me." She stepped inside the apartment and closed the door at her back, leaned against it heavily.

"I was stupid and weak, Pam. That's all I know to tell you. I regretted it every damn day of my life and I still do. You don't know how many nights I sat up, hating myself and cursing myself for being so damn stupid. I never should've went along with it. You can't hate me no more than I already hate myself."

His words hit Pam like a speeding train. She'd said something eerily similar to Nikki a little while ago and the irony of the situation wasn't lost on her. Still, this was Jasper, the same man who had taught her right from wrong and never given up on her when she strayed from those teachings. The same man who had come running when she fell off her bike and tore the skin on her knees open. He had fussed the whole time, blown cool air on her knees when the alcohol burned, and tenderly applied bandages to her scrapes. He was the one who'd given her and Paris matching bikes for their tenth birthdays.

She flipped through the memories in her mind and searched for the times when Jasper hadn't been there, lurking around a corner, looking on, and couldn't find enough of them to add up to the fingers on one hand. She tried like hell to hate him, but the feeling defied her and wouldn't come.

"I don't hate you."

He released the breath he was holding in one huge whoosh. "I tried to always be there," Jasper told her.

"At the school and around town, everywhere I could. Moira, she . . ." a shaky chuckle escaped his lips, "she used to say that I was obsessed with you and Paris, but I couldn't help myself. Wasn't no piece of paper gone tell me I couldn't be a daddy to my girls. And hell, she wasn't no better. Always running up to the home and drawing ya'll out to her house every other day." He rubbed his face roughly. "I guess we both knew we fucked up big time. We was crazy about you girls."

"You know what's funny, Jasper? I always said that if I'd had a daddy, I'd want him to be just like you," Pam admitted. A sob rose in her throat and she slapped a hand over her mouth to keep it in.

"You did have one, you just didn't know it."

"I wish I would've known it."

"I do, too." He came away from the sofa and walked over to her, stopping a few feet away. "You got my mama's forehead, you know that? Got them green eyes from Moira, but the shape of them, that's my mama, too. You never knew her cause she was long gone by the time you and Paris was born, but so many times I looked at you and had to go in my office, lock the door and cry."

"I want to be so angry with you." Pam's fists balled at her sides and she pressed them to her mouth as she walked away from him. Her feet took her to the window, where she stood looking down on a deserted Main Street. Neither of them spoke for several minutes. Behind her, she heard the flicker of a lighter and seconds later cigarette smoke reached her nose. The smell of a burning Viceroy was steady and familiar to her, reminding her of all the years she'd been close enough to him to breathe in his second-hand smoke. "I always wondered why we seemed to have more things than the other kids, clothes and toys and shit. I always wondered where they came from. It was you, wasn't it?"

Jasper studied Pam's back through the smoke he sent into the air. Part of him wanted to lie, for fear that she'd think he was bragging or trying to excuse himself, but he felt that enough lies had been told to last a lifetime. "Me and Moira," he said. "She did just as much as I did. We fixed it so we was you and Paris's sponsors. We would sit up all night going over your Christmas lists, trying to figure out where we was gone find all the stuff you wanted. Liked to drove me to drink a few times."

"You and Moira . . ."

"We carried on for a few months, long enough to make you and Paris, but it was what it was. We never had no problems with you and Paris though. We both loved you two, Pam. Don't ever doubt that."

"I told you I don't want to hear about Moira," she said, glancing over her shoulder at him.

"She's part of this, too. You can't ignore her forever and I decided that I ain't gone let you ignore me. You planning on talking to her anytime soon?"

"I wasn't planning on talking to you, Jasper. I haven't thought far enough ahead to even consider Moira."

"It wasn't all her fault. I'm to blame too. You want to cuss me some more, go ahead."

Now she turned from the window and faced him. "I said some things to you that I didn't really mean to say."

He chuckled and shook his head. "You forget who you're talking to, gal? You said what you meant and meant what you said. You must be getting old if you all of a sudden trying to apologize for speaking your mind. I thought I taught you better than that?"

"You taught me a lot of things, Jasper. You know you did."

Jasper approached Pam slowly, his eyes steady on hers. When he was close enough to touch her he reached out and took her hand, held it between both of his in the space that separated them. "You and Paris, ya'll was my heart, my babies. I used to come to the home and hold you in my arms when you was too little to know it was me and you used to laugh when I would bite your toes. Paris, she didn't like her feet to be fooled with too much, but she cracked up when I got my fingers under her arms and tickled her. You reckon she's somewhere in heaven cursing me straight to hell?"

The sight of Jasper crying humbled Pam. His nostrils flared as tears slowly tracked down his cheeks. "I don't think so." Because she couldn't help herself, she used her free hand to wipe the tears from his face.

"What about you? You cursing me to hell?"

She looked everywhere, but at him. He released her hand when she tugged on it and she pretended not to hear him moan when she stepped back from him. "I have to go," she told him.

"I'm going back to California."

"Pam . . . I . . ." He lifted a hand, then let it drop. His lips were moving before he found his voice. "I love you."

"I know you do, Jasper." She had no trouble telling the truth. He'd always made her feel loved, even when he was fussing. "I always knew that." The scent of Old Spice mingled with tobacco assaulted her senses. Drawn to it, Pam moved closer to him and laid her head on his chest, slid her arms around his waist and squeezed. "I love you too."

Overwhelmed with relief, his arms were slow to respond. A little at a time, they came around Pam, closed her in and held her to him. He palmed her head and buried his nose in her hair. He placed a kiss there, then rested his cheek on the top of her head. "I'm so sorry."

"Me too."

"You gone forgive me, Pam? That's all I'm asking you, is to forgive me and let me be in your life some kind of way."

"Time, Jasper," she whispered. "I need some time."

"I ain't giving you eighteen more years," he vowed solemnly. "The last eighteen just about killed me. Don't go off and stay that long, you hear?"

"I hear."

"But are you listening?"

"I don't know," she sighed.

EPILOGUE

Dear Diary,

I thought it would be weird seeing my dad and Pam together, but it's actually not. What's weird is that my dad is like a totally different person. I've never heard him laugh so much and he's all of a sudden so talkative. I mean, he always talked about stuff like school and what I was doing, but other than that he was kind of quiet. Now he's always talking and laughing with people. I didn't know he had such a funny sense of humor. I didn't know being with another person could bring that out of you or that being with the wrong person could keep it hidden inside. It makes me sad to think that he kept all that life inside of him for so long.

We live in California now and so far I like it. My school is huge, like a stadium with walls and doors, but it's cool. I was nervous about starting at a new school in my senior year, but Pam introduced me to Winnie Freeman's daughter, who turned out to be really nice and down to earth. Then Winnie's daughter introduced me around school on the first day. I never thought I would be hanging out and going to slumber parties at Winnie Freeman's house. You know who she is, she's the famous actress I used to want to be like when I grew up. Now Pam complains about the phone ringing all night long and she finds something wrong with every guy who asks me out. (Sigh)

I'm making friends and having fun, but I still can't wait for Christmas break when Kelli comes to stay with me for a week. She'll get a kick out of me having a skylight in my room and my own car.

Me and Pam spend a lot of time together. I try not to follow her everywhere she goes, but I can't help myself. If I am home and she is going somewhere I want to go, too. My favorite place to follow her is to the recording studio. She's working on another CD, and sometimes we're there late into the night. I fall asleep on the sofa in the studio, listening to her sing and wondering if I have inherited her voice. It is high and light, low and smoky, thick and then smooth. She can make it be whatever she wants it to be and she looks so free and happy when she sings.

She still wears those dark glasses, though, when we go out and a few times I have found her in her attic room, lost inside her head. She is remembering everything, I think. Remembering that my mom is gone, and feeling sad. Probably wishing the same thing that I wish, that we could rewind time and make everything go the way it was supposed to go. I miss my mom. A lot. It seems like she should be here with us enjoying life, too. I remember that when I had my mom, I always missed Pam and wanted her to be there with us. Things have flip-flopped, I guess. Maybe God felt I needed to let one mom go, so I could learn to make room in my heart for another one. I don't know, but I am making room. I can't stop myself from loving Pam like crazy. I always did love her, but finding out that she gave birth to me changed the way I feel about her. Finding out about everything she went through made me see that she isn't just some glamorous, rich woman. She is human. If it's possible, I think I love her even more. The diary started all this. Mom's diary. If I hadn't read it, I wouldn't have found out all I did. Dad wouldn't be happy and neither would I, not really. Mom would still be gone, but Dad and I would still be in Mercy, alone. I'm gladder that we're here in California, instead of in Mercy every day.

The other day I was sitting in Economics class, scribbling in my notebook because Mr. Delaney is sooooo boring and I started thinking. I wonder if it was meant for me to have mom's diary. Maybe mom had something to do with Pam giving it to me, like she wanted me to read it and know the truth. Why else would she have written everything down?

I guess I'll never know . . .

Nikki

November 18th

Dear Diary,

Where to begin? So much has happened that I can't decide what to tell you first and what to save *for last. It's all so important. Thanksgiving is just around the corner and Chad is driving me crazy with his constant recipe taste testing and meal planning discussions. This will be our second Thanksgiving together as a couple and our first as husband and wife. Last year the three of us cooked the meal together, with Nate here to give directions and restore order when things got crazy. He brought a woman with him, and I have to admit I liked her far better than I did the last one I met, the previous Christmas. Mimi, I think her name was. For starters, this one was actually old enough to drink. Still, I shudder to think of what he will turn up with this year. Or I should say, who. I won't be disappointed if he comes solo, because then I won't have to share his lap or his lips with anyone. Nikki says that I am possessive of Nate and that I make his dates uncomfortable, but I don't care. I had first dibs. Chad says that I do it on purpose, to intimidate Nate's dates, and maybe I do. And Nate, when he should be making me get out of his lap and giving his dates his undivided attention, just laughs and whispers to me that we had a deal. Share, he says.*

This year Chad is handling all the cooking himself. Nikki has decided she has no interest in being domesticated and she's using the fact that she has two term papers due after the break to weasel her way out of helping. She is a freshman in college this year and I'm so proud of her I can hardly stand myself. Now if I could just keep her out of my closet . . .

I offered to help Chad with Thanksgiving dinner, but he won't hear of it. He says I need to rest and rejuvenate myself. I have been running around like crazy, trying to wrap up my second album in as many years, and I won't lie and say I'm not worn out. *This album has to be perfect, though. I want to leave my fans with something special to tide them over while I'm on hiatus. I need a break. I'm nowhere near as young and tireless as I used to be. Also, my son is becoming more and more demanding as the days go by. He seems to think that my breasts belong solely to him and wants to suckle them all day and night. He's such a greedy little thing, already twice the size he should be at two-months-old!*

Oh, but he's gorgeous. Brown like Nikki and Chad, with his father's dreamy eyes and long legs. He has my lips, though, and my hair. Chad is always the first to rise from bed to get him when he cries in the middle of the night. As a father, he is everything I knew he would be; patient and soothing, affectionate and loving. I love to see him pick up his son first thing in the morning and kiss his lips like he's never kissed them before, like they are the sweetest things he's ever tasted. He likes to lie in bed and watch as I breast-feed his son or else he will be right there with him, willing to give up the breast he is pleasuring and trade places on demand. I don't think you can fathom how much I love Chad. Sometimes even I can't. All I know is that I feel whole now.

Nikki calls me Pam. Not Aunt Pam. Just Pam. I'm okay with that, just like I'm okay with the way our relationship is progressing. We've grown even closer than before, if that's possible and I cherish each second I have with her. She's a beautiful girl and I'm thankful Paris loved her enough to do such a wonderful job raising her. I almost wish she was here to see what a lovely person Nikki is, but then if she were here I wouldn't have Chad or Nikki or my newest Chad. That feels so wrong to say to you, but it's the truth. I miss Paris every day, and I pray she is at peace, wherever she is, looking down on us with love and wishing us all well.

I hope she understands what I have decided to do where Jasper and Moira are concerned. They are joining us here in California for Thanksgiving and then for a week or so afterward. We've been in touch a lot lately, since I finally worked up the nerve to respond to one of Moira's letters. Of course, everyone in Mercy knows now that they are mine and Paris's birth parents. They are like minor celebrities there, which is strange and kind of funny. The book is now in its third printing and they are constantly refusing offers to appear on television to talk about their roles in our lives. Me? I still don't do interviews. Everyone is curious about Chad and of course, there's talk that he was once married to my sister, but I don't give a shit. I don't have to explain myself to anyone. Not anymore.

I have to find it in my heart to completely forgive them, though, don't I? How can I expect Nikki to do the same for me otherwise? And truthfully, it's not as hard as I thought it would be. I just take it day by day and go with the flow. I believe that everything is going to work out the way it should and that makes all of this so much easier. I could dwell on the past and go on mourning everything I had and lost, but what's the point? Being angry with Paris won't get me back all the years I lost, and now that I know about Jasper and Moira, ignoring them only hurts me more.

I have to let go of the past so I can concentrate on the future.

I didn't know life could be this good, could feel this good, but I'm so glad it is and does.

Pam

"What are you writing about?"

Pam looked up from her diary and focused on Chad's face. He pulled up an ottoman and took a seat in front of her. She let herself get lost in his eyes and smiled. "Everything that's happened so far. Does the baby need me?"

"I just put him down for a nap," Chad said, spreading his hands out on her thighs and kneading the skin there. "He wouldn't let me put him down before that, so I had to walk around with him until he finally dropped off."

"It's your fault for carrying him around all the time. He doesn't pull that shit with me." Pam's tone was knowingly amused. Chad was letting the baby manipulate the hell out of him.

"It's my fault and I'm loving every minute of it, too." He took the book from her hands and laid it on the floor beside her chair. Slid to the edge of the ottoman and stared at her lips until she leaned forward and gave them to him. He kissed her long and deep. "Nikki just left with that bow-legged boy you love to hate and that little monster you gave birth to should sleep for at least another hour."

She cocked a brow. "And?"

"And . . ." Chad slid his tongue up the length of her neck and bit into the spot just behind her ear. "I was wondering if I could talk you into getting naked with me, so I can love every minute of you?"

She drew back and palmed his cheeks, indulged herself in another kiss. "I thought you had some paper-

work to look over?" He was the dean of a private
school for boys and he always brought paperwork
home with him to review. She was hoping he was all
done with that now.

"To hell with the paperwork. I'd rather be looking
you over," he said.

"Oh . . . well, in that case . . ." Pam hopped up from
the chaise and hurried over to the door. They were in
the attic studio and she turned the lock to keep anyone
from interrupting them. She wasn't aware of Chad following her to the door until she turned and found him
right there. "What are you doing?" His hands shot out
and tugged impatiently on the drawstring of her
lounging pants.

Chad backed Pam against the wall and caged her in.
He gave up on her pants for a moment and whipped
her shirt up and over her head so fast she barely had
time to blink. His mouth was everywhere at once. On
hers, stretching it wide for his tongue, on her neck, her
shoulders and nibbling at her breasts. He remembered
that he was still fully dressed and set about remedying
the situation, starting with his pants.

Pam was taking too long dealing with her own pants
and he brushed her hands aside to speed the process
up. She giggled under her breath. "You act like you're
starving or something." She stepped out of her pants
and kicked them out of the way.

"I am starving." Chad moved back and pulled his
shirt over his head; then he zoomed in for her mouth
again. "Come on, come on, come on," he chanted impatiently. "Hurry *up*, Pam."

And then he was inside her and she was the one
doing the chanting. She was saying to him, "Oh, that
feels *so* good. Please don't stop."

And he was telling her, "I'm never stopping, Pam.

You hear me? I'm *never stopping . . ."* He had no intention of letting another eighteen years pass without her in his world and him in hers. It was going to be whatever they wanted it to be forever.

They both giggled when the baby's soft whines filled the room via the monitor set up on the desk. Chad pressed Pam against the wall and continued loving her, hissing from behind his teeth as the whines grew more insistent. "That little monster," he panted in her ear without breaking stride. "I think I might have to kill him. Does he know who he's messing with?"

Pam threw her head back and laughed long and hard. She palmed the back of Chad's head and brought his mouth to hers. "Kill him later," she whispered. "See about me now."

Reading Group Guide

The following discussion questions are intended to enhance your group's reading of Terra Little's *Running from Mercy*. It is our hope that they stimulate insightful discussion and broaden your group's reading experience.

Discussion Questions:

1) Because of the circumstances of their births, Pam and Paris were extremely close. Was their relationship unnaturally close or was it simply indicative of the often talked about bond between twins?

2) Were Pam and Chad really in love with each other or were they just children who thought they were in love? If things hadn't happened the way they did, do you think they would've ended up together?

3) Nate and Pam have been best friends since they were children. Was it natural that they would end up being more to each other? Given that Nate and Chad are best friends and Pam was involved with Chad, is Pam and Nate's relationship inappropriate? How does her relationship with both men factor into your response?

4) Throughout much of the book Paris comes across as being passive and gentle. In the end, does she still come across this way? If not, how has your

perception of her changed? What do you think
her true feelings were toward Pam and why?

5) What is your reaction to Paris's deception? Why
   do you think she chose to keep Pam's secret, even
   after it became obvious that speaking up might
   help rather than hurt those around her? Was she
   jealous of Pam and Chad's relationship, or did her
   actions have more to do with not wanting anyone
   to come between her and Pam? If this is the case,
   why didn't she have issues with Pam and Nate's
   relationship?

6) When Nikki learns the truth about Pam, she is
   angry and confused. Why is she only angry with
   Pam and not with Chad, Nate, or Paris? She says
   that she's always wanted more of Pam. Why do
   you think she's always wanted this and how does
   it tie into the true nature of Pam's relationship to
   her?

7) Pam was violently attacked. Do you blame her for
   running from Mercy? Do you think she could or
   should have kept Nikki with her? She says that
   she was sick and that depression is the reason she
   sent Nikki away. Based on what you may or may
   not know about depression, is this a valid reason
   for doing what she did? Could she have cared for
   Nikki and dealt with the aftermath of her attack
   simultaneously?

8) Nate could've told Chad the truth, too. What is
   your reaction to the fact that he kept quiet for as
   long as he did? Was he being a good friend to Pam

or doing Chad a disservice? How does your response tie in to the fact that he and Pam have
been lovers as well as friends?

9) Take a moment to consider Moira and her reasons for doing what she did. Do they ring true to
you or do you think her own race related issues
played a part in her decision?

10) Jasper was a father without really being a father.
Why is forgiving him easier for Pam than forgiving Moira? How does your response tie into soci-
ety's role expectations of mothers versus fathers?

11) Are the circumstances of Pam's birth in any way
similar to Nikki's birth? Does Pam have the right
to be angry with Moira and Jasper, given the circumstances of Nikki's birth?

12) Who do you think Pam should've ended up with,
Chad or Nate? Why? What is your reaction to the
fact that Pam and Chad resumed their relationship after Paris's death? Was it inevitable?

13) Pam admits that she's in love with both Chad and
Nate, but for different reasons. Think about the
future and speculate on how things will play out.
Will Pam and Nate continue an intimate relationship? Are they capable of just being friends or will
their past come back to haunt them?

14) Will Nikki ever be able to completely forgive
Pam? Will Pam ever be able to completely forgive
Moira and Jasper? Why or why not?

15) When Pam left Mercy she also left Chad. How do
    you feel about his marriage to Paris and are his
    reasons for doing so justified? Could he have
    played a more active role in learning the truth
    earlier on? If so, what could he have done differ-
    ently?

Sneak Preview

WHERE THERE'S SMOKE, THERE'S FIRE

by Terra Little

Coming in January 2009 from Q-Boro Books

ALEC

I was erasing yesterday's lecture material from the blackboard when the process server walked into my classroom. I thought he was one of my students' parents and I automatically put on my best *welcome to my class* smile. "Can I help you?" Several of my students were struggling in my class and if this was a concerned parent, wanting to know how he could help, I was more than willing to discuss his son's or daughter's progress at length.

"Are you Alec Avery?"

I looked at the lanky white man curiously. Short and bushy looking about the head, middle of the road clothes and heavy soled, thick leather shoes laced too tight. I thought he might be Byron Tardell's father, a kid in my fifth hour with a propensity toward sneaking his IPod past me and sitting in the very back of the class, listening to it while I lectured. Just yesterday I had finally confiscated it and I had to admit, the kid had some smooth grooves on that thing, if the sampling I'd treated myself to was any indication.

"Let me guess, you're Byron's dad and you're here to pick up his iPod, right?" I moved from the board to my desk and pulled out a drawer, dug around under some papers. "I have to tell you, this thing is very disruptive in class. I've asked Byron to leave it at home on several occasions, but—"

"I'm not Byron's father, Mr. Avery," the man said, coming toward me with a thick envelope extended. Reflexively, I took it. "In fact, I don't have any children. Never really cared for them, you know? Anyway, I'm a process server and you should consider yourself served. Have a nice day."

With that, he was gone. I looked down at the envelope in my hand as if I had no idea how it got there. *Served?* I'd never been served with anything in my life. Oh yeah, divorce papers but that was different. I had been expecting them, elated with the prospect of finally receiving them, even. This was something else altogether.

I tossed the envelope on my desk and returned to the board. Five seconds later, I was back at my desk, staring at the envelope. I couldn't think of anyone I owed money and, that I knew of, I didn't have any wives left to divorce. So what the hell was this? I sat at my desk and ripped the envelope open, unable to wait another minute. I scanned the cover sheet carefully, my eyes growing wider and wider as the seconds passed. After about five minutes of reading, I mentally reminded myself to breathe.

In my hand I was holding a petition for child support. Some woman, whom I had no knowledge or recollection of, was claiming that I had fathered a child with her over sixteen years ago and, after all these years, she wanted financial compensation. *What the hell?*

I read the plaintiff's name again and searched my memory. Breanne Phillips. The name didn't ring a bell with me, not even remotely. I had done more than my share of traveling while I was in the Marines and, of course, I'd sampled some of the ladies, but I hadn't left any babies behind, that I knew of. But that was how things worked, wasn't it? You didn't know you'd left babies behind until you got hit for child support out of the blue. Like this. Like now. Possibly this was a case of mistaken identity. There were stories of women who had nothing to go on except the name of their child's father. Every guy in the state with the name in question was summoned to appear, so that the woman could point out the right one, the man she had screwed without bothering to learn anything other than his name. This might be one of those situations. It had to be.

I was in the military for twelve years and married for nine of those years. There was no way I had fathered a child. Well, I mean, there was a *way*, but this had to be a mistake.

My students began trickling into class, each looking more harried and harassed than the last, and none of them looking like they were in the mood for Geometry. I shoved the papers in a drawer, put my game face on and went to stand at the door. The first bell of the day would be ringing shortly.

"Miss Jacobs, I thought I asked you to start giving serious thought to the types of shirts you wore to school from now on," I reminded a female student as she sidled past me wearing a sheer looking shirt, unbuttoned to show ample cleavage. Where was her mother when this girl was buying or stealing her clothing?

"You lucky I didn't wear the first one I put on, Mr. Avery," she came back.

"No, I think you might be the lucky one. Go to the office and see if they have a

sweater in the lost and found you can borrow please, Miss Jacobs." The rest of the class burst out laughing and I couldn't resist chuckling myself. The look on her face was truly a Kodak moment.

"You kidding, right?"

"I wish I was. You'd better hurry up because I'm not giving you a pass. You get caught roaming the halls and it's an automatic detention. *Go*." I pointed out the door and raised my eyebrows meaningfully. As soon as she huffed out the door, breasts bouncing all over the place, I pulled it closed and lifted a silencing hand. "Turn to page one-eighty-eight in your books class."

A resounding "*aawww*" filled the room and I silently commiserated as I scooped up the teaching manual and turned to the board, chalk in hand. Whoever this child was that I didn't know and that I was supposed to have fathered, wouldn't be too much older than the hooligans I taught on a daily basis. *God please let this whole thing be a terrible mistake*, I prayed.

It wasn't until the end of the day, when I was picking up wads of paper from the classroom floor and using them to toss free-throws at the trashcan, that I re-membered where I knew the name Breanne Phillips. I froze like a poster of Jordan, flying midair, in the midst of a slam-dunk, and rolled the name around on my tongue for long seconds. It couldn't be. I hoped like hell it wasn't. But it would be just my luck if it was.

Damn.

About the Author

Terra Little holds Bachelor of Science Degrees in Criminology and Sociology, respectively, and a Master's Degree in Professional Counseling. Currently, she is a community-based corrections professional and a crisis intervention counselor. She is a native of St. Louis, Missouri, where she lives with her teenage daughter.

NOW AVAILABLE FROM

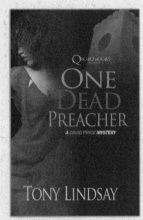

COMING SOON FROM

Q-BORO
BOOKS

FEBRUARY 2008
1-933967-31-5

COMING SOON FROM

Q-BORO
BOOKS

MARCH 2008
1-933967-39-0